MAVERICKS

WILLIAM MACLEOD RAINE

1st WORLD
LIBRARY
Literary Society

Mavericks

William MacLeod Raine

© 1st World Library, 2008
PO Box 2211
Fairfield, IA 52556
www.1stworldlibrary.com
First Edition

LCCN: 2007940236

Softcover ISBN: 978-1-4218-9374-7
Hardcover ISBN: 978-1-4218-9474-4
eBook ISBN: 978-1-4218-9274-0

Purchase *"Mavericks"*
as a traditional bound book at:
www.1stWorldLibrary.com/purchase.asp?ISBN=978-1-4218-9374-7

1st World Library is a literary, educational organization
dedicated to:

- Creating a free internet library of downloadable ebooks

- Hosting writing competitions and offering book publishing
scholarships.

1ˢᵗ World Library Literary Society

Giving Back to the World

"If you want to work on the core problem, it's early school literacy."

- James Barksdale, former CEO of Netscape

"No skill is more crucial to the future of a child, or to a democratic and prosperous society, than literacy."

- Los Angeles Times

"Literacy... means far more than learning how to read and write... The aim is to transmit... knowledge and promote social participation."

- UNESCO

"Literacy is not a luxury, it is a right and a responsibility. If our world is to meet the challenges of the twenty-first century we must harness the energy and creativity of all our citizens."

- President Bill Clinton

"Parents should be encouraged to read to their children, and teachers should be equipped with all available techniques for teaching literacy, so the varying needs and capacities of individual kids can be taken into account."

- Hugh Mackay

TO MY MOTHER

"In vain men tell us time can alter
Old loves, or make old memories falter."

CONTENTS

CHAPTER I

PHYLLIS

Phyllis leaned against the door-jamb and looked down the long road which wound up from the valley and lost itself now and again in the land waves. Miles away she could see a little cloud of dust travelling behind the microscopic stage, which moved toward her almost as imperceptibly as the minute-hand of a clock. A bronco was descending the hill trail from the Flagstaff mine, and its rider announced his coming with song in a voice young and glad.

"My love has breath o' roses,
O' roses, o' roses,
And cheeks like summer posies
All fresh with morning dew,"

floated the words to her across the sunlit open.

If the girl heard, she heeded not. One might have guessed her a sullen, silent lass, and would have done her less than justice. For the storm in her eyes and the curl of the lip were born of a mood and not of habit. They had to do with the gay vocalist who drew his horse up in front of her and relaxed into the easy droop of the experienced rider at rest.

"Don't see me, do you?" he asked, smiling.

Her dark, level gaze came round and met his sunniness without response.

"Yes, I see you, Tom Dixon."

"And you don't think you see much then?" he suggested lightly.

She gave him no other answer than the one he found in the rigor of her straight figure and the flash of her dark eyes.

"Mad at me, Phyl?" Crossing his arms on the pommel of the saddle he leaned toward her, half coaxing, half teasing.

The girl chose to ignore him and withdrew her gaze to the stage, still creeping antlike toward the hills.

"My love has breath o' roses,
O' roses, o' roses,"

he hummed audaciously, ready to catch her smile when it came.

It did not come. He thought he had never seen her carry her dusky good looks more scornfully. With a movement of impatience she brushed back a rebellious lock of blue-black hair from her temple.

"Somebody's acting right foolish," he continued jauntily. "It was all in fun, and in a game at that."

"I wasn't playing," he heard, though the profile did not turn in the least toward him.

"Well, I hated to let you stay a wall-flower."

"I don't play kissing games any more," she informed him with dignity.

"Sho, Phyl! I told you 'twas only in fun," he justified himself. "A kiss ain't anything to make so much fuss over. You ain't the first girl that ever was kissed."

She glanced quickly at him, recalling stories she had heard of his boldness with girls. He had taken off his hat and the golden locks of the boy gleamed in the sunlight. Handsome he surely was, though a critic might have found weakness in the lower part of the face. Chin and mouth lacked firmness.

"So I've been told," she answered tartly.

"Jealous?"

"No," she exploded.

Slipping to the ground, he trailed his rein.

"You don't need to depend on hearing," he said, moving toward her.

"What do you mean?" she flared.

"You remember well enough—at the social down to Peterson's."

"We were children then—or I was."

"And you're not a kid now?"

"No, I'm not."

"Here's congratulations, Miss Sanderson. You've put away childish things and now you have become a woman."

Angrily the girl struck down his outstretched hand.

"After this, if a fellow should kiss you, it would be a crime, wouldn't it?" he bantered.

"Don't you dare try it, Tom Dixon," she flashed fiercely.

Hitherto he had usually thought of her as a school girl, even though she was teaching in the Willow's district. Now it came to him with what dignity and unconscious pride her head was poised, how little the home-made print could conceal the long, free lines of her figure, still slender with the immaturity of youth. Soon now the woman in her would awaken and would blossom abundantly as the spring poppies were doing on the mountain side. Her sullen sweetness was very close to him. The rapid rise and fall of her bosom, the underlying flush in her dusky cheeks, the childish pout of the full lips, all joined in the challenge of her words. Mostly it was pure boyishness, the impish desire to tease, that struck the audacious sparkle to his eyes, but there was, too, a masculine impulse he did not analyse.

"So you won't be friends?"

If he had gone about it the right way he might have found forgiveness easily enough. But this did not happen to be the right way.

"No, I won't." And she gave him her profile again.

"Then we might as well have something worth while to quarrel about," he said, and slipping his arm round her neck, he tilted her face toward him.

William MacLeod Raine

With a low cry she twisted free, pushing him from her.

Beneath the fierce glow of her eyes his laughter was dashed. He forgot his expected trivial triumph, for they flashed at him now no childish petulance, but the scorn of a woman, a scorn in the heat of which his vanity withered and the thing he had tried to do stood forth a bare insult.

"How dare you!" she gasped.

Straight up the stairs to her room she ran, turned the lock, and threw herself passionately on the bed. She hated him...hated him...hated him. Over and over again she told herself this, crying it into the pillows where she had hidden her hot cheeks. She would make him pay for this insult some day. She would find a way to trample on him, to make him eat dirt for this. Of course she would never speak to him again—never so long as she lived. He had insulted her grossly. Her turbulent Southern blood boiled with wrath. It was characteristic of the girl that she did not once think of taking her grievance to her hot-headed father or to her brother. She could pay her own debts without involving them. And it was in character, too, that she did not let the inner tumult interfere with her external duties.

As soon as she heard the stage breasting the hill, she was up from the bed as swift as a panther and at her dressing-table dabbing with a kerchief at the telltale eyes and cheeks. Before the passengers began streaming into the house for dinner she was her competent self, had already cast a supervising eye over Becky the cook and Manuel the waiter, to see that everything was in readiness, and behind the official cage had fallen to arranging the mail that had just come up from Noches on the stage.

From this point of vantage she could cast an occasional look into the dining-room to see that all was going well there. Once, glancing through the window, she saw Tom Dixon in conversation with a half-grown youngster in leathers, gauntlets, and spurs. A coin was changing hands from the older boy to the younger, and as soon as the delivery window was raised little Bud Tryon shuffled in to get the family mail and that of Tom. Also he pushed through the opening a folded paper evidently torn from a notebook.

"This here is for you, Phyl," he explained.

She pushed it back. "I'm too busy to read it."

"It's from Tom," he further volunteered.

"Is it?"

She took the paper quietly but with a swift, repressed passion, tore it across, folded the pieces together, rent them again, and tossed the fragments through the window to the floor.

"Do you want the mail for the Gordons, too, Mr. Purdy?" she coolly asked the next in line over the tow head of Bud.

The boy grinned and ducked from his place through the door. Through the open window there drifted to her presently the sound of a smothered curse, followed by the rapid thud of a horse's hoofs. Phyllis did not look, but a wicked gleam came into her black eyes. As well as if she had seen him she beheld a picture of a sulky youth spurring home in dudgeon, a scowl of discontent on his handsome, boyish face. He had come down the mountain trail singing, but no music travelled with him on his return journey. Nor had she alone known this. Without deigning to notice it, she caught a wink and a nod from one vaquero to another. It was certain they would not forget to "rub it in" when next they met Master Tom. She promised herself, as she handed out newspapers and letters to the cowmen, sheep-herders, and miners who had ridden in to the stage station for their mail, to teach that young man his place.

"I'll take a dollar's worth of two's."

Phyllis turned her head in the slow, disdainful fashion she had inherited from her Southern ancestors and without a word pushed the sheet of stamps through the window. That voice, with its hint of sardonic amusement, was like a trumpet call to battle.

"Any mail for Buck Weaver?"

"No," she answered promptly without looking.

"Sure?"

"Yes."

"Couldn't be overlooking any, could you?"

Her eyes met his with the rapier steel of hostility. He was mocking her, for his mail all came to Saguaro. The man was her father's enemy. He had no business here. His coming was of a piece with all the rest of his insolence. Phyllis hated him with the lusty healthy hatred of youth. She had her father's generosity and courage, his quick indignation against wrong and injustice, and banked within her much of his passionate lawlessness.

"I know my business, sir."

Weaver turned from the window and came front to front with

old Jim Sanderson. The burning black eyes of the Southerner, set in sockets of extraordinary depths, blazed from a ´grim, hostile face. Always when he felt ugliest Sanderson's drawl became more pronounced. His daughter, hearing now the slow, gentle voice, ran quickly round the counter and slipped an arm into that of her father.

"This hyer is an unexpected pleasure, Mr. Weaver," he was saying. "It's been quite some time since I've seen you all in my house before, makin' you'self at home so pleasantly. It's ce'tainly an honor, seh."

"Don't get buck ague, Sanderson. I'm here because I'm here. That's reason a-plenty for me," Weaver told him contemptuously.

"But not for me, seh. When you come into my house—"

"I didn't come into your house."

"Why—why—"

"Father!" implored the girl. "It's a government post-office. He has a right here as long as he behaves."

"H'm!" the old fire-eater snorted. "I'd be obliged just the same, Mr. Weaver, if you'd transact your business and then light a shuck."

"Dad!" the girl begged.

He patted her head awkwardly as it lay on his arm. "Now don't you worry, honey. There ain't going to be any trouble— leastways none of my making. I ain't a-forgettin' my promise to you-all. But I ain't sittin' down whilst anybody tromples on me neither."

"He wouldn't try to do that here," Phyllis reminded him.

Weaver laughed in grim irony. "I'm surely much obliged to you for protecting me." And to the father he added carelessly: "Keep your shirt on, Sanderson. I'm not trying to break into society. And when I do I reckon it won't be with a sheep outfit I'll trail."

With which parting shot he turned on his heel, arrogant and imperious to the last virile inch of him.

CHAPTER II

THE NESTER

With the jingle of trailing spur Buck Weaver passed from the post-office to the porch, where public opinion was wont to formulate itself while waiting for the mail to be distributed. Here twice a week it had sat for many years, had heard evidence, passed judgment, condemned or acquitted. For at this store the Malpais country bought its ammunition, its tobacco, and its canned goods; and on this porch its opinions had sifted down to convictions. From this common meeting ground the gossip of Cattleland was scattered far and wide.

Weaver filled the doorway while he drew on his gauntlets. He was the owner of the Twin Star outfit, the biggest cattle company in that country. Nearly twenty years ago, while still a boy of eighteen, he had begun in a small way. The Malpais had been a wild and lawless place then, but in all the turbid days that followed Buck Weaver had held his own ruthlessly by adroit manipulation, shrewd sense, and implacable daring. Some outfits he had bought out; others he had driven away. Those that survived were at a respectable distance from him. Only the settlers in the hills remained to trouble him. He had come to be the big man of the district, dominating its social, business, and political activities.

William MacLeod Raine

"What's this I hear about another settler up on Bear Creek?" he asked curtly after he had gathered up his bridle and swung to the saddle.

"That's the way Jim Budd's telling it, Mr. Weaver. Another nester homesteaded there," old Joe Yeager answered casually, chewing tobacco with a noncommittal air.

"Fine! There'll soon be a right smart settlement up near the headwaters of the creeks, I shouldn't wonder. The cow business is getting to be a mighty profitable one when you don't own any," Buck said dryly.

The others laughed, but with small merriment. They were either small cattle owners themselves or range riders whose living depended on the business, and during the past two years a band of rustlers had operated so boldly as to have wiped out the profits of some of the ranchers. Most of them disliked Buck extremely for his overbearing ways. But they did not usually tell him so. On this particular subject, too, they joined hand with him.

"You're dead right, Mr. Weaver. It ce'tainly must be stopped."

The man who spoke rolled a cigarette and lit it. Like the rest he was in the common garb of the plains. The broad-brimmed felt hat, the shiny leather chaps, the loosely knotted bandanna, were as much a matter of course as the hard-eyed, weather-beaten look that comes of life under an untempered sun. But Brill Healy claimed a distinction above his fellows. He was a black-haired, picturesque fellow, as supple as a panther, reckless and yet wary.

"We'll have rustling as long as we have nesters, Brill," Buck told him.

"If that's the case we'll serve notice on the nesters to get out," Healy replied.

Buck grinned. Indomitable fighter though he was, he had been unable to roll back the advancing tide of settlement. Here and there homesteaders had taken up land and had brought in small bunches of cattle. Most of these were honest men, others suspected rustlers. But Buck's fiat had not sufficed to keep them out. They had held stoutly to their own and—he suspected—a good deal more than their own. Calves had been branded secretly and cows killed or driven away.

"Go to it, Brill," Weaver jeered. "I'm wishing you all the luck in the world."

He touched his pony with the spur and swept up the road in a cloud of white dust.

Not till he had disappeared did conversation renew itself languidly, for Seven Mile Ranch was lying under the lethargy of a summery sun.

"I expect Buck's got the right of it," volunteered a brawny youth known as Slim. "All you got to do is to take up a claim near a couple of big outfits with easy brands, then keep your iron hot and industrious. There's sure money in being a nester."

Despite the soft drawl of his voice, he spoke with bitterness, as did the others. Every day the feeling was growing stronger that the rustling must be stopped if they were going to continue to run cattle. The thieves had operated with a boldness and a shrewdness that fairly outwitted the ranchers. Enough horses and cattle had been driven across the line to stock a respectable ranch. Not one of the established ranches had escaped heavy losses; so heavy, indeed, that the owners faced the option of going broke or of exterminating the rustlers. Once or twice the thieves had nearly been caught red-handed, but the leader of the outlaws had saved the men by the most daring strategy.

Healy, until lately foreman of the Twin Star outfit, had organized the ranchmen as a protective association. In this he had represented Weaver, himself not popular enough to cooeperate with the other ranchmen. Once Brill had led the pursuit of the rustlers and had come back furious from a long futile chase. For among the cattle being driven across to Sonora were five belonging to him.

Other charges also lay against the hill outlaws. A stage had been robbed with a gold shipment from the Diamond Nugget mine. A cattleman had been held up and relieved of two thousand dollars, just taken as part payment for a sale of beef steers. The sheriff of Noches County, while trying to arrest a rustler, had been shot dead in his tracks.

Brill Healy leaned forward, gathered the eyes of those present, and lowered his voice to a whisper. "Boys, this thing has got to stop. I've sent for Bucky O'Connor. If anybody can run the coyotes to earth he can. Anyhow, that's the reputation he's got."

Yeager nodded. "Good for you, Brill. He's ce'tainly got an A-one rep. as a cattle detective, and likewise as a man hunter. When is he coming?"

"He writes that he's got a job on hand that will keep him busy a couple of weeks, anyhow. After that we'll hear from him. I'm going to drop everything else, if necessary, and stay right with him on this job till he finishes it right," Healy promised.

"Now you're shoutin', Brill. Here, too. It's money in our pocket to stop this thing right now, even if we pay big for it. No use jest sittin' around till we're stole blind," assented Slim.

"It won't cost us anything. Buck, he pays the freight. The waddies have been hitting him right hard lately and he figures it will be up to him to clean them out. Course we expect help from you boys when we call on you."

"Sure. We'll all be with you till the cows come home, Brill," nodded one little fellow called Purdy. He was looking at a dust patch rising from the Bear Creek trail, and slowly moving toward them. "What's the name of this new nester, Jim?"

Budd, by way of being a curiosity on the range, was a fat man with a big double chin. He was large as well as fat, and, by queer contrast, the voice that came from that mountain of flesh was a small falsetto scarce above a whisper.

"Didn't hear his name. Had no talk with him. Hear he is called Keller," he said.

"What's he look like?"

"You-all can see for yourself. This here's the gent rolling a tail this way."

The little cloud of dust had come nearer and disclosed as its source a rider on a rangy roan with four white-stockinged feet. Drawing up in front of the porch, the man swung himself easily from the saddle and glanced around.

"Evening, gentlemen," he said pleasantly.

Some nodded grimly, some growled an acknowledgment of his greeting. But the lack of cordiality, the presence of hostility, could not be doubted. The young man stood at supple ease before them, one hand resting on his hip and the other on the saddle. He let his unabashed gaze travel from one to another, understood perfectly what those expressionless eyes of stone were telling him, and, with a little laugh of light derision, trailed debonairly into the store.

"Any mail for Larrabie Keller?" he inquired of the postmistress.

The girl at the window glanced incuriously at him and turned to look. When she pushed his letter through the grating he met for an instant a flash of dark eyes from a mobile face which the sun and superb health had painted to a harmony of gold and russet, with the soft glow of pink pushing through the tan. The unexpectedness of the picture magnetized his gaze. Admiration, frank and human, shone from the steel-gray eyes that had till now been only a mask. Beneath his steady look she flushed indignantly and withdrew from the window.

Convicted of rudeness, the last thing he had meant, Keller returned to the porch and leaned against the door jamb while he opened his letter. His appearance immediately sand-bagged conversation. Stony eyes were focused upon him incuriously, with expressionless hostility.

He noted, however, an exception. Another had been added to the group, a lad of about eighteen, slim and swarthy, with the same dark look of pride he had seen on the face at the stamp window. It was easy to guess that they were brother and sister, very likely twins, though he found in the boy's expression a sulky impatience lacking in hers. Perhaps the lad needed the discipline that life hammers into those who want to be a law unto themselves.

With an insolence extremely boyish, the lad turned to Healy. "I'm for running out a few of these nesters. We've got more than we can use, I reckon. The range is overstocked now— both with them and cows. Come a bad year and half of our cattle will starve."

There was a moment of surcharged silence. Phil Sanderson had voiced the growing feeling of them all, but he had flung it out as a stark challenge before the time was ripe. It was one thing to resent the coming of settlers; it was quite another to set themselves openly against the law that allowed these men to homestead the natural parks in the hills.

Brill Healy laughed. "The fat's in the fire now, sure enough. Just the same, I back your play, Phil."

He turned recklessly to the man in the doorway. "You may tell your friends up on Bear Creek that we own this range and mean to hold it. We don't aim to let our cattle be starved, and we don't aim to lie down before rustlers. Understand?"

The nester smiled, but there was no gayety in his eyes. They met those of the cattleman with a grip of steel, and measured strength with him. Each knew the other would go the limit before Keller made quiet answer:

"I think so."

And with that he dismissed the subject and his unfriendly audience. With perfect ease, he read his letter, pocketed it, and whistled softly as he impassively took stock of the scenery. Apparently he had wiped Public Opinion from his map, and was interested only in the panorama before him.

Seven Mile Ranch lay rooted at the desert terminus among the foothills, a gateway between the mountains and the Malpais Plain. Below was a shimmering stretch of sand and cactus tortured beneath a blazing sun. Into that caldron with its furnace-cracked floor the sun had poured itself torridly for countless eons. It was a Sahara of mirage and desolation and death.

To the left was a flat-topped mesa eroded to fantastic mockery of some bastioned fort. In the round-topped hills behind it was Noches, fifty miles away. Beyond lay the tangle of hills, rising to the saw-toothed range now painted with orange and mauve and a hint of deepening purple. For dusk was already slipping down over the peaks.

"Mail's been open half an hour, boys," Phyllis announced through the open window.

They dropped in to the store, as noisy as schoolboys, but withal deferential. It was clear the young postmistress reigned a queen among the younger ones, but a queen that deigned to friendship with her subjects. Some of them called her Miss Sanderson, one or two of them Phyllie.

Among these last was Healy, who appeared on very good terms with her indeed. He appointed himself a sort of master of ceremonies, and handed to each man his mail with appropriate jocular comments designed to embarrass the recipient. He knew them all, and his hits were greeted with gay laughter. To the man standing in the doorway with his back to them, they seemed all one happy family—and himself a rank outsider. He trailed down the steps and swung himself to the saddle. As he loped away the sound of her warm, clear laughter floated after him.

CHAPTER III

CAUGHT RED-HANDED

From a cleft in the hills two riders emerged, following a little gulch to the point where it widened into a draw. The alkali dust of Arizona lay thick upon their broad-brimmed Stetsons and every inch of exposed surface, but through the gray coating bloomed the freshness of youth. It rang from their voices, was apparent in the modelling and carriage of their figures. The young man was sinewy and hard as nails, the girl supple and wiry, of a slender grace, straight-backed as an Indian in the saddle.

Just where the draw dipped down into the grassy park they drew rein an instant. Faint and far a sound drifted to them. Somebody down in the park had fired a rifle.

"I don't agree with you, Phil," the girl said, picking up the thread of their conversation where they had dropped it some minutes earlier. "The nesters have as much right here as we have. They come here to settle, and they take up government land. Why shouldn't they?"

"Because we got here first," he retorted impatiently. "Because our cattle and sheep have been feeding on the land they are fencing. Because they close the water holes and the creeks and claim they are theirs. It means the end of the open range. That's what it means."

"Of course that's what it means. We'll have to adapt ourselves to it. You talk foolishness when you make threats to drive out the nesters. That is the sort of thing Buck Weaver has been trying to do. It's absurd. The law is back of them. You would only come to trouble, and if you did succeed others would take their places."

"And rustle our cattle," he added sullenly.

"It isn't proved they are the rustlers. You haven't a shred of evidence. Perhaps they are, but you should prove it before you make the charge."

"If they aren't, who is?" he flared up.

"I don't know. But whoever it is will be caught and punished some day. There is no doubt at all about that."

"You talk a heap of foolishness, Phyl," he answered resentfully. "My notion is they never will be caught. What makes you so sure they will?"

They had been riding down the draw, and at this moment Phyllis looked up, to see a rider silhouetted against the sky line on the ridge above.

"Oh, you Brill!" she cried, with a wave of her quirt.

The man turned, saw them, and rode slowly down. He nodded, after the fashion of the range, first to the girl, and then to her brother.

"Morning," he nodded. "Headed for Mesa? Here, too."

He fell in with them and rode beside the girl. Presently they topped a little hillock, and looked down into the park. It had about the area of a mile, and was perhaps twice as long as broad. Wooded spurs ran down from the hills into it here and there, and through the meadow leaped a silvery stream.

"Hello! Wonder where that smoke comes from?"

It was Healy that spoke. He pointed to a faint cloud rising from a distance. Even before he began to speak, however, Phyllis had her field glasses out, and was adjusting them to her eyes.

"There's a fire there and a man standing over it," she presently announced. "There's something else there, too. I can't make it out—something lying down."

The men glanced at each other, and in the meeting of their eyes some intelligence passed between them. It was as if the younger accused and the older sullenly denied.

"Lemme have the glasses," Phil said to his sister almost roughly.

Healy glanced at Phil swiftly, covertly, as the latter adjusted the glasses. "She's right about the fire and the man. I can see as much with my naked eyes," he cut in.

The boy looked long, lowered the glasses, and met his friend's eye with a kind of shamefaced hesitation. But apparently he gathered reassurance from the quiet steadiness with which the other's gaze met him. He handed the glasses to Healy. When the latter lowered them his face was grave. "There's a man and a fire and a cow and a calf. When these four things meet up together, what does it mean?"

"Branding!" cried the girl.

"That's right—branding. And when the cow is dead what does it mean?" Brill asked, his eyes full on Phil.

"Rustling!" she breathed again.

"You've said it, Phyl. We've got one of them at last," he cried jubilantly.

Phil, hanging between doubt and suspicion and shame, brightened at the enthusiasm of the other.

"Right you are, Brill. We'll solve this mystery once for all."

Healy, unstrapping the case in which lay his rifle, shot a question at the boy. "Armed, Phil?"

The lad nodded. "I brought my six-gun for rattlesnakes."

"Are you going to—to—" cried Phyllis, the color gone from her face.

"We're going to capture him alive if we can, Phyl. You're to wait right here till we come back. You may hear shooting. Don't let that worry you. We've got the drop on him, or will have. Nobody is going to get hurt if he acts sensible," Healy reassured.

"Don't you move from here. You stay right where you are," her brother ordered sharply.

"Yes," she said, and was aware that her throat was suddenly parched. "You'll be careful, won't you, Phil?"

"Sure," he called back, as he put his horse at a canter to

follow his friend up the draw.

The sound of the hoofs died away, and she was alone. That they were going to circle in and out among the tangle of hills until they were opposite the miscreant, she knew, but in spite of Brill's promise she had a heart of water. With trembling fingers she raised the glasses again, and focused them on that point which was to be the centre of the drama.

The man was moving about now, quite unconscious of the danger that menaced him. What she looked at was the great crime of Cattleland. All her life she had been taught to hold it in horror. But now something human in her was deeper than her detestation of the cowardly and awful thing this man had just done. She wanted to cry out to him a warning, and did in a faint, ineffective voice that carried not a tenth of the distance between them.

She had promised to remain where she was, but her tense interest in what was doing drew her forward in spite of herself. She rode along the ridge that bordered the park, at first slowly and then quicker as the impulse grew in her to be in at the finish.

The climax came. She saw him look round quickly, and in an instant his pony was at the gallop and he was lying low on its neck. A shot rang out, and another, but without checking his flight. He turned in the saddle and waved a derisive hand at the shooters, then plunged into a wash and disappeared.

What inspired her she could never tell. Perhaps it was her indignation at the thing he had done, perhaps her anger at that mocking wave of the hand with which he had vanished. She wheeled her horse, and put it at a canter down the nearest draw so as to try to intercept him at right angles. Her heart beat fast with excitement, but she was conscious of no fear.

William MacLeod Raine

Before she had covered half the distance, she knew she was going to be too late to cut off his retreat. Faintly, she heard the rhythm of hoofs striking the rocky bottom of the draw. Abruptly they ceased. Wondering what that could mean, she found her answer presently. For the pounding of the galloping broncho had renewed itself, and closer. The man was riding up the gulch toward her. He had turned into its mesquite-laced entrance for a hiding place. Phyllis drew rein, and waited quietly to confront him, but with a pulse that hammered the moments for her.

A white-stockinged roan, plowing a way through heavy sand, labored into view round the bend, its rider slewed in the saddle with his whole attention upon the possible pursuit. Not until he was almost upon her did the man turn. With a startled exclamation at sight of the motionless figure, he pulled up sharply. It was the nester, Keller.

"You," she cried.

"Happy to meet you, Miss Sanderson," he told her jauntily.

His revolver slid into its holster, and his hat came off in a low bow. White, even teeth gleamed in a sardonic smile.

"So you are a—rustler," she told him scornfully.

"I hate to contradict a lady," he came back, with a kind of bitter irony.

She saw something else, a deepening stain that soaked slowly down his shirt sleeve.

"You are wounded."

"Am I?"

"Aren't you?"

"Come to think of it, I believe I am," he laughed shortly.

"Badly?"

"I haven't got the doctor's report yet." There was a gleam of whimsical gayety in his eyes as he added: "I was going to find him when I had the good luck to meet up with you."

He was a hunted miscreant, wounded, riding for his life as a hurt wolf dodges to shake off the pursuit, but strangely enough her gallant heart thrilled to the indomitable pluck of him. Never had she seen a man who looked more the vagabond enthroned. His crisp bronze curls and his superb shoulders were bathed in the sunpour. Not once, since his eyes had fallen on her, had he looked back to see if his hunters had picked up the lost trail. He was as much at ease as if his whole thought at meeting her were the pleasure of the encounter.

"Can you ride?" she demanded.

"I can stick on a hawss if it's plumb gentle. Leastways I've been trying to for twenty years," he drawled.

Her impatient gesture waved his flippancy aside. "I mean, are you too much hurt to ride? I'm not going to leave you here like a wounded coyote. Can you follow me if I lead the way?"

"Yes, ma'am."

She turned. He followed her obediently, but with a ghost of a smile still flickering on his face.

"Am I your prisoner, Miss Sanderson?" he presently wanted to know.

"I'm not thinking of prisoners just now," she answered shortly, with an anxious backward glance.

Presently she pulled up and wheeled her horse, so that when he halted they sat facing each other.

"Let me see your arm," she ordered.

Obediently he held out to her the one that happened to be nearest. It was the unwounded one. An angry spark gleamed in her eye.

"This is no time to be fresh. Give me the other."

"Yes, ma'am." he answered, with deceptive meekness.

Without comment, she turned back the sleeve which came to the wrist gauntlet, and discovered a furrow ridged by a rifle bullet. It was a clean flesh wound, neither deep nor long enough to cause him trouble except for the immediate loss of blood. To her inexperience it looked pretty bad.

"A plumb scratch," he explained.

She took the kerchief from her neck, and tied it about the hurt, then pulled down the sleeve and buttoned it over the brown forearm. All this she did quite impersonally, her face free of the least sympathy.

"Thank you, ma'am. You're a right friendly enemy."

"It isn't a matter of friendship at all. One couldn't leave a wounded jack rabbit in pain," she retorted coldly, taking up the trail again.

There was room for two abreast, and he chose to ride beside her. "So you tied me up because it was your Christian duty," he soliloquized aloud. "Just the same as if I had been a mangy coyote that was suffering."

"Exactly."

He let his cool eyes rest on her with a hint of amusement. "And what were you thinking of doing with me now, ma'am?"

"I'm going to take you up to Jim Yeager's mine. He is doing his assessment work now, and he'll look out for you for a day or two."

"Look out for me in a locked room?" he wanted to know casually.

"I didn't say so. It isn't my business to arrest criminals," she told him icily.

His eyes gleamed mischief. "Is it your business to help them to escape?"

"I'm not helping you to escape. I'll not risk your dying in the hills alone. That is all."

"Jim Yeager is your friend?"

"Yes."

"And you guarantee he'll keep his mouth padlocked and not betray me?"

"He'll do as he pleases about that," she said indifferently.

"Then I don't reckon I'll trouble his hospitality. Good-by, Miss Sanderson. I've enjoyed meeting you very much."

He checked his pony and bowed.

"Where are you going?" the girl exclaimed.

"Up Bear Creek."

"It's twenty miles. You can't do it."

"Sure I can. Thanks for your kindness, Miss Sanderson. I'll return the handkerchief some day," and with a touch swung round his pony.

"You're not going. I won't have it, and you wounded!"

He turned in the saddle, smiling at her with jaunty insouciance.

"I'll answer for Jim. He won't betray you," she promised, subduing her pride.

"Thanks. I'll take your word for it, but I won't trouble your friend. I've had all the Christian charity that's good for me this mo'ning," he drawled.

At that she flamed out passionately: "Do you want me to tell you that I *like* you, knowing what you are? Do you want me to pretend that I feel friendly when I hate you?"

"Do you want me to be under obligations to folks that hate me?" he came back with his easy smile.

"You have lost a lot of blood. Your arm is still bleeding. You know I can't let you go alone."

"You're ce'tainly aching for a chance to be a Good Samaritan, Miss Sanderson."

With this he left her. But he had not gone a hundred yards before he heard her pony cantering after his. One glance told him she was furious, both at him and at herself.

"Did you come after your handkerchief, ma'am? I'm not through with it yet," he said innocently.

"I'm going with you. I'm not going to leave you till we meet some one that will take charge of you," she choked.

"It isn't necessary. I'm much obliged, ma'am, but you're overestimating the effect of this pill your friend injected into me."

"Still, I'm going. I won't have your death on my hands," she told him defiantly.

"Sho! I ain't aimin' to pass over the divide on account of a scratch like this. There's no danger but what I can look out for myself."

She waited in silence for him to start, looking straight ahead of her.

He tried in vain to argue her out of it. She had nothing to say, and he saw she was obstinately determined to carry her point.

Finally, with a little chuckle at her stubbornness, he gave in and turned round.

"All right. Yeager's it is. We're acting like a pair of kids, seems to me." This last with a propitiatory little smile toward her which she disdained to answer.

Yeager saw them from afar, and recognized the girl.

"Hello, Phyllis!" he shouted down. "With you in a minute."

The girl slipped to the ground, and climbed the steep trail to meet him. Her crisp "Wait here," flung over her shoulder with the slightest turn of the head, kept Keller in the saddle.

Halfway up she and the man met. The one waiting below could not hear what they said, but he could tell she was explaining the situation to Yeager. The latter nodded from time to time, protested, was vehemently overruled, and seemed to leave the matter with her. Together they retraced their way. Young Yeager, in flannel shirt and half-leg miner's boots, was a splendid specimen of bronzed Arizona. His level gaze judged the man on horseback, approved him, and met him eye to eye.

"Better light, Mr. Keller. If you come in we'll have a look at your arm. An accident like that is a mighty awkward thing to happen to a man on the trail. It's right fortunate Miss Sanderson found you so soon after it happened."

The nester knew a surge of triumph in his blood, but it did not show in the impassive face which he turned upon his host.

"It was right fortunate for me," he said, swinging from the saddle. Incidentally he was wondering what story had been narrated to Yeager, but he took a chance without hesitation. "A fellow oughtn't to be so careless when he's got a gun in his hand."

"You're right, seh. In this country of heavy underbrush a man's gun is liable to go off and hit somebody any time if he ain't careful. You're in big luck you didn't shoot yourself up a heap worse."

Yeager led the way to his cabin, and offered Phyllis the single chair he boasted, and the nester a seat on the bed. Sitting beside him, he examined the wound and washed it.

"Comes to being an invalid I'm a false alarm," Keller said apologetically. "I didn't want to come, but Miss Sanderson would bring me."

"She was dead right, too. Time you had ridden twenty miles through the hot sun with that wound you would have been in a raging fever."

"One way and another I'm quite in her debt."

"That's so," agreed Yeager, intent on his work.

She refused to meet the nester's smile. "Fiddlesticks! You talk mighty foolish, Jim. I wouldn't go away and leave a wounded dog if I could help it."

"Suppose the dog were a sheep-killer?" Keller asked with his engaging, impudent smile.

A dust cloud rose from her skirt under a stroke of the restless quirt. "I'd do my best for it and let it settle with the law afterward."

"Even if it were a wolf caught in a trap?"

"I should put it out of its pain. No matter how much I detested it, I wouldn't leave it there to suffer."

"I'm quite sure you wouldn't," the wounded man agreed.

Yeager looked from one to the other, not quite catching the drift of the underlying meaning. Another thing puzzled him, too. But, like most men of the unfenced Southwest, Yeager had a large capacity for silence. Now he attended strictly to his business, without mentioning what he had noticed.

The wound dressed, Phyllis rose to leave. "You'll be down for your mail to-morrow, Jim," she suggested, as she sauntered toward the door.

"Sure. I'll let you know how our patient is getting along."

"Oh, he's yours. I don't want any of the credit," she returned carelessly.

Then, the words scarce off her lips, she gave a little cry of alarm, and stepped quickly back into the room. What she had seen had sapped the color from her face. Yeager started forward, but she waved him back.

"It's Phil and Brill Healy. You've got to hide us, Jim," she told him tensely.

The nester began to grin. He always did when he faced a difficulty apparently insurmountable. Also his fingers slid toward the butt of his revolver.

CHAPTER IV

"I'M A RUSTLER AND A THIEF, AM I?"

Jim swept the cabin with a gesture. "Where can I hide you? Anyhow, there are the horses in plain sight."

Phyllis took imperious control. "Get a coat on him, Jim," she ordered.

At the same time she caught up the basin of bloodstained water and flung its contents through the open window. The torn linen and the stained handkerchief she tossed into a corner and covered with a gunny sack.

"Not a word about the wound, Jim. Mr. Keller is here to help you do your assessment work, remember. And whatever I say, don't give me away."

Yeager nodded. He had manoeuvred the wounded arm through the coat sleeve and was straightening out the shoulders. The nester's eyes were shining with excitement. Alone of the three, he was enjoying himself.

"Remember now. Don't talk too much. Let me run this," the girl cautioned, and with that she stepped to the door, caught sight of her brother with a glad little cry of apparent relief,

William MacLeod Raine

and ran swiftly to him.

"Oh, Phil!" she almost sobbed, and the stress of her emotion was genuine enough, even if she dissembled as to the cause.

The boy patted her dark hair gently. They were twins, without other near relatives except their father, and the tie between them was close.

"What is it, Phyllie? Why didn't you stay where we left you?"

"I was afraid for you. And I rode a little nearer. Then he came straight toward me—and I rode away. I could hear him crashing through the mesquite. When I reached the trail of Jim's mine, I followed it, for I knew he would be here."

"Sure. Course she was scared. What woman wouldn't be? We oughtn't both to have left her. But there wasn't one chance in a thousand of his stumbling on the very spot where she was," said Healy.

Phil gentled her with a caressing hand. "It's all right now, sis. Did you happen to see the fellow at all?"

"Yes. At a distance."

"I don't suppose you would know him," Healy said.

She gave a strained little laugh. "I didn't wait to get a description of him. Didn't you boys recognize him?"

After Phil's answer she breathed freer. "We did not get near enough, though Brill got two shots at him as he pulled out. He was going hell-for-leather and Brill missed both times." He lowered his voice and asked angrily: "What's *he* doing here?"

For Keller had followed Yeager from the cabin and was standing in the doorway with his hands in his pockets. He wore no hat, and had the manner of one very much at home.

"He's helping Jim with his assessment work," she answered in the same low tone. "It's too bad you lost the rustler. He must have broken for the hills."

Healy's eyes had narrowed to slits. Now he murmured a question: "What about this man Keller? Was he here when you came, Phyl?"

The girl turned to Yeager, who had sauntered up. "Didn't you say he came this morning, Jim?"

Yeager's eyes were like a stone wall. "Yep. This mo'ning. I needed some husky guy to help me, so I got him."

"Funny you had to get a fellow from Bear Creek to help you, Jim."

"Are you looking for a job, Brill?"

"No. Why?"

"Because I ain't noticed any stampede this way among the boys to preempt this job. I take a man where I can find him, Brill, and I don't ask you to O.K. him."

"I see you don't, Jim. The boys aren't going to like it very well, though."

"Then they know what they can do about it," Yeager answered evenly, level eyes steadily on those of his critic.

"What time did this nester get here, Jim?" broke in Phil.

Yeager's opaque eyes passed from Healy to Sanderson. "It might have been about eight."

"Then he couldn't be the man," the boy said to Healy, almost in a whisper.

"What man?" Jim asked.

"We ran on a rustler branding a C.O. calf. We got close enough to take a shot at him. Then he slid into some arroyo, and we lost him," Phil exclaimed.

"How long ago was this?" asked Yeager.

"About an hour since we first saw him. Beats all how he ever made his getaway. We were right after him when he gave us the slip."

"Oh, he gave you the slip, did he?"

"Dropped into some hole and pulled it in after him. These hills are built for hide and seek, looks like."

"Notice the color of his horse?"

"It was a roan, Jim. Something like that nester's." Phil nodded toward the animal Keller had ridden.

All eyes focused hard on the horse with the white stockings.

"What brand was he putting on the calf? That'll tell you who the man was."

Phil and Healy looked at each other, and the latter laughed. "That's one on us. We didn't stay to look, but got right out for Mr. Rustler."

"Did he kill the cow?"

Phil nodded.

"Then you'll find the calf still hanging around there unless he had a pal to drive it away."

"That's right. We'll go back now and look. Ready, Phyl?"

"Yes." She stepped to her horse, and swung to the saddle.

Meanwhile Healy rode forward to the cabin. Through narrowed lids he looked down at the man standing in the doorway. "Give that message to your friends?" he demanded insolently.

There are men who have to look at each other only once to know that there is born between them a perpetual hostility. Each of these men had felt it at the first shock of meeting eyes. They would feel it again as often as they looked at each other.

"No," the nester answered.

"Why not?"

"I didn't care to. You may carry your own messages."

"When I do I'll carry them with a gun."

"Interesting if true." Keller's gaze passed derisively over him and dismissed the man.

"And I hope when I come I'll meet Mr. Keller first."

The nester's attention was focused indolently upon the hills.

He seemed to have forgotten that the cattleman was in Arizona.

Healy ripped out a sudden oath, drove the spurs in, and went down the trail with his broncho on the buck.

Keller looked at Yeager and laughed, but that young man met him with a frosty eye.

"I've got some questions to ask you, Mr. Keller," he said.

"Unload 'em."

Yeager led the way inside, offered his guest the chair, and sat down on the bed with his arms on the table which had been drawn close to it.

"In the first place, I'll announce myself. I don't hold with rustlers or waddies. I'm a white man. That being understood, I want to know where we're at."

"Meaning?"

"Miss Phyllis unloads a story on me about you shooting yourself up accidental. Soon as I looked at you that looked fishy to me. You ain't that kind of a durn fool. Would you mind handing me a dipper of water? Thanks." Yeager tossed the water out of the window, and the dipper back into the pail. "I noticed you handed me that water with your right hand. Your gun is on your right side. Then how in Mexico, you being right-handed, did you manage to shoot yourself *in the right arm below the elbow?*"

Keller laughed dryly, and offered no information. "Quite a Sherlock Holmes, ain't you?"

"Hell, no! I got eyes in my head, though. Moreover, that bullet went in at right angles to your arm. How did you make out to do that?"

"Sleight of hand," suggested the other.

"No powder marks, either. And, lastly, it was, a rifle did it, not a revolver."

"Anything more?"

"Some. That side talk between you and Miss Phyllis wasn't over and above clear to me then. I *savez* it now. She hates you like p'ison, but she's too tender-hearted to give you up. Ain't that it?"

"That's it."

"She lied for you to me. She lied again to Phil. So did I. Oh, we didn't lie in words, but it's the same thing. Now, I wouldn't lie to save my own skin. Why then should I for yours, and you a rustler and a thief?"

"I'm a rustler and a thief, am I?"

"Ain't you?"

"Would you believe me if I said I wasn't?"

Yeager debated an instant before he answered flatly, "No."

"Then I won't say it."

The wounded man tossed his answer off so flippantly that Yeager scowled at him. "Mr. Keller, you're a newcomer here. I wonder if you know what the Malpais country would be liable to do to a man caught rustling now."

"I can guess."

"Let me tell what I know and your life wouldn't be worth a plugged quarter."

"Why didn't you tell?"

Yeager brought his big fist down heavily on the table. "Because of Phyl Sanderson. That's why. She put it up to me, and I played her game. But I ain't sure I'm going to keep on playing it. I'm a Malpais man. My father has a ranch down there, and I've rode the range all my life. Why should I throw down my friends to save a rustler caught in the act?"

"You've already tried and convicted me, I see."

"The facts convict you, seh."

"Your understanding of the facts, I reckon you mean."

"I haven't noticed that you're giving me any chance to understand them different," Yeager cut back dryly.

The nester took from his pocket a little pearl-handled knife, picked up a potato from a basket beside him, and began to whittle on it absently. He looked across the table at the man sitting on the bed, and debated a question in his mind. Was it best to confess the whole truth? Or should he keep his own counsel?

"I see you've got Miss Sanderson's knife. Did you forget to return it?" Yeager made comment.

For just an instant Keller's eye confessed amazement. "Miss

Sanderson's knife! Why—how did you know it was hers?" he asked, gathering himself together lamely.

"I ought to know, seeing as I gave it to her for a Christmas present. Sent to Denver for that knife, I did. Best lady's knife in the market, I'm told. Made in Sheffield, England."

"Ye-es. It's sure a good knife. I'll ce'tainly return it next time I see her."

"Funny she ever let you get away with it. She's some particular who she lends that knife to," Jim said proudly.

Keller wiped the blade carefully, shut it, and put the knife back in his pocket. Nevertheless, he was worried in his mind. For what Yeager had told him changed wholly the problem before him. It suggested a possibility, even a probability, very distasteful to him. He was in trouble himself, and before he was through he expected to get others into deep water, too. But not Phyllis Sanderson—surely not this impulsive girl with the blue-black hair and dark, scornful eyes. Wherefore he decided to keep silent now and let Yeager do what he would.

"I reckon, seh, you'll have to do your own guessing at the facts," he said gently.

"Just as you say, Mr. Keller. I reckon if you had anything to say for yourself you would say it. Now, I'll do what talking I've got to do. You may stay here twenty-four hours. After that you may hit the trail for Bear Creek. I'm going down to Seven Mile to tell what I know."

"That's all right. I'll go along and return the pocketknife."

Yeager viewed him with stern disgust. "Don't make any

William MacLeod Raine

mistake, seh. If you go down it's an even chance you'll never go back."

"Sure. Life's full of chances. There's even a chance I'm not a rustler."

"Then I'd advise you not to go down to Seven Mile with me. I'd hate to find out too late I'd helped hang the wrong man," Yeager dryly answered.

CHAPTER V

AN AIDER AND ABETTOR

Having come to an understanding, Yeager and Keller wasted no time or temper in acrimony. Both of them belonged to that big outdoors West which plays the game to the limit without littleness. They were in hostile camps, but that did not prevent them from holding amiable conversation on the common topics of Cattleland. Only one of these they avoided by mutual consent. Neither of them had anything to say about rustling.

Together they ate and smoked and slept, and in the morning after breakfast they saddled and set out for Seven Mile. A man might have traveled far without seeing finer specimens of the frontier, any more competent, self-restrained, or fitter for emergency. They rode with straight back and loose seat, breaking long silences with occasional drawling comment. For in the cow country strong men talk only when they have something to say.

The stage had just left when they reached Seven Mile, and Public Opinion was seated on the porch as per custom. It regarded Keller with a stony, expressionless hostility. Yeager with frank disapprobation.

William MacLeod Raine

Just before swinging from the saddle, Jim turned to the nester. "I'm giving you an hour, seh. After that, I'm going to speak my little piece to the boys."

"Thank you. An hour will be plenty," Keller answered, and passed into the store, apparently oblivious of the silent observation focused upon him.

Phyllis, busy unwrapping a package of papers, glanced up to see his curly head in the stamp window.

"Anything for L. Keller?" he wanted to know, after he had unburdened himself of a friendly "Mornin', Miss Sanderson."

Her impulse was to ask him how his wound was, but she repressed it sternly. She took the letters from the K pigeonhole and found two for him.

"Thank you, I'm feeling fine," he laughed, gathering up his mail.

"I didn't ask you how you were feeling," she answered, turning coldly to her newspapers.

"I thought mebbe you'd want to know about my punctured tire."

"It's very good of you to relieve my anxiety."

"Let me relieve it some more, Miss Sanderson. Here's the knife you lost."

She glanced up carelessly at the pearl-handled knife he pushed through the window. "I didn't know it was lost."

"Well, now you know it's found. When do you remember

seeing it last, ma'am?"

"I lent it to a friend two days ago."

"Oh, to a friend—two days ago."

His eyes were on her so steadily that the girl was aware of some significance he gave to the fact, some hidden meaning that escaped her.

"What friend did you say, Miss Sanderson?"

He asked it casually, but his question irritated her.

"I didn't say, sir."

"That's so. You didn't."

"Where did you get it?" she demanded.

He grinned. "I'll tell you that if you'll tell me who you lent it to."

Her curt answer reminded him that he was in her eyes a convicted criminal. "It's of no importance, sir."

"That's what you think, Miss Sanderson."

She sorted the newspapers in the bundle, and began to slip them into the private boxes where they belonged. Presently, however, her curiosity demanded satisfaction. Without looking at him, she volunteered information.

"But there's no mystery about it. Phil borrowed the knife to fix a stirrup leather, and forgot to give it back to me."

"Your brother?"

"Yes."

He was taken aback. There was nothing for it but a white lie. "I found it near Yeager's mine yesterday. I reckon he must have dropped it on his way there."

"I don't see anything very mysterious about that," she said frostily.

She looked so definitely unaware of him as she worked that he fell back from the window and passed out to the porch. He had found out more than he wanted to know.

Jim Yeager's drawling voice came to him, gentle and low as usual, but with an edge to it. "I been discoverin' I'm some unpopular to-day, Brill. Malpais has been expressin' its opinion right plain. You've arrived in time to chirp in with a 'Me, too.'"

Healy had evidently just ridden up, for he was still in the saddle. He relaxed into one of the easy attitudes used by men of the plains to rest themselves without dismounting.

"You know my sentiments, Jim," he replied, not unamiably.

"Sure I know them. Plumb dissatisfied with me, ain't you? Makes me feel awful bad." Jim was sailing into the full tide of his sarcasm when Keller touched him on the shoulder.

"I'd like to see you for a moment, Mr. Yeager, if you can give me the time," he said.

Healy took in the nester with an eye of jade. "Your twin brother wants you, Jim. Run along with him. Don't mind us."

"I won't, Brill."

The young man rose, and sauntered off with the Bear Creek
settler. At the corral fence, some fifty yards from the house,
he stopped under the shade of a live oak, and put his arms on
the top rail. He had allowed himself to show no sign of it, but
he resented this claim upon him that seemed to ally him
further with the enemy.

"Here I am, Mr. Keller. What can I do for you?"

"You're a friend of Miss Sanderson. You would stand
between her and trouble?" the other demanded abruptly.

"I expect."

"Then find out for me what Phil Sanderson did with the knife
his sister lent him two days ago. Find out whether he lent it
to anybody, and, if so, who."

"What for?"

It had come to a show-down, and the other tabled his cards.

"I found that knife yesterday mo'ning. It was lying beside the
dead cow in the park where your friends happened on me. I
reckon the rustlers must have heard me coming and drove
the calf away just before I arrived. In his hurry one of them
forgot that knife. If you'll tell me the man who had it in his
pocket yesterday when he left-home, I'll tell you who one of
the Malpais rustlers is."

Jim considered this, his gaze upon the far-away range. When
he brought it back to Keller, he was smiling incredulously.

"I hear you say so, seh. But what a man with, a halter round his neck says don't go far before a court."

"I expected you to say about that."

"Then I haven't disappointed you." He continued presently, with cold hostility: "That story you cooked up is about the only one you could spring. What surprises me is that a man with as good a head as yours took twenty-four hours to figure out your explanation. I want to tell you, too, that it don't make any hit with me that you're trying to throw the blame on a boy I've known all my life."

"Who happens to be a brother of Miss Sanderson," Keller let himself suggest.

Yeager flushed. "That ain't the point."

"The point is that I'm trying to clear this boy, and I want your help."

"Looks to me like you want to clear yourself."

"If I prove to you that I'm not a rustler, will you padlock your tongue and help me clear young Sanderson?"

"I sure will—if you prove it to my satisfaction."

Keller drew from his pocket the two letters he had just received. "Read these."

When he had read, Yeager handed them back, and offered his hand. "That clears you, seh. Truth is, I never was satisfied you was a rustler. My mind was satisfied; but, durn it, you didn't *look* like a waddy. It's lucky I hadn't spoke to the boys yet."

"I want to keep this quiet," the Bear Creek settler explained.

"Sure. I'm a clam, and at your service, seh."

"Then find out the truth about the knife."

Yeager's eye chiselled into that of Keller. "Mind, I ain't going to help you bring trouble to Phyllie, and I ain't going to stand by and see it, either."

The other smiled. "I don't ask it of you. What I want is to clear the boy."

"Good enough," agreed Yeager, and led the way back.

Before they had yet reached the house, a figure dropped from the foliage of the live oak under which they had been standing, and rolled like a ball from the fence into the deep dust of the corral. It picked itself up in a gray cloud, from which shone as a nucleus a black face with beady eyes and flashing-white teeth. Swiftly it scampered across the paddock, disappeared into the rear of the stable, and reappeared at the front door.

"Here you, 'Rastus, where you been?" demanded the wrangler. "Didn't I tell you to clean Miss Phyl's trap? I've wore my lungs out hollering for you. Now, you git to work, or I'll wear you to a frazzle."

'Rastus, general alias for his baptismal name of George Washington Abraham Lincoln Randolph, grinned and ducked, shot out of the stable like a streak of light, and appeared ten seconds later in the kitchen presided over by his rotund mother, Becky.

His abrupt entrance disturbed the maternal after-dinner nap.

From the rocking-chair where she sat Becky rolled affronted eyes at him.

"What you doin' here, Gawge Washington? Ain't I done tole you sebenty times seben to keep outa my kitchen at dis time o' day?"

"I wanter see Miss Phyl."

"Then I low you kin take it out in wantin'. Think she got time to fool away on a nigger sprout like you-all? Light a shuck back to the stable, where you belong."

'Rastus grinned amiably, flung himself at a door, and vanished into that part of the house which was forbidden territory to him, the while Becky stared after him in amazement.

"What in tarnation got in dat nigger child?" she gasped.

Phyllis, having arranged the mail and delivered most of it, had left the store in charge of the clerk and retired to her private den, a cool room finished in restful tints at the northeast corner of the house. She was sitting by a window reading a magazine, when there came a knock. Her "Come in" disclosed 'Rastus and the whites of his rolling eyes.

She nodded and smiled. "What can I do for you, George Washington Abraham Lincoln Randolph?"

"I done come to tell you somepin I heerd whilst I was asleep in de live oak at the corral."

"Something you dreamed. It is very good of you, George Wash—"

"Now, don't you call me all dat again, Miss Phyl. And I didn't dream it nerrer. I woke up and heerd it. Mr. Jim Yeager and dat nester they call Keller wuz a-talkin', and Mr. Jim he allowed dat Keller wuz a rustler, and den Keller he allowed dat Mr. Phil wuz de rustler."

"What!" The girl had sprung to her feet, amazed, her dark eyes blazing indignation.

"Tha's what he said. He went on to tell how he done found a knife by the dead cow, an' 'twuz yore knife, an' you done loan it to Mr. Phil."

"He said that!" She was a creature transformed by passion. The hot blood of Southern ancestors raced through her veins clamorously. She wanted to strike down this man, to annihilate him and the cowardly lie he had given to shield himself. And pat to her need came the very person she could best use for her instrument.

Healy stood surprised in the doorway, confronted by the slender young amazon. The storm of passion in the eyes, the underlying flush in the dusky cheeks, indicated a new mood in his experience of this young woman of many moods.

"Come in and shut the door," she ordered. Then, "Tell him, 'Rastus."

The boy, all smiles gone now, repeated his story, and was excused.

"What do you think of that, Brill?" the girl demanded, after the door had closed on him.

The stockman's eyes had grown hard. "I think Keller's covering his own tracks. Of course we've got no direct proof, but—"

"We have," she broke in.

"I can't see it. According to Jim Yeager—"

"Jim lied. I asked him to."

"You—what?"

"I asked him to say that this man had come there to work for him. Jim was not to blame."

"But—why?"

She threw out a gesture of self-contempt. "Why did I do it? I don't know. Because he was wounded, I suppose."

"Wounded! Then I did hit him?"

"Yes. In the arm—a flesh wound. I met him riding through the mesquite. After I had tied up his wound, I took him to Jim's."

His eyes narrowed slightly. "So you tied up his wound?"

"Yes," she answered defiantly, her head up.

"That tender heart of yours," he murmured, with almost a sneer.

"Yes. I'm a fool."

He shrugged his shoulders. "Oh, well."

"And he pays me back by trying to throw it on Phil. Hunt

him down, Brill. Bring him to me. I'll tell all I know against him," she cried vindictively.

"I'll get him, Phyl," he promised, and the sound of his laughter was not pleasant. "I'll get him for you, or find out why."

"Think of him trying to put it on Phil, and after I stood by him and kept his secret. Isn't that the worst ever?" the girl flamed.

"He rode away not five minutes ago as big as coffee on that ugly roan of his with the white stockings; knew what we thought about him, but didn't pay any more attention to us than as if we were bumps on a log."

Healy strode out to the porch, told his story, and within five minutes had organized his posse and appointed a rendezvous for two hours later at Seven Mile.

At the appointed time his men were on hand, six of them, armed with rifles and revolvers, ready for grim business.

From her window Phyllis saw them ride away, and persuaded herself that she was glad. Vengeance was about to fall upon this insolent freebooter who had not even manhood enough to appreciate a kindness. But as the hours passed she was beset by a consuming anxiety. What more likely than that he would resist! If so, there could be only one end. She could not keep her thoughts from those seven men whom she had sent against the one.

There was nobody to whom she could talk about it, for Phil and her father were away at Noches. Restless as a caged panther, she twice had her horse brought to the door, and rode into the hills to meet her posse. But she could not be sure which way they would come, and after venturing a short distance she would return for fear they might arrive in her absence. Night had fallen over the country, and the stars were out long before she got back the second time. Nine—ten—eleven o'clock struck, and still no sign of those for whom she waited.

At last they came, their prisoner riding in the midst, bareheaded and with his hands tied.

"I've got him, Phyl!" Healy cried in a voice that told the girl he was riding on a wave of triumph.

"I see you have."

Nevertheless she looked not at the victor, but at the vanquished, and never had she seen a man who looked more master of his fate than this one. He was smiling down at her whimsically, and she saw they had not taken him without a struggle. The marks of it were on them and on him. Healy's cheek bone was laid open in a nasty cut, and Slim had a handkerchief tied round his head.

As for Keller, his shirt was in ribbons and dyed with the stains of blood from the wound that had broken out again in the battle. The hair on the left side of his head was clotted with dried blood, and his cheeks were covered with it. Both eyes were blacked, and hands and face were scratched badly. But his mien was as jaunty, his smile as gallant, as if he had come at the head of a conquering army.

"Good evenin', Miss Sanderson," he bowed ironically.

She looked at him, and turned away without answering. She heard Healy curse softly and knew why. This man contrived somehow to rob him of his triumph.

"You are none of you hurt, Brill?" the girl asked in a low voice.

"No. He fought like a wild cat, but we took him by surprise. He had only his bare fists."

"How about him? Is he hurt?"

"I don't know—or care," the man answered sullenly.

"But he must be looked to."

"I don't know why. It ain't my fault we had to beat him up."

"I didn't say it *was* your fault, Brill," she answered gently. "But any one can see he has lost a lot of blood, and his wounds are full of dust. They must be washed. I want him brought into the house. Aunt Becky and I will look after him."

"No need of that. Slim will fix him up."

She shook her head. "No, Brill."

His eyes gave way first, but his surrender came with a bad grace.

"All right, Phyl. But he's going to be covered by a gun all the time. I'm not taking chances on him."

"Then have him taken into my den. I'll wake Aunt Becky and we'll be there in a few minutes."

When Phyllis arrived with Aunt Becky she found the nester sitting on the lounge, Healy opposite him with a revolver close to his hand. The prisoner's arms had been freed. His sardonic smile still twitched at the corners of his mouth.

"You've ce'tainly begun your practice on a disreputable patient, Doctor Sanderson. I haven't had time to comb my hair since that little seance with your friends. We sure did have a sociable time. They're all good mixers." He looked into the long glass opposite, laughed at sight of his swollen face, then rattled into a misquotation of some verses he remembered:

"There's many a black black eye, they say, but none so bright as mine; For I'm to be Queen o' the May, mother, I'm to be Queen o' the May."

"Put the water and things down on that table, Becky," her mistress told her, ignoring the man's blithe folly.

"I'm giving you lots of chances to do the Good Samaritan act," he continued. "Honest, I hate to be so much trouble. You'll have to blame Mr. Healy. He's the responsible party for these little accidents of mine."

"I'm going to be responsible for one more," the stockman told him darkly.

"I understand your intentions are good, but I've noticed that sometimes expectation outruns performance," his prisoner came back promptly.

"Not this time, I think."

Phyllis understood that Brill was threatening the nester and that the latter was defying him lightly, but what either meant precisely she did not know. She proceeded to business without a word except the necessary directions to Becky. Not until the arm was dressed and the wound on the head washed and bandaged did she address Keller.

"I'll send you a powder that will help you get to sleep. The doctor left it here for Phil, and he did not need it," she said.

"Mebbe I won't need it, either." Keller laughed hardily, at his enemy it seemed to the girl, and with some hint of a sinister understanding between them from which she was excluded. "Thanks just the same, for that and for everything else you've done for me."

Phyllis said "Good night" stiffly, and followed the old negress out. She went directly to her bedroom, but not to sleep. The night was hot, and it had been to her a day full of excitement. She had much to think of. Going to the open window, she sat down in a low chair with her arms across the sill.

Two men met beneath her window.

"Gimme the makings, Slim," one said to the other.

While he was shaking the tobacco from the pouch to the paper, Slim spoke. "The boys ought all to be here in another hour, Budd. After that, it won't take us long."

"Not long," the fat man answered uneasily.

There was a silence. Slim broke it. "We got to do it, o' course."

"Looks like. Got to make an example. No peace on the range till we do."

"I hate like sin to, Budd. He's so damn game."

"Me, too. But we got to. No two ways about it."

"I reckon. Brill says so. But I wish the cuss had a chanct to fight for his life."

They moved off together in troubled silence, Budd's cigarette glowing red in the darkness. Behind them they left a girl shocked and rigid. They were going to lynch him! She knew it as certainly as if she had been told it in set words. Her blood grew cold, and she shivered. While the confused horror of it raced through her brain, she noticed subconsciously that her fingers on the sill were trembling violently.

What could she do? She was only a girl. These men deferred to her in the trivial pleasantries, but she knew they would go their grim way no matter how she pleaded. And it would be her fault. She had betrayed the rustler to them. It would be the same as if she had murdered him. He had known while she was tending his wounds that she had delivered him to death, and he had not even reproached her.

Courage flowed back to her heart. She would save him if it were possible. It must be by strategy if at all. But how? For of course he was guarded.

She stepped out into the corridor. All was dark there. She tiptoed along it to the guest room, and found the door unlocked. Nobody was inside. She canvassed in her mind the possibilities. They might have him outdoors or in the men's bunk house with them under a guard, or they might have locked him up somewhere until the arrival of the others. If the latter, it must be in the store, since that was the only safe place under lock and key.

Phyllis slipped out of the back door into the darkness, and

skirted the house at a distance. There were lights in the bunk house of the ranch riders, and through the window she could see a group gathered. Creeping close to the window, she looked in. Their prisoner was not with them. In front of the store two men were seated in the darkness. She was almost upon them before she saw them. Each of them carried a rifle.

"Hello! Who's that?" one of them cried sharply.

It was Tom Dixon.

Phyllis came forward and spoke. "That you, Tom? I suppose you are guarding the prisoner."

"Yep. Can't you sleep, Phyl?" He walked a dozen yards with her.

"I couldn't, but I see you're keeping watch, all right. I probably can now. I suppose I was nervous."

"No wonder. But you may sleep, all right. He won't trouble you any. I'll guarantee that," he promised largely. "Oh, Phyl!"

She had turned to go, but she stopped at his call. "Well?"

"Don't you be mad at me. I was only fooling the other day. Course I hadn't ought to have got gay. But a fellow makes a break once in a while."

Under the stress of her deeper anxiety she had forgotten all about her tiff with him. It had seemed important at the time, but since then Tom and his affairs had been relegated to second place in her mind. He was only a boy, full of the vanity that was a part of him. Somehow, her anger against him was all burnt out.

"If you never will again, Tom," she conceded.

"I'll be good," he smiled, meaning that he would be good as long as he must.

"All right," she said, without much enthusiasm.

She left him and passed into the house without haste. But once inside she fairly flew to Phil's room. On a nail near the head of his bed hung a key. She took this, descended to the kitchen, and from there noiselessly down the stairway to the cellar. She groped her way without a light along the adobe wall till she came to a door which was unlocked. This opened into another part of the cellar, used as a room for storing supplies needed in their trade. Past barrels and boxes she went to another stairway and breathlessly ascended it. At the top of eight or nine steps a door barred progress. Very carefully she found the keyhole, fitted in the key, and by infinitesimal degrees unlocked the door.

The night seemed alive with the noise of her movements. Now the door creaked as it swung open before her. She waited, heart beating like a trip hammer, and stared into the blackness of the store.

"Who is it?" a voice asked in a low tone.

"It's me, Phyl Sanderson. Are you alone?" she whispered.

"Yes. Tied to a chair. Guards are just outside."

She went toward him softly with hands outstretched in the darkness, and presently her fingers touched his face. They travelled downward till they found the ropes which bound him. For a moment she fumbled at the knots before she remembered a swifter way.

"Wait," she breathed, and stole back of the counter to the case where pocketknives were kept.

Finding one, she ran to him and hacked at the rope till he was free.

He rose and stretched his cramped limbs.

"This way." Phyllis took him by the hand, and led him to the stairs. Together they descended, after she had locked the door. Another minute, and they stood in the kitchen, still hand in hand.

The girl released herself. "You will find Slim's horse tied to the fence of the corral. When you reach it, ride for your life," she said.

"Why have you saved me after you betrayed me?" he demanded.

"I save you because I did betray you. I couldn't have your blood on my head. Now, go."

"Not till I know why you betrayed me."

"*You* can ask that." Her indignation gathered and broke. "Because you are what you are. Because I know what you told Jim Yeager this afternoon. Why don't you go?"

"What did I tell Yeager? About the knife, you mean?"

"You tried to lay it on Phil to save yourself."

"Did Yeager tell you that?"

"No, but I know it," She pushed him toward the door. "Go,

while there is still a chance."

"I'm not going—not yet. Not till you promise to ask Yeager what I said."

A footstep sounded, and the door opened. The intruder stopped, his hand still on the handle, aware that there were others in the room.

"Who is it?" Phyllis breathed, stricken almost dumb with terror.

"It's Slim. Hope I ain't buttin' in, Phyllie."

Unconsciously he had given her the cue she needed.

"Well, you are." She laughed nervously, as might a lover caught unexpectedly. "It's—it's Phil," she pretended to pretend.

"Oh, it's Phil." Slim laughed in kindly derision, and declared before he went out: "I expect you would spell his name B-r-i-double l. Don't forget to invite me to the wedding, Phyllie. Meanwhile I'll be mum as a clam till you say the word."

With which he jingled away. The door was scarce closed before the girl turned on Keller.

"There! You see. They may catch you any moment."

"Will you ask Yeager?"

"Yes, if you'll go."

"All right. I'll go."

Still he did not leave. The magic of this slim girl had swept him from his feet. In imagination he still felt the touch of her warm fingers, soft as a caress, the thrill of her hair as it had brushed his cheek when she had stooped over him. The drag of sex was upon him and had set him trembling strangely.

"Why don't you go?" she cried softly.

He snatched himself away.

But before he had reached the door he came back in two strides. Startled and unnerved, she waited on him. He caught both her hands in his, and opened them wide so that she was drawn toward him by the swing of the motion. There for an instant he stood, looking down into her eyes by the faint light that sifted through the window upon her.

"What—what do you want?" she demanded tremulously, emotion flooding her in waves.

"Why are you saving me, girl?"

"I—don't know. I've told you why."

"I'm a villain, by your way of it, yet you save my life even while you think me a skunk. I can't thank you. What's the use of trying?"

He looked down into her eyes, and that gaze did more than thank her. It told her he would never forget and never let her forget. How it happened she could not afterward remember, but she found herself in his arms, his kiss tingling through her blood like wine.

She thrust him from her—and he was gone.

She sank into a chair beside the kitchen table, her pulses athrob with excitement. Scorn herself she might and would in good time, but just now her whole capacity for emotion was keyed to an agony of apprehension for this prince of scamps. By the beating of her galloping heart she timed his steps. He must have reached the horse now. Already he would have it untied, would be in the saddle. Surely by this time he had eluded the sentries and was slipping out of the danger zone. Before him lay the open road, the hills, and safety.

A cry rang out in the stillness—and another. A shot, the beat of running feet, a panted oath, more shots! The silent night had suddenly become vocal with action and the fierce passions of men. She covered her face with her hands to shut out the vision of what her imagination conjured—a horse flying with empty saddle into the darkness, while a huddled figure sank together lifeless by the roadside.

CHAPTER VI

A GOOD FRIEND

How long she remained there Phyllis did not know. Fear drummed at her heart. She was sick with apprehension. At last her very terror drove her out to learn the worst. She walked round to the front of the house and saw a light in the store. Swiftly she ran across and up the steps to the porch. Three men were inside examining the empty chair by the light of a lantern one held in his hand.

"Did—did he get away?" the girl faltered.

The men turned. One of them was Slim. He held in his hand pieces of the slashed rope and the open pocket-knife that had freed the prisoner.

"Looks like it," Slim answered. "With some help from a friend. Now, I wonder who that useful friend was and how in time he got in here?"

Her eyes betrayed her. Just for an instant they swept to the cellar door, to make sure it was still shut. But that one glance was enough. Slim, about to speak, changed his mind, and stared at her with parted lips. She saw suspicion grow in his face and resolve itself to certainty, helped to decision by the telltale color dyeing her cheeks.

"Does the cellar stairway from the store connect with the kitchen cellar, Phyllie?" he asked.

"Ye-es."

He nodded, then laughed without mirth. "I reckon I can tell you, boys, who Mr. Keller's friend in need is."

"Who? I'd like right well to know." Brill Healy, in a pallid fury, had just come in and was listening.

Phyllis turned and faced him. "I was that friend, Brill."

"You!" He stared at her in astonishment. "You! Why, it was you sent me out to run him down."

"I didn't tell you that I wanted you to murder him, did I?"

"I guess there's a lot between him and you that you didn't tell me," he jeered.

Slim grinned, not at all maliciously. "I reckon that's right. I don't need to ask you now, Phyllie, who it was I found with you in the kitchen."

"He was just going," she protested.

"Sure, and I busted into the good-bys right inconsiderate."

"Go ahead, Slim. I'm only a girl. You and Brill say what you like," she flashed at him, the nails of her fingers biting into the palms of her hands.

"Only don't say it out loud," cautioned a new voice. Jim

Yeager was at the door, and he was looking very pointedly at Healy.

"I say what I think, Jim," Brill retorted promptly.

"And you think?"

Healy slammed his fist down hard on the counter. "I think things ain't right when a Malpais girl helps a hawss thief and a rustler to escape twice."

"Take care, Brill," advised Phyllis.

"Not right how?" asked Yeager quietly, but in an ominous tone.

"Don't you two go to twisting my meaning. All Malpais knows that no better girl than Phyl Sanderson ever breathed."

The young woman's lip curled. "I'm grateful for this indorsement, sir," she murmured with mock humility.

"Do I understand that Keller has made his getaway?" Jim Yeager asked.

"He sure has—clean as a whistle."

"Then you idiots want to be plumb grateful to Phyllie. He ain't any more a rustler than I am. If you had hanged him you would have hanged an innocent man."

"Prove it," cried Healy.

Jim looked at him quietly. "I cayn't prove it just now. You'll have to take my word for it."

"Yore word goes with me, Jim, even if I am an idiot by yore say-so," his father announced promptly.

Jim smiled and let an arm fall across the shoulders of James Yeager, Senior. "I ain't countin' you in on that class, dad. You got to trailing with bad company. I'll have to bring you up stricter."

"I hate to be a knocker, Jim, but I've got to trust my own eyes before your indorsement," Healy sneered.

"That's your privilege, Brill."

"I reckon Jim knows what he's talking about," said Yeager, Senior, with intent to conciliate.

"Of course I know you're right friendly with him, Jim. There's nobody more competent to pass an opinion on him. Like enough you know all about his affairs," conceded Healy with polite malice.

The two young men were looking at each other steadily. They never had been friends, and lately they had been a good deal less than that. Rival leaders of the range for years, another cause had lately fanned their rivalry to a flame. Now a challenge had been flung down and accepted.

"I expect I know more about them than you do, Brill."

"Sure you do. Ain't he just got through being your guest? Didn't he come visiting you in a hurry? Didn't you tie up his wound? And when Phil and I came asking questions didn't you antedate his arrival about six hours? I'm not denying you know all about him. What I'm wondering is why you didn't tell all you knew. Of course, I understand they are your reasons, though, not mine."

"You've said it. They're my reasons."

"I ain't saying they are not good reasons. Whyfor should a man round on his friend?"

The innuendo was plain, and Yeager put it into words. "I'd be right proud to have him for a friend. But we all know what you mean, Brill. Go right ahead. Try and persuade the boys I'm a rustler, too. They haven't known me on an average much over twenty years. But that doesn't matter. They're so durned teachable to-day maybe you can get them to swallow that with the rest."

With which parting shot he followed Phyllis out of the store. She turned on him at the top of the porch steps leading to the house.

"Did he tell you that Phil was the rustler?"

"You mean did Keller tell me?" he said, surprised.

"Yes. 'Rastus was in the live oak and heard all you said."

"No. He didn't tell me that. We neither of us think it was Phil. It couldn't be, for he was riding with you at the time. But he found your knife there by the dead cow. Now, how did it come there? You let Phil have the knife. Had he lent his knife to some one?"

"I don't know." She went on, after a momentary hesitation: "Are you quite sure, Jim, that he really found the knife there?"

"He said so. I believe him."

She sighed softly, as if she would have liked to feel as sure.

"The reason I spoke of it was that I accused him of trying to throw the blame on Phil, and he told me to ask you about it."

Jim shook his head. "Nothing to it. If you want my opinion, Keller is white clear enough. He wouldn't try a trick like that."

The girl's face lit, and she held out an impulsive hand. "Anyhow, you're a good friend, Jim."

"I've been that ever since you was knee high to a duck, Phyl."

"Yes—yes, you have. The best I've got, next to Phil and Dad." Her heart just now was very warm to him.

"Don't you reckon maybe a good friend might make a good—something else."

She gasped. "Oh, Jim! You don't mean—"

"Yep. That's what I do mean. Course I'm not good enough. I know that."

"Good. You're the best ever. It isn't that. Only I don't like you that way."

"Maybe you might some day."

She shook her head slowly. "I wish I could, Jim. But I never will."

"Is there—someone else, Phyl?"

If it had been light enough he could have seen a wave of color sweep her face.

"No. Of course there isn't. How could there be? I'm only a girl."

"It ain't Brill then?"

"No. It's—it isn't anybody." She carried the war, womanlike, into his camp. "And I don't believe you care for me—that way. It's just a fancy."

"One I've had two years, little girl."

"Oh, I'm sorry. I *do* like you, better than any one else. You know that, dear old Jim."

He smiled wistfully. "If you didn't like me so well I reckon I'd have a better chance. Well, I mustn't keep you here. Good night."

Her ringers were lost in his big fist. "Good night, Jim." And again she added, "I'm so sorry."

"Don't you be. It's all right with me, Phyl. I just thought I'd mention it. You never can tell, though I most knew how it would be. *Buenos noches, nina.*"

He released her hand, and without once looking back strode to his horse, swung to the saddle, and rode into the night.

She carried into the house with her a memory of his cheerful smile. It had been meant as a reassurance to her. It told her he would get over it, and she knew he would. For he was no puling schoolboy, but a man, game to the core.

The face of another man rose before her, saturnine and engaging and debonair. With the picture came wave on wave of shame. He was a detected villain, and she had let him kiss her. But beneath the self-scorn was something new, something that stung her blood, that left her flushed and tingling with her first experience of sex relations.

A week ago she had not yet emerged fully from the chrysalis of childhood. But in the Southland flowers ripen fast. Adolescence steals hard upon the heels of infancy. Nature was pushing her relentlessly toward a womanhood for which her splendid vitality and unschooled impulses but scantily safeguarded her. The lank, shy innocence of the fawn still wrapped her, but in the heart of this frank daughter of the desert had been born a poignant shyness, a vague, delightful trembling that marked a change. A quality which had lain banked in her nature like a fire since childhood now threw forth its first flame of heat. At sunset she had been still treading the primrose path of youth; at sunrise she had entered upon the world-old heritage of her sex.

CHAPTER VII

A SHOT FROM AMBUSH

From the valley there drifted up a breeze-swept sound. The rider on the rock-rim trail above, shifting in his saddle to one of the easy, careless attitudes of the habitual horseman, recognized it as a rifle shot.

Presently, from a hidden wash rose little balloon-like puffs of smoke, followed by a faint, far popping, as if somebody had touched off a bunch of firecrackers. Men on horseback, dwarfed by distance to pygmy size, clambered to the bank—now one and then another firing into the mesquite that ran like a broad tongue from the roll of hills into the valley.

"Looks like something's broke loose," the young man drawled aloud. "The band's sure playing a right lively tune this glad mo'ning."

Save for one or two farewell shots, the firing ceased. The riders had disappeared into the chaparral.

The rider did not need to be told that this was a man hunt, destined perhaps to be one of a hundred unwritten desert tragedies. Some subtle instinct in him differentiated between these hurried shots and those born of the casual exuberance of the cow-puncher at play. He had a reason for taking an interest in it—an interest that was more than casual.

Skirting the rim of the saucer-shaped valley, he rode forward warily, came at length to a canon that ran like a sword cleft into the hills, and descended cautiously by a cattle trail, its scarred slope.

Through the defile ran a mountain stream, splashing over and round boulders in its swift fall.

"I reckon we'll slide down, Keno, and work out close to the fire zone," the rider said to his horse, as they began to slither down the precipitous slope, starting rubble at every motion.

Man and horse were both of the frontier, fit to the minute for any call that might be made on them. The broncho was a roan, with muscles of elastic leather, sure-footed as a mountain goat. Its master—a slim, brown man, of medium height, well knit and muscular—looked on the world, quietly and often humorously, with shrewd gray eyes.

As he reached the bottom of the gulch, his glance fell upon another rider—a woman. She crossed the stream hurriedly, her pony flinging water at every step, and cantered up toward him.

Her glance was once and again over her shoulder, so that it was not until she was almost upon him that she saw the young man among the cottonwoods, and drew her pony to an instant halt. The rifle that had been lying across her saddle leaped halfway to her shoulder, covering him instantly.

"*Buenos dios, senorita.* Are you going for to shoot my head off?" he drawled.

"The rustler!" she cried.

"The alleged rustler, Miss Sanderson," he corrected gently.

"Let me past," she panted.

He observed that her eyes mirrored terror of the scene she had just left.

"It's you that has got the drop on me, isn't it?" he suggested.

The rifle went back to the saddle. Instantly the girl was in motion again, flying up the canon past the white-stockinged roan, her pony's hindquarters gathered to take the sheep trail like those of a wild cat.

Keller gazed after her. As she disappeared, he took off his hat, bowed elaborately, and remarked to himself, in his low, soft drawl:

"Good mo'ning, ma'am. See you again one of these days, mebbe, when you ain't in such a hurry."

But though he appeared to take the adventure whimsically his mind was busy with its meaning. She was in danger, and he must save her. So much he knew at least.

He had scarcely turned the head of his horse toward the mouth of the canon when the pursuit drove headlong into sight. Galloping men pounded up the arroyo, and came to halt at his sharp summons. Already Keller and his horse were behind a huge boulder, over the top of which gleamed the short barrel of a wicked-looking gun.

"Mornin', gentlemen. Lost something up this gulch, have you?" he wanted to know amiably.

William MacLeod Raine

The last rider, coming to a gingerly halt in order not to jar an arm bandaged roughly in a polka-dot bandanna, swore roundly. He was a large, heavy-set man, still on the sunny side of forty, imperious, a born leader, and, by the look of him, not one lightly to be crossed.

"He's our man, boys. We'll take him alive if we can; but, dead or alive, he's ours." He gave crisp orders.

"Oh! It's me you've lost? Any reward?" inquired the man behind the rock.

For answer, a bullet flattened itself against the boulder. The wounded man had whipped up a rifle and fired.

Keller called out a genial warning. "I wouldn't do that. There's too many of you bunched close together, and this old gun spatters like hail. You see, it's loaded with buckshot."

One of the cowboys laughed. He was rather a cool hand himself, but such audacity as this was new to him.

"What's ailing you, Pesky? It don't strike me as being so damned amusing," growled his leader.

"Different here, Buck. I was just grinning because he's such a cheerful guy. Of course, I ain't got one of his pills in my arm, like you have."

"He won't be so gay about it when he's down, with a couple of bullets through him," predicted the other grimly. "But we'll take his advice, just the same. You boys scatter. Cross the creek and sneak up along the other wall, Ned. Curly, you and Irwin climb up this side until you get him in sight. Pesky and I will stay here."

"Hold on a minute! Let's get at the rights of this. What's all the row about?" the cornered man wanted to know.

"You know dashed well what it's about, you blanked bushwhacker. But you didn't shoot straight enough, and you didn't fix it so you could make your getaway. I'm going to hang you high as Haman."

"Thank you. But your intentions aren't directed to the right man. I'm a stranger in this country. Whyfor should I want to shoot you?"

"A stranger. Where from?" demanded Buck Weaver crisply.

"Douglas."

"What doing here?"

"Homesteading."

"Name?"

"Keller."

"Killer, you mean, I reckon. You're a hired assassin, brought in to shoot me. That's what you are."

"No."

"Yes. The man we want came into this gulch, not three minutes ahead of us. If you're not the man, where is he?"

"I haven't got him in my vest pocket."

"I reckon you've got him right there in your coat and pants."

"I ain't so dead sure, Buck," spoke up Pesky. "We didn't see the man so as to know him."

"Riding a roan, wasn't he?" snapped the owner of the Twin Star outfit.

"Looked that way," admitted the cowpuncher.

"Well, then?"

"Keller! Why, that's the name given by the rustler who broke away from us two weeks ago," Curly spoke out.

"No use jawing. I'm going to hang his skin up to dry," Weaver ground out between set teeth.

"By his own way of it, he's only one of them dashed nesters," Irwin added.

Keller was putting two and two together, in amazement. The would-be assassin had, during the past few minutes, been driven into this gulch, riding a roan horse. He could swear that only one person had come in before these pursuers—and that one was a woman on a roan. Her frightened eyes, the fear that showed in every motion, her hurried flight, all contributed to the same inevitable conclusion. It was difficult to believe it, but impossible to deny. This wild, sylvan creature, with the shy, wonderful eyes, had lain in ambush to kill her father's enemy, and was flying from the vengeance on her heels.

His lips were sealed. Even if he were not under heavy obligations to her he could no more save himself at the expense of this brown sylph than he could have testified against his own mother.

"All right. If you feel lucky, come on. You'll get me, of course, but it may prove right expensive," he said quietly.

"That's all right. We're footing our end of the bill," Pesky retorted.

By this time, he and Weaver had dismounted, and were sheltered behind rocks. Already bullets were beginning to spit back and forth, though the flankers had not yet got into action.

"Durn his hide, I hate like sin to puncture it," Pesky told his boss. "I tell you we're making a mistake, Buck. This fellow's a pure—he ain't any hired killer. You can tie to that."

"He's the man that pumped a bullet into my arm from ambush. That's enough for me," the cattleman swore.

"No use being revengeful, especially if it happens he ain't the man. By his say-so, that's a shotgun he's carrying. Loaded with buckshot, he claims. What hit you was a bullet from a Winchester, or some such gun. Mighty easy to prove whether he's lying."

"We'll be able to prove it afterward, all right."

"What's the matter with proving it now? I don't stand for any murder business myself. I'm going to find out what's what."

The cow-puncher tied the red bandanna from his neck round the end of his revolver, and shoved it above the rock in front of him.

"Flag of truce!" he shouted.

"All right. Come right along. Better leave your gun behind,"

William MacLeod Raine

Keller called back.

Pesky waddled forward—a short, thick-set, bow-legged man in chaps, spurs, flannel shirt, and white sombrero. When he took off this last, as he did now, it revealed a head bald as a billiard ball.

"How're they coming?" he inquired genially of the besieged man, as he rounded the rock barricade.

Larrabie's steel eyes relaxed to a hint of a friendly smile. He knew this type of man like a brother.

"Fine and dandy here. Hope you're well yourself, seh."

"Tol'able. Buck's up on his ear, o' course. Can't blame him, can you? Most any man would, with that kind of a pill sent to his address so sudden by special delivery. Wasn't that some inconsiderate of you, Mr. Keller?"

"I thought I explained it was another party did that."

Pesky rolled a cigarette and lit it.

"Right sure of that, are you? Wouldn't mind my taking a look at that gun of yours? You see, if it happens to be what you said it was, that kinder lets you out."

Keller handed over the gun promptly. The cow-puncher broke it, extracted a shell, and with his knife picked out the wad. Into his palm rolled a dozen buckshot.

"Good enough! I told Buck he was barking up the wrong tree. Now, I'll go back and have a powwow with him. I reckon you'll be willing to surrender on guarantee of a square deal?"

"Sure—that's all I ask. I never met your friend—didn't know who he was from Adam. I ain't got any option to shoot all the red-haided men I meet. No, sir! You've followed a cross trail."

"Looks like. Still, it's blamed funny." Pesky scratched his shining poll, and looked shrewdly at the other. "We certainly ran Mr. Bushwhacker into the canon. I'd swear to that. We was right on his heels, though we couldn't see him very well. But he either come in here or a hole in the ground swallowed him."

He waited tentatively for an answer, but none came other than the white-toothed smile that met him blandly.

"I reckon you know more than you aim to tell, Mr. Keller," continued Pesky. "Don't you figure it's up to you, if we let you out of this thing, to whack up any information you've got? The kind of reptile that kills from ambush don't deserve any consideration."

Half an hour ago, the other would have agreed with him. The man that shot his enemy from cover was a coyote—nothing less. But about that brown slip of a creature, who had for three minutes crossed his orbit, he wanted to reserve judgment.

"I expect I haven't got a thing to tell you that would help any," he drawled, his eye full on that of the cowpuncher.

Pesky threw away his cigarette. "All right. You're the doctor. I'll amble back, and report to the boss."

He did so, with the result that a truce was arranged.

Keller gave up his post of vantage, and came forward

to surrender.

Weaver met him with a hard, wintry eye. "Understand, I don't concede your innocence. You're my prisoner, and, by God, if I get any more proof of your guilt, you've got to stand the gaff."

The other nodded quietly, meeting him eye to eye. Nor did his gaze fall, though the big cattleman was the most masterful man on the range. Keller was as easy and unperturbed as when he had been holding half a dozen irate men at bay.

"No kick coming here. But, if it's just the same to you, I'll ask you to get the proof first and hang me afterward."

"If you're homesteading, where's your place?"

"Back in the hills, close to the headwaters of Salt Creek."

"Huh! You'll make that good before I get through with you. And I want to tell you this, too, Mr. Keller. It doesn't make any hit with me that you're one of those thieving nesters. Moreover, there's another charge against you. In the Malpais country we hang rustlers. The boys claim to have you cinched. We'll see."

"Who's that with Curly?" Pesky called out. "By Moses, it's a woman!"

"It is the Sanderson girl," Weaver said in surprise.

Keller swung round as if worked by a spring. The cowpuncher had told the truth. Curly's companion was not only a woman, but *the* woman—the same slim, tanned creature who had flashed past him on a wild race for safety, only a few minutes earlier.

All eyes were focused upon her. Weaver waited for her to speak. Instead, Curly took up the word. He was smiling broadly, quite unaware of the mine he was firing.

"I found this young lady up on the rock rim. Since we were rounding up, I thought I'd bring her down."

"Good enough. Miss Sanderson, you've been where you could see if anyone passed into the canon. How about it? Anybody go up in last ten minutes?"

Phyllis moistened her dry lips and looked at the prisoner. "No," she answered reluctantly.

Weaver wheeled on Keller, his eyes hard as jade. "That ties the rope round your neck, my man."

"No," Phyllis cried. "He didn't do it."

The cattleman's stone wall eyes were on her now.

"Didn't? How do you know he didn't?"

"Because I—I passed him here as I rode up a few minutes ago."

"So you rode up a few minutes ago." Buck's lids narrowed. "And he was here, was he? Ever meet Mr. Keller before?"

"Yes."

"When? Speak up. Mind, no lying."

This, struck the first spark of spirit from her. The deep eyes flashed. "I'm not in the habit of lying, sir."

"Then answer my question."

"I've met him at the office when he came for his mail. And the boys arrested him by mistake for a rustler. I saw him when they brought him in."

"By mistake. How do you know it was by mistake?"

"It was I accused him. But I did it because I was angry at him."

"You accused an innocent man of rustling because you were sore at him. You're ce'tainly a pleasant young lady, Miss Sanderson."

Her look flashed defiance at him, but she said nothing. In her slim erectness was a touch of feminine ferocity that gave him another idea.

"So you just rode into the canon, did you?"

"Yes."

"Meet up with anybody in the valley before you came in?"

"No."

His eyes were like steel drills. They never left her. "Quite sure?"

"Yes."

"What were you doing there?"

She had no answer ready. Her wild look went round in search of a friend in this circle of enemies. They found him in the man who was a prisoner. His steadfast eyes told her to have no fear.

"Did you hear what I said?" demanded Weaver.

"I was—riding."

"Alone?"

The answer came so slowly that it was barely audible. "Yes."

"Riding in Antelope Valley?"

"Yes."

"Let me see that gun." Weaver held out his hand for the rifle.

Phyllis looked at him and tried to fight against his domination; then slowly she handed him the rifle. He broke and examined it. From the chamber he extracted an empty shell.

Grim as a hanging judge, his look chiselled into her.

"I expect the lead that was in here is in my arm. Isn't that right?"

"I—I don't know."

"Who does, then? Either you shot me or you know who did."

Her gaze evaded his, but was forced at last to the meeting.

"I did it."

She was looking at him steadily now. Since the thing must

William MacLeod Raine

be faced, she had braced herself to it. It was amazing what defiant pluck shone out of her soft eyes. This man of iron saw it, and, seeing, admired hugely the gameness that dwelt in her slim body. But none of his admiration showed in the hard, weather-beaten face.

"So they make bushwhackers out of even the girls among your rustling, sheep-herding outfit!" he taunted.

"My people are not rustlers. They have a right to be on earth, even if you don't want them there."

"I'll show them what rights they have got in this part of the country before I get through with them. But that ain't the point now. What I want to know is how they came to send a girl to do their dirty killing for them."

"They didn't send me. I just saw you, and—and shot on an impulse. Your men have clubbed and poisoned our sheep. They wounded one of our herders, and beat his brother when they caught him unarmed. They have done a hundred mean and brutal things. You are at the bottom of it all; and when I saw you riding there, looking like the lord of all the earth, I just—"

"Well?"

"Couldn't help—what I did."

"You're a nicely brought up young woman—about as savage as the rest of your wolf breed," jeered Weaver.

Yet he exulted in her—in the impulse of ferocity that had made her strike swiftly, regardless of risk to herself, at the man who had hounded and harried her kin to the feud that was now raging. Her shy, untamed beauty would not itself have attracted him; but in combination with her fierce courage it made to him an appeal which he conceded grudgingly.

"What in Heaven's name brought you back after you had once got away?" Weaver asked.

The girl looked at Keller without answering.

"I reckon I can tell you that, seh," explained that young man. "She figured you would jump on me as the guilty party. It got on her conscience that she had left an innocent man to stand for it. I shouldn't wonder but she got to seeing a picture of you-all hanging me or shooting me up. So she came back to own up, if she saw you had caught me."

Weaver nodded. "That's the way I figure it, too. Gamest thing I ever saw a woman do," he said in an undertone to Keller, with whom he was now standing a little apart.

The latter agreed. "Never saw the beat of it. She's scared stiff, too. Makes it all the pluckier. What will you do with her?"

"Take her along with me back to the ranch."

"I wouldn't do that," said the young man quickly.

"Wouldn't you?" Weaver's hard gaze went over him haughtily. "When I want your advice, I'll ask you for it, young man. You're in luck to get off scot-free yourself. That ought to content you for one day."

"But what are you going to do with her? Surely not have her imprisoned for attacking you?"

"I'll do as I dashed please, and don't you forget it, Mr. Keller. Better mind your own business, if you've got any."

With which Buck Weaver turned on his heel, and swung slowly to the saddle. His arm was paining him a great deal, but he gave no sign of it. He expected his men to game it out when they ran into bad luck, and he was stoic enough to set them an example without making any complaints.

The little group of riders turned down the trail, passed through the gateway that led to the valley below, and wound down among the cow-backed hills toward the ranch roofs, which gleamed in the distance. They were the houses of the Twin Star outfit, the big concern owned by Buck Weaver, whose cattle fed literally upon a thousand hills.

It suited Buck's ironic humor to ride beside the girl who had just attempted his life. He bore her no resentment. Had the offender been a man, Buck would have snuffed out his life with as little remorse as he would a guttering candle. But her sex and her youth, and some quality of charm in her, had altered the equation. He meant to show her who was master, but he would choose a different method.

What sport to tame the spirit of this wild desert beauty until she should come like one of her own sheep dogs at his beck and call! He had never yet met the woman he could not dominate. This one, too, would know a good many new emotions before she rejoined her tribe in the hills.

He swung from the saddle at the ranch plaza, and greeted her with a deep bow that mocked her.

"Welcome, Miss Sanderson, to the best the Twin Star outfit has to offer. I hope you will enjoy your visit, which is going to be a long one."

To a Mexican woman, who had come out to the porch in answer to his call, he delivered the girl, charging her duty in two quick sentences of Spanish. The woman nodded her understanding, and led Phyllis inside.

Weaver noticed with delight that his captive's eye met his steadily, with the defiant fierceness of some hunted wild thing. Here was a woman worth taming, even though she was still a girl in years. His exultant eye, returning from the last glimpse of the lissom figure as it disappeared, met the gaze of Keller. That young man was watching him with an odd look of challenge on his usually impassive face.

The cattleman felt the spur of a new antagonism stirring his blood. There was something almost like a sneer on his lips as he spoke:

"Sorry to lose your company, Mr. Keller. But if you're homesteading, of course, we'll have to let you go back to the hills right away. Couldn't think of keeping you from that spring plowing that's waiting to be done."

"You're putting up a different line of talk from what you did. How about that charge of rustling against me, Mr. Weaver? Don't you want to hold me while you investigate it?"

"No, I reckon not. Your lady friend gives you a clean bill of health. She may or may not be lying. I'm not so sure myself. But without her the case against you falls."

Keller knew himself dismissed cavalierly, and, much as he would have liked to stay, he could find no further excuse to urge. He could hardly invite himself to be either the guest or the prisoner of a man who did not want him.

"Just as you say," he nodded, and turned carelessly to his pony.

Yet he was quite sure it would not be as Weaver said if he could help it. He meant to take a hand in the game, no matter what the other might decree. But for the present he acquiesced in the inevitable. Weaver was technically within his rights in holding her until he had communicated with the sheriff. A generous foe might not have stood out for his pound of flesh, but Buck was as hard as nails. As for the reputation of the girl, it was safe at the Twin Star ranch. Buck's sister, a maiden lady of uncertain years, was on hand to play chaperone.

Larrabie swung to the saddle. His horse's hoofs were presently flinging dirt toward the Twin Star as he loped up to the hills.

CHAPTER VIII

MISS-GOING-ON-EIGHTEEN

Time had been when the range was large enough for all, when every man's cattle might graze at will from horizon to horizon. But with the push of settlement to the frontier had come a change. The feeding ground became overstocked. One outfit elbowed another, and lines began to be drawn between the runs of different owners. Water holes were seized and fenced, with or without due process of law.

With the establishment of forest reserves a new policy dominated the government. Sanderson had been one of the first to avail himself of it by leasing the public demesne for his stock. Later, learning that the mountain parks were to be thrown open as a pasturage for sheep, he had bought three thousand and driven them up, having first arranged terms with the forestry service.

Buck Weaver, fighting the government reserve policy with all his might, resented fiercely the attitude of Sanderson. A sharp, bitter quarrel had resulted, and had left a smoldering bad feeling that flamed at times into open warfare. Upon the wholesome Malpais country had fallen the bitterness of a sheep and cattle feud.

William MacLeod Raine

The riders of the Twin Star outfit had thrice raided the Sanderson flocks. Lambing sheep had been run cruelly. One herd had been clubbed over a precipice, another decimated with poison. In return, the herders shot and hamstrung Twin Star cows. A herder was held up and beaten by cowboys. Next week a vaquero galloped home to the Twin Star ranch with a bullet through his leg. This was the situation at the time when the owner of the big ranch brought Phyllis a prisoner to its hospitality.

Nothing could have been more pat to his liking. He was, in large measure, the force behind the law in San Miguel county. The sheriff whom he had elected to office would be conveniently deaf to any illegality there might be in his holding the girl, would if necessary give him an order to hold her there until further notice. The attempt to assassinate him would serve as excuse enough for a proceeding even more highhanded than this. Her relatives could scarce appeal to the law, since the law would then step in and send her to the penitentiary. He could use her position as a hostage to force her stiff-necked father to come to terms.

But it was characteristic of the man that his reason for keeping her was, after all, less the advantage he might gain by it than the pleasure he found in tormenting her and her family. To this instinct of the jungle beast was added the interest she had inspired in him. Untaught of life she was, no doubt, a child of the desert, in some ways primitive as Eve; but he perceived in her the capacity for deep feeling, for passion, for that kind of fierce, dauntless endurance it is given some women to possess.

Miss Weaver took charge of the comfort of her guest. Her manner showed severe disapproval of this girl so lost to the feelings of her sex as to have attempted murder. That she was young and pretty made matters worse. Alice Weaver always had worshipped her brother, by the law of opposites perhaps. She was as drab and respectable as Boston. All her tastes ran to humdrum monotony. But turbulent, lawless Buck, the brother whom she had brought up after the death of their mother, held her heart in the hollow of his hard, careless hand.

"Have you had everything you wish?" she would ask Phyllis in a frigid voice.

"I want to be taken home."

"You should have thought of that before you did the dreadful thing you did."

"You are holding me here a prisoner, then?"

"An involuntary guest, my brother puts it. Until the sheriff can make other arrangements."

"You have no right to do it without notifying my father. He is at Noches with my brother."

"Mr. Weaver will do as he thinks best about that." The spinster shut her lips tight and walked from the room.

Supper was brought to Phyllis by the Mexican woman. In spite of her indignation she ate and slept well. Nor did her appetite appear impaired next morning, when she break-fasted in her bedroom. Noon found her promoted to the family dining room. Weaver carried his arm in a sling, but made no reference to the fact. He attempted conversation, but Phyllis withdrew into herself and had nothing more friendly than a plain "No" or "Yes" for him. His sister was presently called away to arrange some household difficulty. At once Phyllis attacked the big man lounging in his chair at his ease.

"I want to go home. I've got to be at the schoolhouse to-morrow morning," she announced.

"It won't hurt you any to miss a few days' schooling, my dear. You'll learn more here than you will there, anyhow," he assured her pleasantly. Buck was cracking two walnuts in the palm of his hand and let his lazy smile drift her way only casually.

She stamped her foot. "I tell you I'm the teacher. It is necessary I should be there."

"You a schoolmarm!" he repeated, in surprise. "How old are you?"

Her dress was scarcely below her shoe tops. She still had the slimness of immature girlhood, the adorable shy daring of some uncaptured wood nymph.

"Does that matter to you, sir?"

"How old?" he reiterated.

"Going-on-eighteen," she answered—not because she wanted to, but because somehow she must. There was something compelling about this man's will. She would have resisted it had she not wanted to gain her point about going home.

"So you teach the kids their A B C's, do you? And you just out of them yourself! How many scholars have you?"

"Fourteen."

"And they all love teacher, of course. Would you take me for a scholar, Miss Going-On-Eighteen?"

"No!" she flamed.

"You'd find me right teachable. And I would promise to love you, too."

Color came and went in her face beneath the brow. How dared he mock her so! It humiliated and embarrassed and angered her.

"Are you going to let me go back to my school?" she demanded.

"I reckon your school will have to get along without you for a few days. Your fourteen scholars will keep right on loving you, I expect. 'To memory dear, though far from eye.' Or, if you like, I'll send my boys up into the hills, and round up the whole fourteen here for you. Then school can keep right here in the house. How about that? Ain't that a good notion, Miss Going-On-Eighteen?"

She could stand his ironic mockery no longer. She faced him, fearless as a tiger: "You villain!"

With that, turning on her heel, she passed swiftly into her little bedroom, and slammed the door. He heard the key turn in the lock.

"She's sure got some devil in her," he laughed appreciatively, and he cracked another walnut.

Already he had struck the steel of her quality. She would be his prisoner because she must, but the "no compromise" flag was nailed to her masthead.

"I wonder why you are so fond of me?" he mused aloud next day when he found her as unresponsive to his advances as a block of wood.

He was lying in the sand at her feet, his splendid body relaxed full length at supple ease. Leaning on an elbow, he had been watching her for some time.

Her gaze was on the distant line of hills; on her face that far-away expression which told him that he was not on the map for her. Used as he was to impressing himself upon the imagination of women, this stung his vanity sharply. He liked better the times when her passion flamed out at him.

Now he lost his sardonic mockery in a flash of anger.

"Do you hear me? I asked you a question."

She brought her head round until her eyes rested upon him.

"Will you ask it again, please? I wasn't listening."

"I want to know what makes you hate me so," he demanded roughly.

"Do I hate you?"

He laughed irritably. "What else do you call it? You won't hardly eat at the same table with me. Last night you wouldn't come down to supper. Same way this morning. If I sit down near you, soon you find an excuse to leave. When I speak, you don't answer."

"You are my jailer, not my friend."

"I might be both."

"No, thank you!"

She said it with such quick, instinctive certainty that he ground his teeth in resentment. He was the kind of man that always wanted what he could not get. He began to covet this girl mightily, even while he told himself that he was a fool for his pains. What was she but an untaught, country schoolgirl? It would be a strange irony of fate if Buck Weaver should fall in love with a sheepman's daughter.

"Many people would go far to get my friendship," he told her.

Quietly she looked at him. "The friends of my people are my friends. Their enemies are mine."

"Yet you said you didn't hate me."

"I thought I did, but I find I don't."

"Not worth hating, I suppose?"

She neither corrected nor rejected his explanation.

He touched his wounded arm as he went on: "If you don't hate me, why this compliment to me? I reckon good, genuine hate sent that bullet."

The girl colored, but after a moment's hesitation answered:

"Once I shot a coyote when I saw it making ready to pounce on one of our lambs. I did not hate that coyote."

"Thank you," he told her ironically.

Her gaze went back to the mountains. She had always had a

William MacLeod Raine

capacity for silence. But it was as extraordinary to her as to him how, in the past few days, she had sloughed the shy timidity of a mountain girl and found the enduring courage of womanhood. Her wits, too, had taken on the edge of maturity. He found that her tongue could strike swiftly and sharply. She was learning to defend herself in all the ways women have acquired by inheritance.

Weaver's jaw set like a vise. Getting to his feet, he looked down at her with the hard, relentless eyes that had made his name a terror.

"Good enough, Miss Phyllis Sanderson. You've chosen your way. I'll choose mine. You've got to learn that I'm master here; and, by God, I'll teach it to you. Before I get through with you, young woman, you'll come running when I snap my fingers. From to-day things will be different. You'll eat your meals with us and not in your room. You'll speak when you're spoken to. Set yourself up against me, and I'll bring you to your knees fast enough. There's no law on the Twin Star Ranch but Buck Weaver's will."

He strode away, almost herculean in figure, and every inch of him forceful. She had never seen such a man, one so virile and, at the same time, so wilful and so masterful. Before he was out of her sight, she got an instance of his recklessness.

A Mexican vaquero was driving some horses into a corral. His master strode up to him, and dragged him from the saddle.

"Didn't I tell you to take the colts down to the long pasture?"

"*Si, senor,*" answered the trembling native.

Weaver's great fist rose and fell once. The Mexican sank

limply down. Without another glance at him, the cattleman flung him aside, and strode to the house.

As the owner of the Twin Star had said, so it was. Thereafter Phyllis sat at the table with him and his sister, while Josephine, the Mexican woman, waited upon them. The girl came and went at his bidding. But she held herself with such a quiet aloofness that his victory was a barren one.

"Do you want to go home?" he taunted her one morning, while at breakfast.

"Is it likely I would want to stay here?" she retorted.

"Why not? What have you to complain of? Aren't you treated well?"

"Yes."

"What, then? Are you afraid?"

"No!" she answered, with a flash of her fine eyes.

"That's good, because you've got to stay here—or go to the pen. You may take your choice."

"You're very generous. I suppose you don't expect to keep me here always," she said scornfully.

"Until my arm gets well. Since you wounded it you ought to nurse it."

"Which I am not doing, even while I am here."

"Anyhow it soothes the temper of the invalid to have you around." He grinned satirically.

"So I judge, from the effects."

"Meaning that I'm always in a rage when I leave you?"

"I notice your men are marked up a good deal these days."

"I'll tell them to thank you for it," he flung back.

Two days later, he scored on her hard for the first time. She came down to breakfast just as two of the Twin Star riders brought a boy into the hall.

She flew instantly into his arms, thereby embarrassing him vastly.

"Phil! How did you come here?"

Her brother nodded toward Curly and Pesky. "They found me outside and got the drop on me."

"You were here looking for me?"

"Yes. Just got back from Noches. Dad is still there. He don't know."

"But—what are they going to do with you?"

"What would you suggest, Miss Phyllis?" a voice behind her gibed.

The speaker was Weaver. He filled the doorway of the dining room triumphantly. She had had no fears for herself; he would see if she had none for her brother.

The boy whirled on the ranchman like a tiger whelp. "I don't care what you do. Go ahead and do your worst."

Weaver looked him over negligently, much as he might watch a struggling calf. To him the boy was not an enemy—merely a tool which he could use for his own ends. Phyllis, watching anxiously the hard, expressionless face, felt that it was cruel as fate. She knew that somehow she would be made to suffer through her love for her brother.

"You daren't touch him. He's done nothing," she cried.

"He shot at one of my riders. I can't have dangerous characters around. I'm a peaceable man, me," grinned Buck.

"You didn't, Phil," his sister reproached.

"Sure I did. He tried to take my gun from me," the boy explained hotly.

"Take him out to the bunk house, boys. I'll attend to him later," nodded Buck, turning away indifferently.

Stung to fury by the cavalier manner of his enemy, the boy leaped at him like a wild cat. Weaver whirled round again, caught him by the shoulder with his great hand, and shook him as if he had been a puppy. When he dropped him, he nodded again to his men, who dragged out the struggling boy.

Phyllis stood straight as an arrow, but white to the lips. "What are you going to do to him?" she asked.

"How would a good chapping do, to start with? That is always good for an unlicked cub."

"Don't!" she implored.

"But, my dear, why not—since it's for his good?"

Passion unleashed leaped from her. "You coward!"

He shrugged his shoulders. "I'm right desolated to have your bad opinion. But you say it almost as if you did hate me. That's a compliment, you know. You didn't hate the coyote, you mentioned."

Her eyes flamed. "Hate you! If wishes could kill, you would be a thousand times dead!"

"You disappoint me, my dear. I expected more than wishes from you. There's a loaded revolver in that table drawer. It's yours, any time you want it," he derided.

"Don't tempt me!" she cried wildly. "If you lay a hand on Phil, I'll use it—I surely will."

His eyes shone with delight. "I wonder. By Jove, I've a mind to flog the colt and see. I'll do it."

The passion sank in her as suddenly as it had risen. "No—you mustn't! You don't know him—or us. We are from the South."

"That settles it. I will," he exulted. "You have called me a coward. Would a coward do this, and defy your whole crew to its revenge?"

"Would a brave man break the pride of a high-spirited boy for such a mean motive?" she countered.

"His pride will have to look out for itself. He took his chance of it when he tried to assault me. What he'll get is only what's coming to him."

"Please don't! I'll—I'll be different to you. Take it out on me," she begged.

He laughed harshly. "Do you suppose I'm such a fool as not to know that the way to take it out on you is to take it out of him?"

She had come nearer, a step at a time. Now she threw her hand out in a gesture of abandon.

"Be generous! Don't punish me that way. Something dreadful will come of it."

She broke down and struggled with her tears. He watched her for a moment without speaking.

"Good enough. I'll be generous and let you pay his debt for him, if you want to do it."

Her eyes were glad with the swift joy that leaped into them.

"That is good of you! And how shall I pay?" she cried.

"With a kiss."

She drew back as if he had struck her, all the sparkling eagerness driven from her face.

"Oh!" she moaned.

"Just one kiss—I don't ask anything more. Give me that, and I'll turn him loose. Honor bright."

He held her startled gaze as a snake holds that of a fascinated bird.

"Choose," he told her, in his masterful way.

Her imagination conceived a vision of her young brother being tortured by this man. She had not the least doubt that he would do what he said, and probably would think the boy got only what he deserved.

"Take it," she told him, and waited.

Perhaps he might have spared her had it not been for the look of deep contempt that bit into his vanity.

He kissed her full on the lips.

Instantly she woke to life, struck him on the cheek with her little, brown fist, and, with a sob of woe, turned and ran from the room.

Weaver cursed himself in a fury of anger. He felt himself to be a hound because of the thing he had done, and he hated the instinct in him that drove him to master her. He had insulted and trampled on her. Yet he knew in his heart that he would have killed another man for doing it.

CHAPTER IX

PUNISHMENT

The cattleman strode into the bunk house, where young Sanderson sat sulkily on a bed under the persuasion of Curly's rifle.

"Have this boy's horse saddled and brought around, Curly."

"You're the doctor," answered the cowboy promptly, and forthwith vanished outdoors to obey instructions.

Phil looked sullenly at his captor, and waited for him to begin. One of his hands was under the pillow of the cot upon which he sat. His fingers circled the butt of a revolver he had found there, where one of the riders had chanced to leave it that morning.

"I'm going to turn you loose to go home to the hills," Weaver told him.

"And my sister?"

"She stays here."

"Then so do I."

"That's up to you. There's no law against camping on the plains—that is, out of range of the Twin Star."

"What are you going to do with her?" the boy demanded ominously.

"If you ask no questions, I'll tell you no lies."

"You'll let her go home with me—that's what you'll do," cried Phil.

"I reckon not. You've got a license to feel lucky you're going yourself."

"By God, I say you shall!"

The cattleman's eyes took on their stony, snake-like look. His hand did not move by so much as an inch toward the scabbarded revolver at his side.

"All right. Come a-shooting. I see you've got a gun under that pillow."

The weapon leaped into sight. "You're right I have! I'll drill you full of holes as soon as wink."

Weaver laughed contemptuously. "Begin pumping, son."

"I'm going to take my sister home with me. You'll give orders to your men to that effect."

"Guess again."

"I tell you I'll shoot your hide full of holes if you don't!" cried the excited boy.

"Oh, no, you won't."

Buck Weaver was flirting with death, and he knew it. The very breath of it fanned his cheek. During that moment he lived gloriously; for he was a man who revelled in his sensations. He laughed into the very muzzle of the six-shooter that covered him.

"Quit your play acting, boy," he jeered.

"I give you one more chance before I blow out your brains."

The cattleman put his unwounded hand into his trousers pocket and lounged forward, thrusting his smiling face against the cold rim of the blue barrel.

"I reckon you'll scatter proper what few brains I've got."

With a curse, the boy flung the weapon down on the bed. He could not possibly kill a man so willing as this. To draw guns with him, and chance the issue, would have suited young Sanderson exactly. But this way would be no less than murder.

"You devil!" he cried, with a boyish sob.

Weaver picked up the revolver, and examined it. "Mighty careless of Ned to leave it lying around this way," he commented absently, as if unaware of the other's rage. "You never can tell when a gun is going to get into the wrong hands."

"What are you letting me go for? You've got a reason. What is it?" Phil demanded.

Weaver looked at him through narrowed, daredevil eyes.

"The ransom price has been paid," he explained.

"Paid! Who paid it?"

"Miss Phyllis Sanderson."

"Phyllis?" repeated the boy incredulously. "But she had no money."

"Did I say she paid it in money?"

"What do you mean?"

"She asked me to set you free. I named my price, and she agreed."

"What was your price?" the boy asked hoarsely.

"A kiss."

At that, Phil struck him full in the sardonic, mocking face. Blood crimsoned the lips that had been crushed against the strong, white teeth.

"Again," said Weaver.

The brown fist went back and shot forward like a piston rod. This time it left an ugly gash over the cheek bone.

"Much obliged. Once more."

The young man balanced himself carefully, and struck hard and true between the eyes.

A third, a fourth, and a fifth time Phil lashed out at the disfigured, grinning face.

"Let's make it an even half dozen," the cattleman suggested.

But Phil had had enough of it. This was too much like butchery. His passion had spent itself. He struck, but with no force behind the blow.

Weaver went to the washstand, dashed some water on his face, and pressed a towel against the raw wounds. He flung the red-soaked towel aside just as Curly cantered up on Sanderson's horse. The cow-puncher stared at his boss in amazement, opened his lips to speak, and thought better of it. He looked at Phil, whose knuckles were badly barked and bleeding.

Curly had seen his master marked up before, but on such occasions the other man was a sight for the gods to wonder at. Now Weaver was the spectacle, and the other was untouched. In view of Buck's reputation as a rough-and-tumble fighter, this seemed no less than a miracle. Curly departed with the wonder unexplained, for Weaver dismissed him with a nod.

"Like to see your sister before you go?" the cattleman asked curtly of Phil, over his shoulder.

"Yes."

Buck led the way across the plaza to the house, and clapped his hands in the hall. Josephine answered the summons.

"Tell Miss Sanderson that her brother would like to see her."

The woman vanished up the stairway, and the two men waited in silence. Presently Phyllis stood in the door. Her eyes ignored Weaver, and were only for her brother. Her first glance told her that all was well so far as he was concerned, even though it also let her know that the boy was anxious.

"Phil!" she breathed.

"So you bought my freedom for me, did you?" the boy said, his voice trembling.

Phyllis answered in the clearest of low voices. "Yes. Did he tell you?"

"You oughtn't to have done it. I'll have no such bargains made. Understand that!" cried her brother, emotion in his high tones.

"I couldn't help it, Phil. I did it for the best. You don't know."

"I know that you're to keep out of this. I'll fight my own battles. In our family the girls don't sell kisses. Remember that."

Phyl hung her head. She felt herself disgraced, but she knew that she would do it again in like circumstances.

Weaver broke in roughly: "You young fool! She's worth a dozen of you, who haven't sense enough to *sabe* her kind."

The girl glanced at him involuntarily. At sight of his swollen and beaten face, she started. Her gaze clung to him, eyes wild and fluttering with apprehension.

"I've been taking a massage treatment," he explained.

Phyllis looked at her brother, then back at the ranchman. The thing was beyond comprehension. Ten minutes ago, this ferocious Hercules had left her, sound and unscratched. Now he returned with a face beaten and almost beyond recognition from bloodstains.

"What—what is it?" The appeal was to her brother.

"He let me beat him," Phil explained.

"Let you beat him! Why?"

"I don't know."

What the boy said was true, yet it was something less than the truth. He was dimly aware that this man knew himself to have violated the code, and that he had submitted to punishment because of the violation.

"Tell me," Phyllis commanded.

Phil told her in three sentences. She looked at Weaver with eyes that saw him in a new light. He still sneered, but behind the mask she got for the first time a glimpse of another man. Only dimly she divined him; but what she visioned was half devil and half hero, capable of things great as well as of deeds despicable.

"I'm not going to leave you here in this house," young Sanderson told her. "I'll not go. If you stay, I stay."

She shook her head. "No, Phil—you must go. I'm all right here—as safe as I would be at home. You know, he has a right to send me to prison if he wants to. I suppose he is holding me as a hostage against our friends in the hills."

The boy accepted her decree under protest. He did not know what else to do. Decision comes only with age, and he could hit on no policy that would answer. Reluctantly he gave way.

"If you so much as touch her, you'll die for it," he gulped at Weaver, in a sudden boyish passion. "We'll shoot you down like a dog."

"Or a coyote," suggested Buck, with a swift glance at Phyllis. "It seems to be a family habit. I'm much obliged to you."

Phyl was in her brother's arms, frankly in tears.

It was all very well to tell him to go; it was quite another thing to let him go without a good cry at losing him.

"Just say the word, and I'll see it out with you, sis," he told her.

"No, no! I want you to go. I wouldn't have you stay. Tell the boys it's all right, and don't let them do anything rash."

Sanderson clenched his teeth, and looked at Weaver. "Oh, they'll do nothing rash. Now they know you're here, they won't do a thing but sit down and be happy, I expect."

The twins whispered together for a minute, then the boy kissed her, put her from him suddenly, and strode away. From the door he called back two words at the cattleman.

"Don't forget."

With that, he was gone. Yet a moment, and they heard the clatter of his horse's hoofs.

"Why did you tell him?" Phyllis asked. "It will only anger them. Now they will seek vengeance on you."

The man shrugged his shoulders. "Search me. Perhaps I

wanted to prove to myself that a man may be a mean bully, and not all coyote. Perhaps I wanted to get under his hide. Who knows?"

She knew, in part. He had treated her abominably, and wanted blindly to pay for it in the first way that came to his mind. Half savage as he sometimes was, that way had been to stand up to personal punishment, to invite retaliation from his enemies.

"You must have your face looked to. Shall I call Josephine?"

"No," he answered harshly.

"I think I will. We can help it, I'm sure."

That "we" saved the day. He let her call the Mexican woman, and order warm water, towels, dressings, and adhesive plaster. It seemed to him more than a fancy that there was healing in the cool, soft fingers which washed his face and adjusted the bandages. His eyes, usually so hard, held now the dumb hunger one sees in those of a faithful dog. They searched hers for something which he knew he would never find in them.

CHAPTER X

INTO THE ENEMY'S COUNTRY

A man lay on the top of Flat Rock, stretched at supple ease. By his side was a carbine; in his hand a pair of field glasses. These last had been trained upon Twin Star Ranch for some time, but were now focused upon a pair of approaching riders. At the edge of the young willow grove the two dismounted and came forward leisurely.

"Looks like the mountains are coming to Mahomet this trip," the watcher told himself.

One figure was that of a girl—a brown, light-stepping nymph, upon whom the checkered sunlight filtered through the leaves. The other was a finely built man, strong as an ox, but with the sap of youth still in his blood and the spring of it in his step, in spite of his nearly twoscore years. He stopped at the foot of Flat Rock, and turned to his companion.

"I've been wondering why you went riding with me yesterday and again to-day, Miss Phyllis. I reckon I've hit on the reason."

"I like to ride."

"Yes, but I expect you don't like to ride with me so awful much."

"Yet you see I do," answered the girl with her swift, shy smile.

"And the reason is that you know I would be riding, anyway. You don't want any of your people from the hills to use me as a mark. With you along, they couldn't do it."

"My people don't shoot from ambush," she told him hotly. It was easy to send her gallant spirit out in quick defense of her kindred.

He looked at his arm, still resting in a sling, and smiled significantly.

She colored. "That was an impulse," she told him.

"And you're guarding me from any more family impulses like it." He grinned. "Not that it flatters me so much, either. I've got a notion tucked in the back of my head that you're watching me like a hen does her one chick, for their sake and not for mine. Right guess, I'll bet a dollar. How about it, Miss Sanderson?"

"Yes," she admitted. "At least, most for them."

"You'd like to call the chase off for the sake of the hunters, and not for the sake of the coyote."

"I wish you wouldn't throw that word up to me. I oughtn't to have said that. Please!"

"All right—I won't. It isn't your saying it, but thinking it, that hurts."

"I don't think it."

"You think I'm entirely to blame in this trouble with your people. Don't dodge. You know you think I'm a bully."

"I think you're very arbitrary," she replied, flushing.

"Same thing, I reckon. Maybe I am. Did you ever hear my side of the story?"

"No. I'll listen, if you will tell me."

Weaver shook his head. "No—I guess that wouldn't be playing fair. You're on the other side of the fence. That's where you belong. Come to that, I'm no white-winged angel, anyhow. All that's said of me—most of it, at least—I sure enough deserve."

"I wonder," she mused, smiling at him.

Scarcely a week before, she had been so immature that even callow Tom Dixon had seemed experienced beside her. Now she was a young woman in bloom, instinctively sure of herself, even without experience to guide her. Though he had never said so, she knew quite well that this berserk of the plains had begun to love her with all the strength of his untamed heart. She would have been less than human had it not pleased her, even though, at the same time, it terrified her.

Buck swept his hand around the horizon. "Ask anybody. They'll all give me the same certificate of character. And I reckon they ain't so far out, either," he added grimly.

"Perhaps they are all right, and yet all wrong too."

He looked at her in surprise. "What do you mean?"

"Maybe they don't see the other side of you" said Phyllis gently.

"How do you know there's another side?"

"I don't know how, but I do."

"I reckon it must be a right puny one."

"It has a good deal to fight against, hasn't it?"

"You're right it has. There's a devil in me that gets up on its hind legs and strangles what little good it finds. But it certainly beats me how you know so much that goes on inside a sweep like me."

"You forget. I'm not very good myself. You know my temper runs away with me, too."

"You blessed lamb!" she heard him say under his breath; and the way he said it made the exclamation half a groan.

For her naive confession emphasized the gulf between them. Yet it pleased him mightily that she linked herself with him as a fellow wrongdoer.

"I suppose you've been wondering why your people have made no attempt to rescue you," he said presently; for he saw her eyes were turned toward the hills beyond which lay her home.

"I'm glad they haven't, because it must have made trouble; but I *am* surprised," she confessed.

"They have tried it—twice," he told her. "First time was Saturday morning, just before daylight. We trapped them as they were coming through the Box Canon. I knew they would come down that way, because it was the nearest; so I was ready for them."

"And what happened?" Her dilated eyes were like those of a stricken doe.

"Nothing that time. I let them see I had them caught. They couldn't go forward or back. They laid down their arms, and took the back trail. There was no other way to escape being massacred."

"And the second time?"

Buck hesitated. "There was shooting that time. It was last night. My riders outnumbered them and had cover. We drove them back."

"Anybody hurt?" cried Phyllis.

"One of them fell. But he got up and ran limping to his horse, I figured he wasn't hurt badly."

"Was he—could you tell—" She leaned against the rock wall for support.

"No—I didn't know him. He was a young fellow. But you may be sure he wasn't hit mortally. I know, because I shot him myself."

"You!" She drew back in a sudden sick horror of him.

"Why not?" he answered doggedly. "They were shooting at me—aiming to kill, too. I shot low on purpose, when I might have killed him."

"Oh, I must go home—I must go home!" she moaned.

"I've got the sheriff's orders to hold you pending an investigation. What harm does it do you to stay here a while?" he asked doggedly.

"Don't you see? When my father hears of it he will be furious. I made Phil promise not to tell him. But he'll hear when he comes back. And then—there will be trouble. He'll drag me from you, or he'll die trying. He's that kind of man."

A pebble rolled down the face of the wall against which she leaned. Weaver looked up quickly—to find himself covered by a carbine.

"Hands up, seh! No—don't reach for a gun."

"So it's you, Mr. Keller! Homesteading up there, I presume?"

"In a way of speaking. You remember I asked you a question."

"And I told you to go to Halifax."

"Well, I came back to answer the question myself. You're going to turn the young lady loose."

"If you say so." Weaver's voice carried an inflection of sarcasm.

"That's what I say. Miss Sanderson, will you kindly unbuckle that belt and round up the weapons of war? Good enough! I'll drift down that way now myself."

Keller lowered himself from Flat Rock, keeping his prisoner covered as carefully as he could the while. But, though Keller came down the steep bluff with infinite pains, the rough going offered a chance of escape to one so reckless as Weaver, of which he made not the least attempt to avail himself. Instead, he smiled cynically and waited with his hand in the air, as bidden. Keller, coming forward with both eyes on his prisoner, slipped on a loose boulder that rolled beneath his foot, stumbled, and fell, almost at the feet of the cattleman. He got up as swiftly as a cat. Weaver and his derisive grin were in exactly the same position.

Keller lowered his carbine instantly. This plainly was no case for the coercion of arms.

"We'll cut out the gun play," he said. "Better rest the hand that's reaching for the sky. I expect hostilities are over."

"You certainly had me scared stiff," Weaver mocked.

From the first roll of the pebble that had announced the presence of a third party, Phyl had experienced surprise after surprise. She had expected to see one of the Seven Mile boys or her brother instead of Keller—had looked with a quaking heart for the cattleman to fling back the swift challenge of a bullet. His tame surrender had amazed her, especially when Keller's fall had given him a chance to seize the carbine. His drawling, sarcastic badinage pointed to the same conclusion. Evidently he had no desire to resist. Behind this must be some purpose which she could not fathom.

"Elected yourself chaperon of the young lady, have you, Mr. Keller?" Buck asked pleasantly.

The young man smiled at the girl before he answered. "You've been losing too much time on the job, Mr. Weaver.

Subject to her approval, I got a notion I'd take her back home."

"Best place for her," assented Weaver promptly. "I've been thinking for a day or two that she ought to get back to those school kids of hers. But I'm going to take her there myself."

"Yourself!" Phyllis spoke up in quick surprise.

"Why not?" The cattleman smiled.

"Do you mean with your band of thugs?"

"No, ma'am. You and I will be enough."

The suggestion was of a piece with his usual audacity. The girl knew that he would be quite capable of riding with her into the hills, where he had a score of bitter, passionate enemies, and of affronting them, if the notion should come into his head, even in their stronghold. Within twenty-four hours he had shot one of them; yet he would go among them with his jaunty, mocking smile and that hateful confidence of his.

"You would not be safe. They might kill you."

"Would that gratify you?"

"Yes!" she cried passionately.

He bowed. "Anything to give pleasure to a lady."

"No—you can't go! I won't go with you. I wouldn't be responsible for what might happen."

"What might happen—another family impulse?"

"You know as well as I do—after what you've done. And there's bad blood between you already. Besides, you are so reckless, so intemperate in what you say and do."

"All right. If you won't go with me, I'll go alone," he said.

She appealed to Keller to support her, but the latter shook his head.

"No use. A wilful man must have his way. If he says he's going, I reckon he'll go. But whyfor should I be euchred out of my ride. Let me go along to keep the peace."

Her eyes thanked him. "If you are sure you can spare the time."

"Don't incommode yourself, if you're in a hurry. We won't miss you." Weaver's cold stare more than hinted that three would be a crowd.

The younger man ignored him cheerfully. "Time to burn, Miss Sanderson."

"You don't want to let that spring plowing suffer," the cattleman suggested ironically.

"That's so. Glad you mentioned it. I'll try to pick up some one to do it at the store," returned the optimist.

"Seems to me there are a pair of us, Mr. Keller, who may not be welcome at Seven Mile. Last time you were down there, weren't you the guest of some willing lads who were arranging a little party for you?"

"Mr. Weaver," reproached Phyllis, flushing.

But the reference did not embarrass the nester in the least. He laughed hardily, meeting his rival eye to eye. "The boys did have notions, but I expect maybe they have got over them."

"Nothing like being hopeful. Now I'd back my show against yours every day in the week."

The girl handed his revolver back to Weaver, after first asking a question of the homesteader with her eyes.

"Oh, I get my hardware back, do I?" Buck grinned.

Keller brought his horse round from back of Flat Rock, where it had been picketed. They started at once, cutting across the plain to a flat butte, which thrust itself out from the hills into the valley. Two hours of steady travel brought them to the butte, behind which lay Seven Mile ranch.

At the first glimpse of the roofs shining in the golden sunlight Phyllis gave a cry of delight.

"Home again. I wonder whether Father's here."

"I wonder," echoed Weaver grimly.

"That little fellow riding into the corral is one of my scholars," she told them.

"One of the fourteen that loves you, Miss Going-On-Eighteen. My, there'll be joy in Israel over the lost that is found. I reckon by to-morrow you'll be teaching the young idea how to shoot." He glanced down at his bandaged arm with a malicious grin.

Phyllis looked at him without speaking. It was Keller who

made application of the remark.

"There are others here beside her pupils. Some of them are right quick and straight on the shoot, Mr. Weaver. Now you've seen Miss Sanderson home, there's still time to make your getaway without trouble. How about hitting the trail while travelling is good, seh?"

"What's the matter with you taking your own advice, Keller?"

"I don't figure the need is pressing in my case. Different with you."

"I told you I would back my chances against yours. Well, I'm standing pat on that."

"The road will be open to me to-morrow. I wonder will it be open to you then."

"My friend, who elected you guardeen to Buck Weaver?" drawled the big man carelessly.

"I wish you would go," Phyllis pleaded, plainly troubled over his obstinacy.

"Me, I always hated to disoblige a lady," Buck admitted.

"Then go," she cried eagerly.

"But I hate still more to go back on my word. So I'll stay."

There was nothing more to be said. They rode forward to the ranch. 'Rastus, at the stables, raised a shout and broke for the store on the run.

"Hyer's Miss Phyl done come home."

At his call light-stepping dusty men poured from the building like seeds from a squeezed orange. There was a rush for the girl. She was lifted from her saddle and carried in triumph to the porch. Jim Sanderson came running from the cellar in the rear and buried her in his arms.

She broke down and began to cry a little. "Oh, Dad—Dad, I'm so glad to be home."

The old Confederate veteran was close to tears himself.

"Honey, I jes' got back from town. Phil, he done wrong not letting me know. I come pretty nigh giving that boy the bud. Wait till I meet up with Buck Weaver. It's him or me for suah this time."

"No, Dad, no! You must let me explain. I've been quite safe, and it's all over now. Everything is all right."

"Is it?" Sanderson laughed harshly.

"The sheriff telephoned him to keep me, but you see he brought me home."

"Brought you home?" The sheepman's black eyes lifted quickly and met those of his enemy.

"So you're there, Buck Weaver. I reckon you and I will settle accounts."

Phil and Tom Dixon had quietly circled round so as to cut off Weaver's retreat in case he attempted one.

"He's got the rustler with him," Tom Dixon cried quickly.

"Goddlemighty, so he has. We'll make a clean sweep," the Southerner cried, his eyes blazing.

"Then you'll destroy the man who was ready to give his life for mine," his daughter said quietly.

"What's that? How's that, Phyllie?"

"It's a long story. I want you to hear it all. But not here."

Her voice fell. A sudden memory had come to her of one thing at least that she could not tell even to him—the story of that moment when she had lain in the arms of the nester with his heart beating against her breast.

The old man caught her by the shoulder, holding her at arm's length, while the deep eyes under his shaggy, grizzled brows pierced her.

"What have you got to tell me, gyurl? Out with it!"

But on the heels of his imperative demand came reassurance. A tide of color poured into her face, but her eyes met his quietly. They let him understand, more certainly than words, that all was well with his ewe lamb. Putting her gently to one side, he strode toward his enemy.

"What are you doing here, Buck Weaver?"

The cattleman swept the circle of lowering faces, and laughed contemptuously. "A man might think I wasn't welcome if he didn't know better."

"Oh, you're welcome—I reckon nobody on earth is more welcome right now," retorted Sanderson grimly. "We were starting right out after you, seh. But seeing you're here it saves trouble. Better 'light, you and your friend, both."

The declining sun flashed on three weapons that already covered the cattleman. He looked easily from one to another, without the least concern, and swung lightly from his horse.

"Much obliged. Glad to accept your hospitality. But about this young man here—he's not exactly a friend of mine—a mere pick-up acquaintance, in fact. You mustn't accept him on my say-so. Of course, you know *I'm* all right, but I can't guarantee *him*," Buck drawled, with magnificent effrontery.

Phyllis spoke up unexpectedly. "*I* can."

Keller looked at her gratefully. It was not that he cared so much for the certificate of character as for the friendly spirit that prompted it. "That's right kind of you," he nodded.

"We haven't heard yet what you are doing here, Buck Weaver," old Jim Sanderson said, holding the cattleman with a hard and hostile eye. "And after you've explained that, there are a few other things to make clear."

"Such as—" suggested the plainsman.

"Such as keeping my daughter a captive and insulting her while she was in your house," the father retorted promptly.

"I held her captive because it was my right. She admitted shooting me. Would you expect me to turn her loose, and thank her right politely for it? I want to tell you that some folks would be right grateful because I didn't send her to the penitentiary."

"You couldn't send her there. No jury in Arizona would convict—even if she were guilty," Tom Dixon broke out.

"That's a frozen fact about the Arizona jury," the cattleman agreed, with a swift, careless look at the boy. "Just the same, I had a license to hold her. About the insult—well, I've got nothing to say. Nothing except this, that I wouldn't be wearing these decorations"—he touched the scars on his face—"if I didn't agree with you that nobody but a sweep would have done it."

"Everybody unanimous on that point, I reckon," said Jim Yeager promptly.

Phyllis had been speaking to her father in a low voice. The old man listened with no great patience, but finally nodded a concession to her importunity.

"We'll waive the matter of the insult just now. How about that boy you shot up? Looks like you're a fool to come drilling in here, with him still lying there on his bed."

"He took his fighting chance. You ain't kicking because I played out the game the way you-all started to play it? If you are, I'll have to say I might have expected a sheep herder to look at it that way," Weaver retorted insolently.

The old man took a grip on his rising wrath. "No—we're not kicking, any more than you've got a right to kick when we settle accounts with you."

"As we're liable to do right shortly, now we've got you," said Dixon, vindictively.

"All right—go ahead with the indictment," Weaver acquiesced quietly, ignoring the boy.

"Keep still, Tom," Sanderson ordered, and went on with his grievance. "You try to run this valley as if you were God

Almighty. By your way of it, a man has to come with hat in hand to ask you if he may take up land here. The United States says we may homestead, but Buck Weaver says we shan't. Uncle Sam says we may lease land to run sheep. Buck Weaver has another notion of it. We're to take orders from him. If we don't he clubs our sheep and drives off our cattle."

"Cattle were here first," retorted Weaver. "The range is overstocked, and they've got a prior right. Nesters in the hills here are making money by rustling Twin Star calves. That's another thing."

"Some of them. You'll not find any rustled calves with the Seven Mile brand on them. And we don't recognize any prior right. We came here legally. We intend to stay. Every time your riders club a bunch of our sheep, we'll even up on Twin Star cattle. You take my daughter captive; I hold you prisoner."

"You'll be in luck if you get away from here with a whole skin," broke out Phil. "You came here to please yourself, but you'll stay to please us."

"So?" Buck smiled urbanely. He was staying because he wanted to, though they never guessed it.

"Unbuckle his gun belt, Tom," ordered the old man.

"Save you the trouble." Weaver unbuckled the belt and tossed it, revolver and all, to Yeager.

"Now, Mr. Weaver, we'll adjourn to the house."

"Anything to oblige."

"What about Mr. Keller?" Phyllis asked, in a low voice, of

her father.

The old man's keen, hard eyes surveyed the stranger. "Who is he? What do you know about him?"

As shortly as she could, she told what she knew of Keller, and how he had rescued her from captivity.

Her father strode forward and shook hands with the young man.

"Make yourself at home, seh. We'll be glad to have you stay with us as long as you can. What you have done for my daughter puts us everlastingly in your debt."

"Not worth mentioning. And, to be fair, I think Weaver was going to bring her home, anyhow."

"The way the story reached me, he didn't mention it until you had the drop on him," answered Sanderson dryly.

"That's right," nodded the cattleman ironically, from the porch. "You're the curly-haired hero, Keller, and I'm the red-headed villain of this play. You want to beware of the miscreant, Miss Sanderson, or he'll sure do you a meanness."

Tom Dixon eyed him frostily. "I expect you'll not do her any meanness, Buck Weaver. From now on, you'll go one way and she'll go another. You'll be strangers."

"You don't say!" Buck answered, looking him over derisively, as he passed into the house. "You're crowing loud for your size. And don't you bet heavy on that proposition, my friend."

CHAPTER XI

TOM DIXON

With whoops and a waving of caps boys burst out of one door, while girls came out of the opposite one more demurely, but with the piping of gay soprano voices. For school was out, and young America free of restraint for eighteen hours at least. Resilient youth, like a coiled spring that has been loosed, was off with a bound. Horses were saddled or put to harness. The teacher came to the door, hand in hand with six-year-olds, who clung to her with fond good-bys before they climbed into the waiting buggies. The last straggler disappeared behind the dip in the road.

The girl teacher turned from waving her fare-wells—to meet the eyes of a young man fastened upon her. Light-blue eyes they were, set in a good-looking, boyish face, that had somehow an effect of petulancy. It was not a strong face, yet it was no weaker than nine out of ten that one meets daily.

"Got rid of your kiddies, Phyl?" the young man asked, with an air of cheerful confidence that seemed to be assumed to cover a doubt.

Her eyes narrowed slightly. "They have just gone—all but little Jimmie Tryon. He rides home with me."

"Hang it! We never seem to be alone any more since you came back," complained the man.

"Why should we?" asked the young woman, her gaze apparently as frank and direct as that of a boy.

But he understood it for a challenge. "You didn't use to talk that way. You used to be glad enough to see me alone," he flung out.

"Did I? One outgrows childish follies, I suppose," she answered quietly.

"What's the matter with you?" he cried angrily. "It's been this way ever since—"

He broke off.

A faint, scornful smile touched her lips. "Ever since when, Tom?"

"You know when well enough. Ever since I shot Buck Weaver."

"And left me to pay forfeit," she suggested quickly, and as quickly broke off. "Hadn't we better talk of something else? I've tried to avoid this. Must we thrash it out?"

"You can't throw me over like that, after what's been between us. I reckon you pretend to have forgotten that I used to keep company with you."

A flush of annoyance glowed through the tan of her cheeks, but her eyes refused to yield to his. "Nonsense! Don't talk foolishness, Tom. We were just children."

"Do you mean that everything's all off between us?"

"We made a mistake. Let us be good friends and forget it, Tom," she pleaded.

"What's the use of talking that way, Phyl?" He swung from the saddle, and came toward her eagerly. "I love you— always have since I was knee-high to a grasshopper. We're going to be married one of these days."

She held up a hand to keep him back. "No—we're not. I know now that you're not the right man for me, and I'm not the right girl for you."

"I'm the best judge of that," he retorted.

She shook her head with certainty. It seemed a lifetime since this boy had kissed her at the dance and she had run, tingling, from his embrace. She felt now old enough in experience to be his mother.

"No, Tom—let us both forget it. Go back to your other girls, and let me be just a friend."

"I haven't any other girls," he answered sullenly. "And I won't be put off like that. You've got to tell me what has come between us. I've got a right to know, and I'm going to know."

"Yes, you have a right—but don't press it. Just let it go at this: I didn't know my own mind then, and I do now."

"It's something about the shooting of Buck Weaver," he growled uneasily.

She was silent.

"Well?" he demanded. "Out with it!"

"I couldn't marry a man I don't respect from the bottom of my heart," she told him gently.

"That's a dig at me, I reckon. Why don't you respect me? Is it because I shot Weaver?"

"You shot him from ambush."

"I didn't!" he protested angrily. "You know that ain't so, Phyl. I saw him riding down there, as big as coffee, and I let him have it. I wasn't lying in wait for him at all. It just came over me all of a heap to shoot, and I shot before—"

"I understand that. But you shouldn't have shot without giving warning, even if it was right to shoot at all—which, of course, it wasn't."

"Well, say I did wrong. Can't you forgive a fellow for making a mistake?"

"It isn't a question of forgiveness, Tom. Somehow it goes deeper than that. I can't tell you just what I mean."

"Haven't I told you I'm sorry?" he demanded, with boyish impatience.

"Being sorry isn't enough. If you can't see it then I can't explain."

"You're sore at me because I left you," he muttered, and for very shame his eyes could not meet hers.

"No—I'm not sore at you, as you call it. I haven't the least resentment. But there's no use in trying to hide the truth.

Since you ask for it, you shall have it. I don't want to be unkind, but I couldn't possibly marry you after that."

The young man looked sulkily across the valley, his lips trembling with vexation and the shame of knowing that this girl had been a witness of that scene when he had fled like a scared rabbit and left her to bear the brunt of what he had done.

"You told me to go, and now you blame me for doing what you said," he complained bitterly.

She realized the weakness of his defense—that he had saved himself at the expense of the girl he claimed to love, simply because she had offered herself as a sacrifice in his place. She thought of another man, who, at the risk of his life, had held back the half dozen pursuers just to give a better chance to a girl he had not known a week. She thought of the cattleman who had ridden gayly into this valley of enemies, because he loved her, and was willing to face any punishment for the wrong he had done her. Her brother, too, pointed the same moral. He had defied the enemy, though he had been in his power. Not one of them would have done what Tom Dixon, in his panic terror, had allowed himself to do. But they were men, all of them—men of that stark courage that clings to self-respect rather than to life. This youth had met the acid test, and had failed in the assay. She had no anger toward him—only a kindly pity, and a touch of contempt which she could not help.

"No—I don't blame you, Tom," she told him, very kindly. "But I can't marry you. I couldn't if you explained till Christmas. That is final. Now let us be friends."

She held out her hand. He looked at it through the tears of mortification that were in his eyes, dashed it aside with an oath, swung to the saddle, and galloped down the road.

Phyllis gave a wistful sigh. Tears filmed her eyes. He was her first lover, had given her apples and candy hearts when he was in the third grade and she learning her A, B, C. So she felt a heartache to see him go like this. Their friendship was shattered, too. Nor had she experience enough to know that this could not have endured, save as a form, after the wrench he had given it. Yet she knew him well enough now to be sure that it was his vanity and self-esteem that were hurt, and not his love. He would soon find consolation among the other ranch girls, upon whom he had been used to lavish his attentions at intervals when she was not handy to receive them.

"Was Tom Dixon mean to you, teacher?"

Little five-year-old Jimmie Tryon was standing before her, feet apart, fists knotted, and brow furrowed. She swooped upon her champion and snatched him up for a kiss.

"Nobody has been mean to teacher, Jimmie, you dear little kiddikins," she cried. "It's all right, honey. Tom thinks it isn't, but before long he'll know it is."

"Who'll tell him?" Jimmie wanted to know anxiously.

"Some nice girl, little curiosity box. I don't know who yet, but it will be one of two or three I could name," she laughed.

She harnessed the horse and hitched it to the trap in which Jimmie and she came to school. But before she had gathered up the reins to start, another young man strolled upon the scene.

This one was walking and carried a rifle.

At sight of him a glow began to burn through her dark cheeks. They had not been alone together before since that moment when the stress of their emotion had swept them to a meeting of warm lips and warm bodies that had startled her by the electric pulsing of her blood.

Her eyes could not hold to his. Shame dragged the lashes down.

With him it was not shame. The male in him rode triumphant because he had moved a girl to the deeps of her nature. But something in him, some saving sense of embarrassment, of reverence for the purity and innocence he sensed in her, made him shrink from pressing the victory. His mind cast about for a commonplace with which to meet her.

He held up as a trophy of his prowess two cottontails. "Who says I can't shoot?" he wanted to know boisterously.

"Where did you buy them?" she scoffed, faintly trying for sauciness.

"That's a fine reward for honest virtue, after I tramped five miles to get them for your supper," protested Keller.

She recovered her composure quickly, as women will.

"If they are for my supper, we'll have to ask him to ride home with us—won't we, Jimmie? It would never do to have them reach the ranch too late," she said, making room for Keller in the seat beside her.

It was after she had driven several hundred yards that he said, with a smile: "I met a young man on horseback as I was coming up. He went by me like a streak of light. Looked like he found this a right mournful world. You had ought to scatter sunshine and not gloom, Miss Phyllis."

"Am I scattering gloom?" she asked demurely.

"Not right now," he laughed. "But looks like you have been."

She flicked a fly from the flank of her horse before she answered: "Some people are so noticing."

"It was hanging right heavy on him. Had the look of a man who had lost his last friend," the young man observed meditatively.

"Dear me! How pathetic!"

"Yes—he sure looked like he'd rejoice to plug another cattleman. I 'most arranged to send for Buck Weaver again," said Keller calmly.

Phyllis turned on him eyes brilliant with amazement. "What's that you say?"

"I said he looked some like he'd admire to go gunning again."

"Yes, but you said too—"

"Sho! I've been using my eyes and ears. I never did find that story of yours easy to swallow. When I discovered from your brother that you was riding with Tom Dixon the day Buck was shot, and when I found out from 'Rastus that the gun that did the shooting was Dixon's, I surely smelt a mouse. Come to mill the thing out, I knew you led Buck's boys off on a blind trail, while the real coyote hunted cover."

"He isn't a coyote," she objected.

Larrabie thought of the youth with a faint smile of scorn. He knew how to respect an out-and-out villain; but there was no bottom to a man who would shoot from cover without warning, and then leave a girl to bear the blame of his wrongdoing. "No—I reckon coyote is too big a name for him," he admitted.

"Buck Weaver ruined his father and drove him from his homestead. It was natural he should feel a grudge."

"That's all right, too. We're talking about the way he settled it. How come you to let him do it?"

"I was riding about twenty yards behind him. Suddenly I saw his gun go up, and stopped. I thought it might be an antelope. As soon as he had fired, he turned and told me he had shot Weaver. The poor boy was crazy with fear, now that he had done it. I took his gun and made him hide in the big rocks, while I cut across toward the canon. The men saw me, and gave chase."

"They fired at you. Thank God, none of them hit you," said Keller, with emphasis.

Her swift gaze appreciated the deep feeling that welled from him. "Of course they did not know I was a woman. All they could see was that somebody was riding through the chaparral."

"Jimmie, what do you think of a girl game enough to take so big a chance to save a friend? Deserves a Carnegie medal, don't you reckon?" Keller put the question to the third passenger, using him humorously as a vent to his feelings.

Phyllis did not look at him, nor he at her. "And what do you think of a man game enough to take the same chance to save a girl who was not even a friend?" the girl asked of little Jimmie, as lightly as she could.

"Wasn't she? Well, if my friends will save my life every time I need them to, like this enemy did, I'll be satisfied with them a-plenty."

"He stood by her, too," she answered, trying to keep the matter impersonal.

"Perhaps he wanted to make her his friend," Larrabie suggested.

"There is no perhaps about his success," she said quietly, her gaze just beyond the ears of her horse. The young man dared now to look at her—a child of the sun despite her duskiness. Eagerly he awaited the deep, lustrous eyes that would presently sweep round upon him, big and dark and sparkling. When she turned her head, they were full of that new womanly dignity that yet did not obscure the shy innocence.

"Look!" Jimmie Tryon pointed suddenly to the figure of a man disappearing from the road into the mesquite two hundred yards in front of them.

"That's odd. I reckon you'd better wait here, and let me investigate a few," suggested Keller.

"Be careful," she said anxiously.

"It's all right. Don't worry," the young man assured her.

He got down from the trap and dived into the underbrush, rifle in hand. The two in the buggy waited a long time. No sound came to them from the cactus-covered waste to indicate what was happening. When Phyllis' watch told her that he had been gone ten minutes, a cheerful hail came from the road in front.

"All right. Come on."

But it was far from all right. Keller had with him an old Mexican herder, called Manuel Quito—a man in the employ of her father. A bandanna was tied round his shoulder, and it was soaked with bloodstains. He told his story with many shrugs and much excited gesticulation. He and Jesus Menendez had been herding on Lone Pine when riders of the Twin Star outfit had descended upon them and attacked the sheep. He and Menendez had elected to fight, and Jesus had been shot down; he himself had barely escaped with his life—and that not without a wound. The cow-punchers had followed him, and continued to fire at him, but he had succeeded in escaping. Yes—he felt sure that Menendez was dead. Even if he had not been dead at first, they would have killed him.

Keller consulted Miss Sanderson silently. He knew that she was thinking the thought that was in his own mind. It would never do to let this story reach her father and her brother, while Buck Weaver was still in their power. Inflamed as they already were against him, they would surely do in hot blood that which they would repent later. Somehow, Keller and she must hold back the news until they could contrive a way to free the cattleman.

"Best leave Manuel at the Tryon place till morning. They will look out for him as well as you can. That will give us twelve hours to work before they hear what has happened."

"But what about poor Jesus, lying out there alone?"

"We'll get Bob Tryon to drive out. But you needn't worry

about Jesus. If they found him still living, the Twin Star boys will attend to him just as kindly as we could. Cowboys have tender hearts, even though they go off at half cock."

They did as Keller had suggested, and left the old Mexican under the care of Mrs. Tryon, having pledged the family to a reluctant silence until morning. Manuel's wound was not a bad one, and there seemed to be no reason why he should not do well.

It was difficult to decide upon a plan for the release of Weaver. He was confined in an old log cabin and watched continually by some one of the riders; but a tentative plan was accepted, subject to revision if a better chance of escape should occur. The success of this depended upon the possibility of Keller drawing off the guard by a diversion, while Phyllis slipped in and freed the prisoner.

The outlook was not roseate, but nothing better occurred to them. One thing was sure—if Buck Weaver was not out of the hands of his enemies before the news of this last outrage of his cowboys reached them, his chance of life was not worth even an odds-on bet. For the hot blood of the South raced through the veins of the sheepmen. They would strike first and think about it afterward. And without doubt that first swift blow would be a deadly one.

CHAPTER XII

THE ESCAPE

For the sixth time since the three-quarters, Phyllis looked at her watch by the light of a full moon, which shone through the window of her bedroom. The hands indicated five minutes to one.

In her stocking feet she stole out of the room, downstairs, and along the porch to the heavy shadows cast by the cucumber vines that screened one end of it. Here she waited, heart in mouth and pulse beating like a trip hammer.

Presently came the mournful hoot of an owl from the live oaks over in the pasture. Softly her clear, melodious voice flung back the signal. Again the minutes drummed eternally in silence.

But when at last this was shattered, it was with a crash to wake the dead. The girl marvelled that one man could fire so rapidly, and so often. The night seemed to crackle with rifle and revolver shots. To judge from the sound, there might be a company engaged.

The expected happened. The door of the cabin, in which lay the prisoner and Tom Dixon, was flung open. A dark form

William MacLeod Raine

filled the doorway, and the moonlight gleamed on the shining barrel of a rifle. For an instant Tom stood so, trying to locate the source of the firing. He disappeared into the cabin, then reappeared. The door was closed and locked. Taking what cover he could find, Tom slipped over the fence, and into the mesquite on the other side of the road.

Phyllis darted forward like a flame. Her trembling fingers fitted a key to the lock of the cabin. Opening the door, she slipped in and closed it behind her.

"Where are you?" her young voice breathed.

"Over here by the fireplace. What is it all about, Miss Sanderson?"

She groped her way to him. "Never mind now. We've got to hurry. Are you tied?"

"Yes—hands and feet."

A beam of light through the window showed the flash of a knife. With a few hacks of the blade, she had freed him. He was about to rise when the door opened and a head was thrust in.

"What's the row, Tom?"

Weaver growled an answer. "He isn't here. Pulled out when the firing began. I wish you'd tell me what it is all about."

But the head was already withdrawn, and its owner scudding toward the fray. Phyllis rose from the foot of the cot, where she had crouched.

"Come!" she told the cattleman imperiously, and led the way

from the cabin in a hurried flight for the porch shadows.

They had scarcely reached these when another half-clad figure emerged from the house, rifle in hand, and plunged across the road into the cacti. He, too, headed for the scene of the now intermittent shooting.

"Now!" cried Phyllis, and gave her hand to the man huddled beside her.

She led him into the dark house, up the stairs, and into her room. He would have prolonged the sweet intimacy of that minute had it been in his power; but, once inside the chamber, she withdrew her fingers.

"Stay here till I come back," she ordered. "I must show myself, so as not to arouse suspicion."

"But tell me—what does it mean?" demanded Buck.

"It means we're trying to save your life. Whatever happens, don't leave this room or let yourself be seen at the window. If you do, we're lost."

With that she was gone, flying down the stairs to show herself as an apparition of terror to learn what was wrong.

She heard the returning warriors as they reached the door of the log cabin. They had thrashed through the live-oak grove and found nothing, and were now hurrying back to the prison house, full of suspicions.

"He's gone!" she heard Phil cry from within. Came then the sound of excited voices, and presently the shaft of light from a kerosene lamp. Feet trampled in the cabin. Phyllis heard the cot being kicked over. This moment she chose for her entrance.

"What in the world is the matter?" she asked innocently, from the doorway.

"He's got away—we've been tricked!" Tom told her furiously.

"But—how?"

"Never mind, Phyl. Go back to your room. There may be trouble yet. By God, there will be if we find him, or his friends!" her father swore.

Another figure blocked the doorway. This time it was Keller, hatless and coatless, as if he had come quickly from a hurried waking. He, too, fired blandly the inevitable: "What's the trouble?"

"Nothing—except that we are a bunch of first-class locoed fools," snapped Tom. "We've lost our prisoner—that's what's the matter."

Larrabie came in and looked inquiringly from one to another. "I thought you kept him guarded."

"We did, but they drew Tom off on a false trail," explained Phil.

"I notice they worked the rest of us, too," retorted his father tartly.

"I heard the shooting," Keller said innocently. His eyes drifted to a meeting with those of Phyllis. His telegraphed a question, and hers answered that the prisoner was safe so far.

"A dead man could have heard it," suggested Phil, not without sarcasm. "Sounded like a battle—and when we got there not a soul could be found. Beats me how they got away so slick."

Annoyance, disappointment, disgust were in the air. Keller remained to be properly sympathetic, while Phyllis slipped back to her room, as she had been told to do.

She found Weaver sitting by the window looking out. He turned his head quickly when she entered.

"Now, if you'll kindly tell me what's doing, I'll not die of curiosity," he began.

"It's all your wicked men," she told him bluntly. "They have killed one of our herders and wounded another. Mr. Keller and I met the wounded man as he was coming back to the ranch. We stopped him and took him to a neighbor's. If they had known, my people would have revenged themselves on you. They are hot-blooded men, quick to strike. I was afraid—we were both afraid of what they would do. So we planned your escape. Mr. Keller slipped into the chaparral, and feigned an attack upon the ranch, to draw the boys off. I had got the other key to the cabin from the nail above father's bed. When Tom left, I came to you. That is all."

"But what am I to do here?"

"They will scour the valley and watch the pass. If we had let you go, the chances are they would have caught you again."

"And if they had caught me, you think they would have killed me?"

"Doesn't the Bible say that he who takes the sword shall perish by the sword? Are you a god, that you should kill when you please and expect to escape the law that has been written?"

"You say I deserve death, yet you save my life."

"I don't want blood on the hands of my people."

"Personally, then, I don't count in the matter," said Weaver, with his old sneer.

She had saved him, but her anger was hot against the slayers of poor Jesus Menendez. "Why should you count? I am no judge of how great a punishment you deserve; but my father and my brother shall not inflict it, if I can help. They must not carry the curse of Cain on them."

"But Cain killed a brother," he jeered. "I am not a brother, but a wolfish Amalekite. Come—the harvest is ripe. Send me forth to the reapers."

He arose as if to go; but she was at the door before him, arms extended to block the way.

"No, no, no! Are you mad? I tell you they will kill you to-morrow, when the news comes."

"The judgment of the Lord upon the wicked," he answered, with his derisive smile.

"You do nothing but mock—at your own death, at that of others. But you shan't go. I've saved you. Your life belongs to me," she cried, a little wildly.

"If you put it that way—"

"You know what I mean," she broke in fiercely. "Don't dare to pretend to misunderstand me. I've saved you from my people. You shan't go back to them out of spite or dare-deviltry."

"Just as you say."

"I should think you'd be ashamed to be so trivial: You seem to think all our lives are planned for your amusement."

"I wish yours were planned—" He pulled himself up short. "You're right, Miss Sanderson, I'm acting like a schoolboy. I'll put myself in your hands. Whatever you want me to do, I'll do."

"I want you to stay here until they come back from searching for you. You may have to spend all day in this room. Nobody will come here, and you will be quite safe. When night comes again, we'll arrange a chance for you to get away."

"But I'll be driving you out," he protested.

"I'm going to sleep with Anna—the daughter of our house-keeper, Mrs. Allan. She'll suppose me nervous on account of the shooting. Lock the door. I'll give three taps when I want to come in. If anybody else knocks, don't answer. You may sleep without fear."

"Just a moment." He flung up a hand to detain her, then poured out in a low voice part of the feeling pent up in him. "Don't think I haven't the decency to appreciate this. I don't care why you do it. The point is that you have saved my life. I can't begin to tell you what I think of this. You'll surely have to take my thanks for granted till I get a chance to prove them."

She nodded, her eyes grown suddenly shy. "That's all right, then." And with that she left him to himself.

Buck Weaver could not sleep for the thoughts that crowded

upon him; but they were not of his danger, great as that still was. The joy of her, and of the thing she had done, flooded him. He might pretend to cynicism to hide his deep pleasure in it; none the less, he was moved profoundly.

The night wore itself away, but before morning had broken he saw her again. She came with her three light taps, and he opened the door to find her in the passage with a tray of food.

"I didn't dare cook you any coffee. There's nothing hot—just what happened to be in the pantry. Mrs. Allan won't miss it, because the boys are always foraging at all hours. She'll think one of them got hungry. Of course, I couldn't wait till morning," she explained, as she put the tray on the table.

Weaver experienced anew the stress of humility and emotion. He caught up her little hand and crushed it with a passion of tenderness in his great fist. She looked at him in the old, startled, shy way; then snatched her hand from him, and, with a wildly beating heart, scudded along the passage and down the back stairs.

He sank into a chair, with a groan. What use? This creature, fine as silk, the heiress of all that youth had to offer in daintiness and charm, was not—could not be for such as he. He had gone too far on the road to hell, ever to find such a heaven open to him.

How long he sat so, he did not know. Probably, not long, but gray morning was sweeping back the curtain of darkness when he came from his absorption with a start. Somebody had tapped thrice for admittance.

He arose and unlocked the door. A young woman stood outside the threshold, peering into the semi-darkness toward him.

"Is it you, Phyl?" she asked.

The cattleman said nothing. On the spur of the moment, he could not think of the fitting speech. The eyes of his visitor, becoming accustomed to the dim light, saw before her the outline of a man. She let out a startled little scream that ended in a laugh of apology.

"It's Phil, isn't it?"

There was no way out of it. "No—it's not Phil. Come in, ma'am, and I'll explain," said Buck Weaver.

Instead, she turned and ran headlong, along the passage, down the stairs, and into the kitchen. Here she came face to face with her young mistress.

"What's the matter? You look as if you had seen a ghost."

"I have! At least, I've seen a man in your room."

"In my room? What were you doing there?" demanded Phyllis sharply.

"Looking for you. I wakened and found you gone. I thought—oh, I don't know what I thought."

Phyllis knew perfectly how it had come about. Anna Allan was a very curiosity box and a born gossip. She had to have her little pug nose in everybody's business.

"So you think you saw somebody in my room?" her mistress said quietly.

"I don't think. I saw him."

"Saw whom? Phil, or was it Father?" suggested the other, with a hint of gentle scorn.

"No—he was a stranger. I think it was Mr. Weaver, but I'm not sure."

"Nonsense, Anna! Don't be foolish. What would he be doing there? I'll go and see myself. You stay here."

She went, and returned presently. "It must have been one of the boys. I wouldn't say anything about it, Anna. No use stirring up bogeys now, when everybody is excited over the escape of that man."

"All right, ma'am. But I saw somebody, just the same," the girl maintained obstinately.

"No doubt it was Phil. He was up to see me."

Anna said no more then; but she took occasion later to find out from Phil, without letting him know that she was pumping him, that he had been searching the hills until after six o'clock. One by one she eliminated every man in the house as a possibility. In the end, she could not doubt her eyes and her ears. Her young mistress had lied to her to save the man in her room.

CHAPTER XIII

A MISTAKE

At breakfast, a ranchman brought in the news of the attack upon the sheep camp, and by means of it set fire to a powder magazine. The Sandersons went ramping mad for the moment. They saw red; and if they could have laid hands on their enemy, they would undoubtedly have made an end of him.

Phyllis, seeing the fury of their passion, trembled for the safety of the man upstairs. He might be discovered at any moment. Yet she must go to school as if nothing were the matter, and leave him to whatever fate might have in store.

When the time came for her to go, she could hardly bring herself to leave.

She was in her room, putting in the few minutes she usually spent there, rearranging her hair and giving the last few touches to her toilet after the breakfast.

"I hate to go," she confessed to Weaver. "Promise me you'll not make a sound or open the door to anybody while I'm away."

"I promise," he told her.

She was very greatly troubled, and could not help showing it. Her face was wan and drawn, all the youthful life stricken out of it.

"It will be all right," he reassured her. "I'll sit here and read, without making a sound. Nothing will happen. You'll see."

"Oh, I hope not—I hope not!" she cried in a whisper. "You *will* be careful, won't you?"

"I sure will. A hen with one chick won't be a circumstance to me."

Larrabie Keller had hitched her horse and brought it round to the front door. She leaned toward him after she had gathered the reins.

"You'll not go far away, will you? And if anything happens—"

"But it won't. Why should it?"

"Anna knows. She blundered upon him."

"Will she keep it quiet?"

"I think so, but she's a born gossip. Don't leave her alone with the boys."

"All right," he nodded.

"I feel as if I ought to stay at home," the young teacher said piteously, hoping that he would encourage her to do so.

He shook his head. "No—you've got to go, to divert suspicion. It will be all right here. I'll keep both eyes open. Don't forget that I'm going to be on the job all day."

"You're so good!"

"After I've been around you a while. It's catching." He tucked in the dust robe, without looking at her.

But she looked at him, as she started, with that swift, shy glance of hers, and felt the pink tint her cheeks beneath the tan. He was much in her thoughts, this slender brown man with the look of quiet competence and strength. Ever since that night in the kitchen, he had impressed himself upon her imagination. She had fallen into the way of comparing him with Tom Dixon, with her own brother, with Buck Weaver— and never to his disadvantage.

He talked with a drawl. He walked and rode with an air of languid ease. But the man himself, behind the indolence that sat upon him so gracefully, was like a coiled spring. Sometimes she could see this force in his eyes, when for the moment some thought eclipsed the gay good humor of them. Winsome he was. He had already won her father, even as he had won her. But the touch of affection in his manner never suggested weakness.

From the porch Tom Dixon watched her departure sullenly. Since he could not have her, he let himself grow jealous of the man who perhaps could. And because he was what he was—a small man, full of vanity and conceit—he must needs make parade of himself with another girl in the role of conquering squire. Larrabie smiled as the young fellow went off for a walk in obviously confidential talk with Anna Allan, but he learned soon that it was no smiling matter.

William MacLeod Raine

Half an hour later, the girl came flying back along the trail the two had taken. Catching sight of Keller, she ran across to him, plainly quivering with excitement and fluttering with fears.

"Oh, Mr. Keller—I've done it now! I didn't think—I thought—"

"Take it easy," soothed the young man, with one of his winning smiles. "Now, what is it you have done?" Already his eyes had picked out Dixon returning, not quite so impetuously, along the trail.

"I told him about the man in Phyllis' room."

Larrabie's eyes narrowed and grew steely. "Yes?"

"I told him—I don't know why, but I never could keep a secret. I made him promise not to tell. But he is going to tell the boys. There he comes now. And I told Phyllis I wouldn't tell!" Anna began to cry, miserably aware that she had made a mess of things.

"I just begged him not to tell—and he had promised. But he says it's his duty, and he's going to do it. Oh, Mr. Keller—if Mr. Weaver is there they will hurt him, and I'll be to blame."

"Yes, you will be," he told her bluntly. "But we may save him yet—if you can go about your business and keep your mouth shut."

"Oh, I will—I will," she promised eagerly. "I'll not say a word—not to anybody."

"See that you don't. Now, run along home. I'm going to have a quiet little talk with that young man. Maybe I can persuade him to change his mind," he said grimly.

"Please—if you could. I don't want to start any trouble."

Larrabie grinned, without taking his eyes from the man coming down the trail. It was usually some good-natured idiot, with a predisposition to gabbling, that made most of the trouble in the world.

"Well, you be a good girl and padlock your tongue. If you do, I'll fix it up with Tom," he promised.

He sauntered forward toward the path. Dixon, full of his news, was hurrying to the ranch. He was eager to tell it to the Sandersons, because he wanted to reinstate himself in their good graces. For, though neither of them knew he had fired the shot that wounded Weaver, he had observed a distinct coolness toward him for his desertion of Phyllis in her time of need. It had been all very well for him to explain that he had thought it best to hurry home to get help. The fact remained that he had run away and left her alone.

Now he was for pushing past Keller with a curt nod, but the latter stopped him with a lift of the hand.

"What's your sweat?"

"Want to see me, do you?"

Keller nodded easily.

"All right. Unload your mind. I can't give you but a minute."

"Press of business on to-day?"

"It's *my* business."

"I'm going to make it mine."

"What do you mean?" came the quick, suspicious retort.

"Let's walk back up the trail and talk it over."

"No."

"Yes."

Their eyes clashed, and those of the stronger man won.

"We can talk it over here," Dixon said sullenly.

"We can, but we won't."

"I don't know as I want to go back up the trail."

"Come." Larrabie let a hand fall on the shoulder of the other man—a brown, strong hand that showed no more uncertainty than the steady eyes.

Dixon cursed peevishly, but after a moment he turned to go back. He did not know why he went, except that there was something compelling about this man. Besides, he told himself, his news would keep for half an hour without spoiling. They walked nearly a quarter of a mile before he stopped.

"Now get busy, Mr. Keller. I've got no time to monkey," he stormed, attempting to regain what he had lost by his concession.

"Sho! You've got all day. This rush notion is the great failing of the American people. We hadn't ought to go through life on the lope—no, sir! We need to take the rest cure for that habit," Larrabie mused aloud, seating himself on a flat boulder between Tom and the ranch.

Dixon let out an oath. "Did you bring me here to tell me that durn foolishness?"

"Not only to tell you. I figured we would try out the rest cure, you and me. We'll get close to nature out here in the sunshine, and not do a thing but rest till the cows come home," Keller explained easily. His voice was indolent, his manner amiable; but there was a wariness in his eyes that showed him prepared for any move.

So it happened that when Dixon made the expected dash into the chaparral Keller nailed him in a dozen strides.

"Let me alone! Let me go!" cried Tom furiously. "You've got no business to keep me here."

"I'm doing it for pleasure, say."

The other tried to break away, but Larrabie had caught his arm and twisted it in such a way that he could not move without great pain. Impotently he writhed and cursed. Meanwhile his captor relieved him of his revolver, and, with a sudden turn, dropped him to the ground and stepped back.

"What's eating you, Keller? Have you gone plumb crazy? Gimme back that gun and let me go," the young fellow screamed.

"You don't need the gun right now. Maybe, if you had it, you might take a notion to plug me the way you did Buck Weaver."

"What—what's that?" Then, in angry suspicion: "I suppose

Phyllis told you that lie."

He had not finished speaking before he regretted it. The look in the face of the other told him that he had gone too far and would have to pay for it.

"Stand up, Tom Dixon! You've got to take a thrashing for that. There's been one coming to you ever since you ran away and left a girl to stand the gaff for you. Now it's due."

"I don't want to fight," Tom whined. "I reckon I oughtn't to have said that, but you drove me to it. I'll apologize—"

"You'll apologize after your thrashing, not before. Stand up and take it."

Dixon got to his feet very reluctantly. He was a larger man than his opponent by twenty pounds—a husky, well-built fellow; but he was entirely without the fighting edge. He knew himself already a beaten man, and he cowered in spirit before his lithe antagonist, even while he took off his coat and squared himself for the attack. For he knew, as did anybody who looked at him carefully, that Keller was a game man from the marrow out.

Men who knew him said of Larrabie Keller that he could whip his weight in wild cats. Get him started, and he was a small cyclone in action. But now he went at his man deliberately, with hard, straight, punishing blows.

Dixon fought back wildly, desperately, but could not land. He could see nothing but that face with the chilled-steel eyes, but when he lashed out it was never there. Again and again, through the openings he left, came a right or a left like a pile driver, with the weight of one hundred and sixty pounds of muscle and bone back of it. He tried to clinch, and was shaken off by body blows. At last he went down from an uppercut, and stayed down, breathing heavily, a badly thrashed man.

"For God's sake, let me alone! I've had enough," he groaned.

"Sure of that?"

"You've pretty near killed me."

Larrabie laughed grimly. "You didn't get half enough. I'll listen to that apology now, my friend."

With many sighs, the prostrate man came through with it haltingly. "I didn't mean—I hadn't ought to have said—"

Keller interrupted the tearful voice. "That'll be enough. You will know better, next time, how to speak respectfully of a lady. While we're on the subject, I don't mind telling you that nobody told me. I'm not a fool, and I put two and two together. That's all. I'm not her brother. It wasn't my business to punish you because you played the coyote. But when you said she lied to me, that's another matter."

For very shame, trampled in the dust as he had been, Tom could not leave the subject alone. Besides, he had to make sure that the story would be kept secret.

"The way of it was like this: After I shot Buck Weaver, we saw they would kill me if I was caught; so we figured I had better hunt cover. 'Course I knew they wouldn't hurt a girl any," he got out sullenly.

"You don't have to explain it to me," answered the other coldly.

"You ain't expecting to tell the boys about me shooting Buck, are you?" Dixon asked presently, hating himself for it. But he was afraid of Phil and his father. They had told him plainly what they thought of him for leaving the girl in the lurch. If they should discover that he had done the shooting and left her to stand the blame for it, they would do more than talk.

"I certainly ought to tell them. Likely they may want to see you about it, and hear the particulars."

"There ain't any need of them knowing. If Phyl had wanted them to know, she could have told them," said Tom sulkily. He had got carefully to his feet, and was nursing his face with a handkerchief.

"We'll go and break our news together," suggested the other cheerfully. "You tell them you think Weaver is in her room, and I'll tell them my little spiel."

"There's no need telling them about me shooting Weaver, far as I can see. I'd rather they didn't know."

"For that matter, there's no need telling them your notions about where Buck is right now."

Tom said nothing, but his dogged look told Larrabie that he was not persuaded.

"I tell you what we'll do," said Keller, then: "We'll unload on them both stories, or we won't tell them either. Which shall it be?"

Dixon understood that an ultimatum was being served on him. For, though his former foe was smiling, the smile was a frosty one.

"Just as you say. I reckon it's your call," he acquiesced sourly.

"No—I'm going to leave it to you," grinned Larrabie.

The man he had thrashed looked as if he would like to kill him. "We'll close-herd both stories, then."

"Good enough! Don't let me keep you any longer, if you're in a hurry. Now we've had our little talk, I'm satisfied."

But Dixon was not satisfied. He was stiff and sore physically, but mentally he was worse. He had played a poor part, and must still do so. If he went down to the ranch with his face in that condition, he could not hope to escape observation. His vanity cried aloud against submitting to the comment to which he would be subjected. The whole story of the thrashing would be bound to come out.

"I can't go down looking like this," he growled.

"Do you have to go down?"

"Have to get my horse, don't I?"

"I'll bring it to you."

"And say nothing about—what has happened?"

"I don't care to talk of it any more than you do. I'll be a clam."

"All right—I'll wait here." Tom sat down on a boulder and chewed tobacco, his head sunk in his clenched palms.

Keller walked down the trail to the ranch. He was glad to go in place of Dixon; for he felt that the young man was unstable and could not be depended upon not to fall into a rage, and, in a passionate impulse, tell all he knew. He saddled the horse, explaining casually to the wrangler that he had lost a bet with Tom, by the terms of which he had to come down and saddle the latter's mount.

He swung to the back of the pony and cantered up the trail. But before he had gone a hundred yards, he was off again, examining the hoofmarks the animal left in the sand. The left hind mark differed from the others in that the detail was blurred and showed nothing but a single flat stamp.

This seemed to interest Keller greatly. He picked up the corresponding foot of the cow pony, and found the cause of the irregularity to be a deformity or swelling in the ball of the foot, which apparently was now its normal condition. The young man whistled softly to himself, swung again to the saddle, and continued on his way.

The owner of the horse had his back turned and did not hear him coming as he padded up the soft trail. The man was testing in his hand something that clicked.

Larrabie swung quietly to the ground, and waited. His eyes were like tempered steel.

"Here's your horse," he said. Before the other man moved, he drawled: "I reckon I'd better tell you I'm armed, too. Don't be hasty."

Dixon turned his swollen face to him in a childish fury. He had picked up, and was holding in his hand, the revolver Larrabie had taken from him and later thrown down. "Damn you, what do you mean? It's my own gun, ain't it? Mean to say I'm a murderer?"

"I happen to know you have impulses that way. I thought I'd check this one, to save you trouble."

He was standing carelessly with his right hand resting on the mane of the pony; he had not even taken the precaution of lowering it to his side, where the weapon might be supposed to lie.

For an instant Tom thought of taking a chance. The odds would be with him, since he had the revolver ready to his fingers. But before that indomitable ease his courage ebbed. He had not the stark fighting nerve to pit himself against such a man as this.

"I don't know as I said anything about shooting. Looks like you're trying to fasten another row on me," the craven said bitterly.

"I'm content if you are; and as far as I'm concerned, this thing is between us two. It won't go any further."

Keller stood aside and watched Dixon mount. The hillman took his spleen out on the horse, finding that the safest vent for his anger. He jerked its head angrily, cursed it, and drove in the spurs cruelly. With a leap, the cow pony was off. In fifty strides it reached the top of the hill and disappeared.

Keller laughed grimly, and spoke aloud to himself, after the manner of one who lives much alone.

"There's a *nice* young man—yellow clear through. Queer thing she could ever have fancied him. But I don't know, either. He's a right good looker, and has lots of cheek; that goes a long way with girls. Likely he was mighty careful before her. And he'd not been brought up against the acid test, then."

His roving eyes took in with disgust the stains of tobacco juice plastered all over the clean surface of the rocks.

"I'll bet a doughnut she never knew he chewed. Didn't know it myself till now. Well, a man lives and learns. Buck Weaver told me he came on a dead cow of his just after the rustlers had left. Fire still smoldering. Tobacco stains still wet on the rocks. And one of the horses had a hind hoof that left a blurred trail. Surely looks like Mr. Tom Dixon is headed for the pen mighty fast."

He turned and strolled back to the house, smiling to himself.

CHAPTER XIV

A DIFFERENCE OF OPINION

Breakfast finished, Weaver cast about for some diversion to help him pass the time.

This room, alone of those he had seen in the house, seemed to reflect something of the teacher's dainty personality. There were some framed prints on the walls—cheap, but, on the whole, well selected. The rugs were in subdued brown tints that matched well the pretty wall paper. To the cattleman, it was pathetic that the girl had done so much with such frugal means to her hand. For plainly her meagre efforts were circumscribed by the purse limitation.

Ranging over the few books in the stand, he selected a volume of verse by Markham, and, turning the leaves aimlessly, chanced on "A Satyr Song."

> I know by the stir of the branches,
>   The way she went;
> And at times I can see where a stem
>   Of the grass is bent.
> She's the secret and light of my life,
>   She allures to elude;
> But I follow the spell of her beauty,

Whatever the mood.

"Knows what he's talking about—some poet, that fellow," Buck cried aloud to himself, for it seemed to him that the Californian had put into words his own feeling. He read on avidly, from one poem to another, lost in his discovery.

It was perhaps an hour later that he came back to a realization of a gnawing desire. He wanted a pipe, and the need was an insistent one. It was of no use to argue with himself. He surely had to have one smoke. Longingly he fingered his pipe, filled it casually with the loose tobacco in his coat pocket, and balanced the pros and cons in his mind. From behind the window curtain he examined the plaza.

"Not a soul in sight. Don't believe there's a man about the place. No risk at all, looks to me."

With that, he swept the match to a flame, and lit the pipe. He sat close to the open window, so that the smoke could drift out without his being seen.

The experiment brought no disaster. He finished his smoke undisturbed, and went back to reading.

The hours dragged slowly past. Noon came and went; mid-afternoon was upon him. His watch showed a few minutes past four when he decided on another smoke. From the corner of his pocket he raked the loose tobacco into the bowl of his pipe, and pressed it down. Presently he was again puffing in pleasant serenity.

Suddenly there came a blinding flash and a roar.

Buck started to his feet in amazement, the stem of the pipe still in his mouth, the bowl shattered into a hundred bits. His first thought was that he had been the target for a sharp-shooter. There was a neat hole through the framework of the window case, showing where the bullet had plowed. But an investigation left him in the air; for the direction of the bullet hole was such that, if anybody from outside had fired it, he must have been up in a balloon.

The explanation came to him like a flash. In raking the tobacco into his pipe with his fingers, he must have pressed into the bowl a stray cartridge left some time in the pocket. This had gone off after the heat had reached the powder.

By the time he had reached this conclusion some one came running along the passage and tried the locked door. After some rattling at the knob, the footsteps retreated. Buck could hear excited voices.

"Coming back in force, I'll bet," he told himself, with a dubious grin.

The fat was surely in the fire now.

Footsteps made themselves heard again, this time in numbers. The door was tried cautiously. A voice demanded admittance sharply.

Buck opened the door and gazed at the intruders in mild surprise. Old Sanderson and Phil were there, together with Slim and a cow-puncher known as Cuffs. All of them were armed.

"Want to come in, gentlemen?" Weaver asked.

"So you're here, are you?" spoke up Phil.

"That's right. I'm here, sure enough."

"How long you been here?"

"Been hanging round the place ever since my escape. You kept so close a watch I couldn't make my getaway. Some time the other side of noon I drifted in here, figuring some of you would drive me from cover by accident during the day if I stayed out in the chaparral. This room looked handy, so I made myself right at home and locked the door. I hate to shoot up a lady's boudoir, but looks like that's what I've done."

"You durn fool! Who were you shooting at?" Phil asked contemptuously.

But his father stepped forward, and with a certain austere dignity, more menacing than threats, took the words out of the mouth of his son.

"I think I'll negotiate this, Phil."

Buck explained the accident amiably, and relieved himself of the imputation of idiocy. "Serves a man right for smoking without permission in a lady's room," he admitted humorously.

A man came up the stairway two steps at a time, panting as if he had been running. It was Keller.

That the cattleman must have been discovered, he knew even before he saw him grinning round on a circle of armed foes. Weaver nodded recognition, and Larrabie understood it to mean also thanks for what he had done for him last night.

"We'll talk this over downstairs," old Sanderson announced grimly.

They went down into the big hall with the open fireplace, and the old sheepman waved his hand toward a chair.

"Thanks. Think I'll take it standing," said Buck, an elbow on the mantel.

He understood fully his precarious situation; he knew that these men had already condemned him to death. The quiet repression they imposed on themselves told him as much. But his gaze passed calmly from one to another, without the least shrinking. All of them save Keller and Phil were unusually tall men—as tall, almost, as he; but in breadth of shoulder and depth of chest he dwarfed them. They were grim, hard men, but not one so grim and iron as he when he chose.

"Your life is forfeit, Buck Weaver," Sanderson said, without delay.

"Made up your mind, have you?"

"Your own riders made it up for us when they murdered poor Jesus Menendez."

"A bad break, that—and me a prisoner here. Some of the boys had been out on the range a week. I reckon they didn't know I was the rat in your trap."

"So much the worse for you."

"Looks like," Weaver nodded. Then he added, almost carelessly: "I expect there wouldn't be any use mentioning the law to you? It's here to punish the man that shot Menendez."

"Not a bit of use. You own the sheriff and half the juries in this county. Besides, we've got the man right here that is responsible for the killing of poor Jesus."

"Oh! If you look at it that way, of course—"

"That's the way to look at it I don't blame your riders any more than I blame the guns they fired. *You* did that killing."

"Even though I was locked up on your ranch, more than twenty miles away."

"That makes no difference."

"Seems to me it makes some," suggested Keller, speaking for the first time. "His riders may have acted contrary to orders. He surely did not give any specific orders in this case."

"His actions for months past have been orders enough," said Cuffs.

"You'd better investigate before you take action," Larrabie urged.

"We've done all the investigating we're going to do. This man has set himself up like a czar. I'm not going through the list of it all, but he has more than reached the limit months ago. He's passed it now. He's got to die, by gum," the old sheepman said, his eyes like frozen stars.

"We all have to do that. Just when does my time come?" Weaver asked.

"Now," cried Sanderson, with a bitter oath.

Phil swallowed hard. He had grown white beneath the tan. The thing they were about to do seemed awful to him.

"Good God! You're not going to murder him, are you?" protested Larrabie.

"He murdered poor Jesus Menendez, didn't he?"

"You mean you're going to shoot him down in cold blood?"

"What's the matter with hanging?" Slim asked brutally.

"No," spoke up Keller quickly.

The old man nodded agreement. "No—they didn't hang Menendez."

"Your sheep herder died—if he died at all, and we have no proof of it—with a gun in his hands," Larrabie said.

"That's right," admitted Phil quickly. "That's right. We got to give him a chance."

"What sort of a chance would you like to give him?" Sanderson asked of the boy.

"Let him fight for his life. Give him a gun, and me one. We'll settle this for good and all."

The eyes of the old Confederate gleamed, though he negatived the idea promptly.

"That wouldn't be a square deal, Phil. He's our prisoner, and he has killed one of our men. It wouldn't be right for one of us to meet him on even terms."

"Give me a gun, and I'll meet all of you!" cried Weaver, eyes gleaming.

"By God, you're on! That's a sporting proposition," Sanderson retorted promptly. "Lets us out, too. I don't fancy killing in cold blood, myself. Of course we'll get you, but you'll have a run for your money first, by gum."

"Maybe you'll get me, and maybe you won't. Is this little vendetta to be settled with revolvers, or rifles?"

"Make it rifles," Phil suggested quickly.

There was always a chance that, if the battle were fought at long range, the cattleman might reach the hill canons in safety.

Keller was helpless. He lived in a man's world, where each one fought for his own head and took his own fighting chance. Weaver had proposed an adjustment of the difficulty, and his enemies had accepted his offer. Even if the Sandersons would have tolerated further interference, the cattleman would not.

Moreover Keller's hands were tied as to taking sides. He could not fight by the side of the owner of the Twin Star Ranch against the father and brother of Phyllis. There was only one thing to do, and that offered little hope. He slipped quietly from the room and from the house, swung to the back of a horse he found saddled in the place and galloped wildly down the road toward the schoolhouse.

Phyllis had much influence over her father. If she could reach the scene in time, she might prevent the duel.

His pony went up and down the hills as in a moving-picture play.

Meanwhile terms of battle were arranged at once, without

haggling on either side. Weaver was to have a repeating Winchester and a belt full of cartridges, the others such weapons as they chose. The duel was to start with two hundred and fifty yards separating the combatants, but this distance could be increased or diminished at will. Such cover as was to be found might be used.

"Whatever's right suits me," the cattleman said. "I can't say more than that you are doing handsomely by me. I reckon I'll make that declaration to some of your help, if you don't mind."

The horse wrangler and the Mexican waiter were sent for, and to them the owner of the place explained what was about to occur. Their eyes stuck out, and their chins dropped, but neither of the two had anything to say.

"We're telling you boys so you may know it's all right. I proposed this thing. If I'm shot, nobody is to blame but myself. Understand?" Weaver drove the idea home.

The wrangler got out an automatic "Sure," and Manuel an amazed "*Si, senor*," upon which they were promptly retired from the scene.

Having prepared and tested their weapons, the parties to the difficulty repaired to the pasture.

"I'd like to try out this gun, if you don't mind. It's a new proposition to me," the cattleman said.

"Go to it," nodded Slim, seating himself tailor-fashion on the ground and rolling a cigarette. He was a black, bilious-tempered fellow, but this particular kind of gameness appealed to him.

Weaver glanced around, threw the rifle to his shoulder, and fired immediately. A chicken, one hundred and fifty yards away, fell over.

"Accidents will happen," suggested Slim.

"That accident happened through the neck, you'll find," Weaver retorted calmly.

"Betcher."

Buck dropped another rooster.

"You ain't happy unless you're killing something of ours," Slim grinned. "Well, if you're satisfied with your gun, we'll go ahead and see how good you are on humans."

They measured the distance, and Sanderson called: "Are you ready?"

"I reckon," came back the answer.

The father gave the signal—the explosion of a revolver. Even as it flashed, Buck doubled up like a jack rabbit and leaped for the shelter of a live oak, some thirty yards distant. Four rifles spoke almost at the same instant, so that between the first and the last not a second intervened. One of them cracked a second time. But the runner did not stop until he reached the tree and dropped behind its spreading roots.

"Hunt cover, boys!" the father gave orders. "Don't any of you expose yourself. We'll have to outflank him, but we'll take our time about it."

He got this out in staccato jerks, the last part of it not until all were for the moment safe. The strange thing was that

Weaver had not fired once as they scurried for shelter, even though Phil's foot had caught in a root and held him prisoner for an instant while he freed it. But as they began circling round him carefully, he fired—first at one of them and then at another. His shooting was close, but not one of them was hit. Recalling the incident of the chickens, this seemed odd. In Slim's phrasing, he did not seem to be so good on "humans."

Behind his live oak, Buck was so well protected that only a chance shot could reach him before his enemies should outflank him. How long that would have taken nobody ever found out; for an intervention occurred in the form of a flying Diana, on horseback, taking the low fence like a huntress.

It was Phyllis, hatless, her hair flying loose—a picture long to be remembered. Straight as an arrow she rode for Weaver, flung herself from the saddle, and ran forward to him, waving her handkerchief as a signal to her people to cease firing.

"Thank God, I'm in time!" she cried, her voice deep with feeling. Then, womanlike, she leaned against the tree, and gave way to the emotion that had been pent within her.

Buck patted her shoulders with awkward tenderness.

"Don't you! Don't you!" he implored.

Her collapse lasted only a short time. She dried her tears, and stilled her sobs. "I must see my father," she said.

The old man was already hurrying forward, and as he ran he called to his boys not to shoot. Phyl would not move a single step of the way to meet him, lest they take advantage of her absence to keep up the firing.

"How under heaven did you get here?" Buck asked her.

"Mr. Keller came to meet me. I took his horse, and he is bringing the buggy. I heard firing, so I cut straight across," she explained.

"You shouldn't have come. You might have been hit."

She wrung her hands in distress. "It's terrible—terrible! Why will you do such things—you and them?" she finished, forgetting the careful grammar that becomes a schoolmarm.

Buck might have told her—but he did not—that he had carefully avoided hitting any of her people; that he had determined not to do so even if he should pay for his forbearance with his life. What he did say was an apologetic explanation, which explained nothing.

"We were settling a difference of opinion in the old Arizona way, Miss Phyl."

"In what way? By murdering my father?" she asked sharply.

"He's covering ground right lively for a dead one," Buck said dryly.

"I'm speaking of your intentions. You can't deny you would have done it."

"Anyhow, I haven't denied it."

Sanderson, almost breathless, reached them, caught the girl by the shoulders, and shook her angrily.

"What do you mean by it? What are you doing here? Goddlemighty, girl! Are you stark mad?"

"No, but I think all you people are."

"You'll march home to your room, and stay there till I come."

"No, father.'"

"Yes, I say!"

"I must see you—alone."

"You can see me afterward. We'll do no talking till this business is finished."

"Why do you talk so? It won't be finished—it can't," she moaned.

"We'll attend to this without your help, my girl."

"You don't understand." Her voice fell to the lowest murmur. "He came here for me."

"For you-all?"

"Oh, don't you see? He brought me back here because he—cared for me." A tide of shame flushed her cheeks. Surely no girl had ever been so cruelly circumstanced that she must tell such things before a lover, who had not declared himself explicitly.

"Cared for you? As a wolf does for a lamb!"

"At first, maybe—but not afterward. Don't you see he was

sorry? Everything shows that."

"And to show that he was sorry, he had poor Jesus Menendez killed!"

"No—he didn't know about that till I told him."

"Till *you* told him?"

"Yes. When I freed him and took him to my room."

"So you freed him—*and took him to your room?*" She had never heard her father speak in such a voice, so full at once of anger and incredulous horror.

"Don't look at me like that, father! Don't you see—can't you see—Oh, why are you so cruel to me?" She buried her face in her forearm against the rock.

Her father caught her arm so savagely that a spasm of pain shot through her. "None of that! Give me the truth. Now—this instant!"

Anger at his injustice welled up in her. "You've had the truth. I knew of the attack on the sheep camp—heard of it on the way home from school, from Manuel. Do you think I've lived with you eighteen years for nothing? I knew what you would do, and I tried to save you from yourself. There was no place where he would be safe but in my room. I took him there, and slept with Anna. I did right. I would do it again."

"Slept with Anna, did you?"

She felt again that furious tide of blood sweep into her face. "Yes. From the time of the shooting."

"Goddlemighty, gyurl, I wisht you'd keep out of my business."

"And let you do murder?"

"Why did you save him? Because you love him?" demanded Sanderson fiercely.

"Because I love *you*. But you're too blind to see it."

"And him—do you love him? Answer me!"

"No!" she flamed. "But if I did, I would be loving a man. He wouldn't take odds of five to one against an enemy."

Her father's great black eyes chiselled into hers. "Are you lying to me, girl?"

Weaver spoke out quietly. "I expect *I* can answer that, Mr. Sanderson. Your daughter has given me to understand that I'm about as mean a thing as God ever made."

But Phyl was beyond caution now. Her resentment against her father, for that he had forced her to drag out the secret things of her heart and speak of them in the presence of the man concerned, boiled into words—quick, eager, full of passion.

"I take it all back then—every word of it!" she cried. "You are braver, kinder, more generous to me than my own people—more chivalrous. You would have gone to your death without telling them that I took you to my room. But my own father, who has known me all my life, insults me grossly."

"I was wrong," Sanderson admitted uneasily.

Keller climbed the pasture fence, and came running up at the same time as Phil and Slim.

"Menendez is alive!" he cried. "He is at the Twin Star Ranch. The boys there are taking care of him, and the doctor says he will pull through."

"Who told you?"

"Bob Tryon. I met him not five minutes ago. He is on his way here."

This put a new face on things. If Menendez were still alive, Weaver could be held to await developments. Moreover, since the sheep herder was a prisoner at the Twin Star Ranch, retaliation would follow any measures taken against the cattleman.

Phyllis gave a glad little cry. "Then it's all right now."

Weaver's face crinkled to a leathery grin. "Mighty unfortunate—ain't it, boys? Puts a kind of a kink in our plans for the little entertainment we were figuring on pulling off. But maybe you've a notion of still going on with it."

"If we don't, it won't be on your account, seh, I don't reckon," Sanderson answered reluctantly.

But though he would not admit it, the old man was beginning to admire this big fellow, who could afford to miss his enemies on purpose even in the midst of a deadly duel. He was coming to a grudging sense of quality in Weaver. The cattleman might be many things that were evil, but undeniably he possessed also those qualities which on the frontier count for more than civilized virtues. He was game to the core. And he knew how to keep his mouth shut at the right time, no matter what it was going to cost him. On the whole Buck Weaver would stand the acid test, the old soldier was coming to think. And because he did not want to believe any good of his enemy, old Jim Sanderson, when he was alone in the corral with the horses or on a hillside driving his sheep, would shake his gnarled fist impotently and swear fluently until his surcharged feelings were relieved.

CHAPTER XV

THE BRAND BLOTTER

Two riders followed the trail to Yeager's Spur—one a man, brown and forceful; the other a girl, with sunshine in her dancing eyes and a voice full of the lilt of laughter. What they might come to be to each other both were already speculating about, though neither knew as yet. They were the best of friends—good comrades, save when chance eyes said unguardedly too much. For the girl that sufficed, but it was not enough for the man. He knew that he had found the one woman he wanted for his wife. But Phyllis only wondered, let her thoughts rove over many things. For instance, why queer throbs and sudden shyness swept her soft young body. She liked Larrabie Keller—oh, so much!—but her untutored heart could not quite tell her whether she loved him. His eyes drilled into her electric pulsations whenever they met hers. The youth in him called to the youth in her. She admired him. He stirred her imagination, and yet—and yet—

They rode through a valley of gold and russet, all warm with yellow sunlight. In front of them, the Spur projected from the hill ridge into the mountain park.

"Then I think you're a cow-puncher looking for a job, but not very anxious to find one," she was hazarding, answering a question.

"No. That leaves you one more guess."

"That forces me to believe that you are what you say you are," she mocked; "just a plain, prosaic homesteader."

She had often considered in her mind what business might be his, that could wait while he lingered week after week and rode trail with the cowboys; but it had not been the part of hospitality to ask questions of her friend. This might seem to imply a doubt, and of doubt she had none. To-day, he himself had broached the subject. Having brought it up, he now dropped it for the time.

He had shaded his eyes, and was gazing at something that held his attention—a little curl of smoke, rising from the wash in front of them.

"What is it?" she asked, impatient that his mind could so easily be diverted from her.

"That is what I'm going to find out. Stay here!"

Rifle in hand, Keller slipped forward through the brush. His imperative "Stay here!" annoyed her just a little. She uncased her rifle, dropped from the saddle as he had done, and followed him through the cacti. Her stealthy advance did not take her far before she came to the wash.

There Keller was standing, crouched like a panther ready for the spring, quite motionless and silent—watching now the bushes that fringed the edge of the wash, and now the smoke spiral rising faintly from the embers of a fire.

Slowly the man's tenseness relaxed. Evidently he had made

up his mind that death did not lurk in the bushes, for he slid down into the wash and stepped across to the fire. Phyllis started to follow him, but at the first sound of slipping rubble her friend had her covered.

"I told you not to come," he reproached, lowering his rifle as soon as he recognized her.

"But I wanted to come. What is it? Why are you so serious?"

His eyes were busy making an inventory of the situation, his mind, too, was concentrated on the thing before him.

"Do you think it is rustlers? Is that what you mean?" she asked quickly.

"Wait a minute and I'll tell you what I think." He finished making his observations and returned to her. "First, I'll tell you something else, something that nobody in the neighborhood knows but you and Jim Yeager. I belong to the ranger force. Lieutenant O'Connor sent me here to clean up this rustling that has been going on for several years."

"And a lot of the boys thought you were a rustler yourself," she commented.

"So did one or two of the young ladies," he smiled. "But that is not the business before this meeting. Because I'm trained to it I notice things you wouldn't. For instance, I saw a man the other day with a horse whose hind hoof left a trail like that."

He pointed to one, and then another track in the soft sand. "Maybe that might be a coincidence, but the owner of that horse had a habit of squirting tobacco juice on clean rocks— like that—and that."

"That doesn't prove he has been rustling."

"No; but the signs here show he has been branding, and Buck Weaver ran across these same marks left by a waddy who surely was making free with a Twin Star calf."

"How long has he been gone?"

"There were two of them, and they've been gone about twenty minutes."

"How do you know?"

He pointed to a stain of tobacco juice still moist.

"Who is he?" she asked.

He knew her stanch loyalty to her friends, and Tom Dixon had been a friend till very lately. He hesitated; then, without answering, made a second thorough examination of the whole ground.

"Come—if we have any luck, I'll show him to you," he said, returning to her. "But you must do just as I say—must be under my orders."

"I will," she promised.

Forthwith, they started. After they had ridden in silence for some distance, covering ground fast, they drew to a walk.

"You know by the trail for where they were heading," she suggested in a voice that was a question.

"I guessed."

Presently, at the entrance to a little canon, Keller swung down and examined the ground carefully, seemed satisfied, and rode with her into the gully. But she noticed that now he went cautiously, eyes narrowed and wary, with the hard face and the look of a coiled spring she had seen on him before. Her heart drummed with excitement. She was not afraid, but she was fearfully alive.

At the other entrance to the canon, Larrabie was down again for another examination. What he seemed to find gave him pleasure.

"They've separated," he told Phyllis. "We'll give our attention to the gentleman with the calf, and let his friend go, to-day."

They swung sharply to the north, taking a precipitous trail of shale that Phyllis judged to be a short cut. It was rough going, but their mountain ponies were good for anything less than a perpendicular wall. They clambered up and down like cats, as sure-footed as wild goats.

At the summit of the ridge, Keller pointed out something in the valley below—a rider on horseback, driving a calf.

"There goes Mr. Waddy, as big as coffee."

"He's going to swing round the point. You mean to drop down the hill and cut him off?"

"That's the plan. Better do no more talking after we pass that live oak. See that little wash? We'll drop into it, and hide among the cottonwoods."

The rustler was pushing along hurriedly, driving the calf at a trot, half the time twisted in the saddle, with anxious eyes to the rear. Revolvers and a rifle garnished him, but quite plainly they gave him no sense of safety.

When the summons came to him to "Drop that gun!" it was only a confirmation of his fears. Yet he jumped as a boy jumps under the unexpected cut of a cane.

The rifle went clattering to the stony trail. Without being ordered to do so, the hands of the waddy were thrust skyward.

"Why, it's Tom Dixon! We've made a mistake," Phyllis discovered; and moved forward from her hiding place.

"We've made no mistake. I told you I'd show you the rustler, and I've shown him to you," Keller answered, as he too stepped forward. And to Tom, whose hands dropped at sight of Phyllis: "Better keep them reaching till I get those guns. That's right. Now, you may 'light."

"What's got into you?" demanded Dixon, his teeth still chattering. "Holding up a man for nothing. Take away that gun you got bent on me!"

"You're under arrest for rustling, seh," the cattle detective told him sternly.

"Prove it. Prove it!" Dixon swung from the saddle, and faced the other doggedly.

"That calf you're driving now is rustled. You branded it less than two hours ago in Spring Valley, right by the three cottonwoods below the trail to Yeager's Spur."

"How do you know?" cried the startled youth. And on the heels of that: "It's a lie!" He was getting a better grip on his courage. He spat defiantly a splash of tobacco juice on a flat pebble which his eye found. "No such thing! This calf was a maverick. Ask Phyl. She'll tell you I'm no rustler."

Phyllis said nothing. Her gaze was very steadily on Tom.

Keller pointed to the evidence which the hoof of the horse had printed on the trail, and to that which the man had written on the pebble. "We found both these signs once before. They were left by one of the rustlers operating in this vicinity. That time it was a Twin Star brand you blotted. You've done a poor job, for I can see there has been another brand there. Your partner left you with the cow at the entrance to the canon. Caught red-handed as you have been driving the calf to your place, you'll find all this aggregates evidence enough to send you to the penitentiary. Buck Weaver will attend to that."

"It's a conspiracy. You and him mean to railroad me through," Tom charged sullenly. "I tell you, Phyllis knows I'm no rustler."

"I've known you were one ever since the day you wanted to go back and tell where Weaver was hidden. You and your pony scattered the evidence around then, just as you're doing here," the ranger answered.

"You've got it cooked up to put me through," Dixon insisted desperately. "You want to get me out of the way, so you'll have a clear track with Phyl. Think I don't *sabe* your game?"

The angry color sucked into Keller's face beneath the tan. He avoided looking at Phyllis. "We'll not discuss that, seh. But I can say that kind of talk won't help buy you anything."

The girl looked at Dixon in silent contempt. She was very

angry, so that for the moment her embarrassment was swamped. But she did not choose to dignify his spleen by replying to it.

There was no iron in Dixon's make-up. When he saw that this attack had reacted against him, he tried whining.

"Honest, you're wrong about this calf, Mr. Keller. I don't say, mind you, it ain't a rustled calf. It may be; but I don't know it if it is. Maybe the rustlers were scared off just before I happened on it."

"We'll see how a jury looks at that. You're going to get the chance to tell that story to one, I expect," Larrabie remarked dryly.

"Pass it up this time, and I'll get out of the country," the youth promised.

"Take care! Whatever you say will be used against you."

"Suppose I did rustle one of Buck Weaver's calves—mind, I don't say I did—but say I did? Didn't he bust my father up in business? Ain't he aiming to do the same by your folks, Phyl?" He was almost ready to cry.

The girl turned her head aside, and spoke in a low voice to Keller. She was greatly angered and disgusted at Tom; but she had been his friend, and on this occasion there had been some justification for him in the wrong the cattleman had done his family.

"Do you have to report him and have him prosecuted?"

"I'm paid to stop the rustling that has been going on," answered Keller, in the same undertone.

"He won't do it again. He has had his scare. It will last him a lifetime." Even while she promised it for him, it was not without contempt for the poor-spirited craven who could be so easily driven from his evil ways. If a man must do wrong, let it be boldly—as Buck Weaver did it.

"Yes, but his pals haven't had theirs."

"But you don't know them."

"I can guess one man in it with him. We've got to root the thing out."

"Why not serve warning on him by Tom? Then they would both clear out."

Dixon divined that she was pleading for him, and edged in another word for himself. "Whatever wrong I've done I've been driven to. There's been an older man to lead me into it, too."

"You mean Red Hughes?" Keller said sharply.

Tom hesitated. He had not got to the point of betraying his accomplice. "I ain't saying who I mean. Nor, for that matter, I ain't admitting I've done any particular wrong—no more than other young fellows."

Keller brought him sharply to time. "You've used your last wet blanket. I've got the evidence that will put you behind the bars. Miss Phyllis wants me to let you off. I can't do it unless you make a clean breast of it. You'll either come through with what I want to know, and do as I say, or you'll have to stand the gaff."

"What do you want to know?"

"How many pals had you in this rustling?"

"You said you would use against me anything I said."

"I say now I'll use it *for* you if you tell the truth and meet my conditions."

"What are your conditions?"

"Never mind. You'll learn them later. Answer my question. How many?"

"One"—very sullenly.

"Red Hughes?"

"That's the one thing I can't tell you," the lad cried. "Don't you see I can't?"

"It's the one thing I don't need to know. I've got Red cinched about as tight as you, my boy. How long has this been going on?"

The information came from Dixon as reluctantly as a tight cork comes from a bottle. "Nearly a year."

Sharp, incisive questions followed, one after another; and at the end of the quiz Tom was pumped nearly dry. Those who heard his confession listened to the story of how and why he had first started rustling—the tale of each exploit, the location of the mountain cache where the calves had been driven, even the name of the Mexican buyer who once had come across the line to receive a bunch of stolen cattle.

Keller laid down his conditions. "You'll go to Red *muy pronto*, and tell him he's got thirty-six hours to get across the line. He and you will go to Sonora, and you'll stay there. We've got you dead to rights. Show up in this country again, and you'll both go to Yuma. Understand?"

Tom understood well enough. He writhed under it, but he was up against the need of surrender. Sullenly he waited until the other had laid down the law, then asked for his weapons. Keller emptied the chambers of the cartridges, and returned the revolvers, looking also to the magazine of the rifle before he handed it back. Without a word, without even a nod or a glance, Dixon rode out of the gulch.

The eyes of the remaining two met, and became tangled at once. Hastily both pairs withdrew.

"We'll have to drive the calf back, won't we?" said Phyllis, seizing on the first irrelevant thing that occurred to say.

"Yes—as far as Tryon's."

Presently she said: "Do you think they will leave the country?"

"No."

Her glance swept him in surprise. "Then—why did you let him go so easily?"

He smiled. "Didn't you ask me to let him off?"

"Yes; but—" How could she explain that by lapsing from his duty so far, even at her request, he had disappointed her!

"No, ma'am! I'm a false alarm. It wasn't out of gallantry I unroped him. Shall I tell you why it was? I kept naming Red as his partner. But Hughes ain't in this. He has been in

Sonora for a year. When Tom goes back all worried and tells what has happened to him, the gentleman who is the brains for the outfit is going to be right pleased I'm following a false trail. That's liable to make him more careless. If we had had the evidence to cinch Dixon it would have been different. But a roan calf is a roan calf. I don't expect the owner could swear to it, even if we knew who he was. So I made my little play and let him go."

"And I thought all the time you were doing it for me," she laughed, and on the heels of it made her little confession: "And I was blaming you for giving way."

"I'll know now that the way to please you is not to do what you want me to do."

"You know a lot about girls, don't you?" she mocked.

"Me, I'm a wiz," he agreed with her derision.

Keller spoke absently, considering whether this might be the propitious moment to try his luck. They had been comrades together in an adventure well concluded. Both were thinking of what Dixon had said. It seemed to Larrabie that it would be a wonderful thing if they might ride back through the warm sunlight with this new miracle of her love in his life. It was at the meeting of their fingers, when he gave her the bridle, that he spoke.

"I've got to say it, Miss Phyllis. I've got to know where I stand."

She understood him of course. The touch of their eyes had warmed her even before he began. But "Stand how?" she repeated feebly.

"With you. I love you! We both know that. What about you? Could you care for me? Do you?"

Her shy, deep eyes met his fairly. "I don't know. Sometimes I think I do, and then sometimes I think I don't—that way."

The touch of affection that made his face occasionally tender as a woman's, lit his warm smile.

"Couldn't you make that first sometimes always, don't you reckon, Phyllis?"

"Ah! If I knew! But I don't—truly, I don't. I—I want to care," she confessed, with divine shyness.

"That's good listening. Couldn't you go ahead on those times you do, honey?"

"No!" She drew back from his advance. "No—give me time. I'm—I'm not sure—I'm not at all sure. I can't explain, but—"

"Can't decide between me and another man?" he suggested, by way of a joke, to lighten her objection.

Then, in a flash, he knew that by accident he had hit the truth. The startled look of doubt in her eyes told him. Perhaps she had not known it herself before, but his words had clarified her mind. There was another man in the running—one not to be thrust aside easily.

Phyllis' first impulse was to be alone. She turned her face away and busied herself with a stirrup leather.

"Don't say anything more now—please. I'm such a little goose! I don't know—yet. Won't you wait and—forget it till—say, till next week?"

He promised to wait, but he did not promise to forget it. As they rode home, he made cheerful talk on many subjects; but the one in both their minds was that which had been banned. Every silence was full charged with it. Its suppression ran like quicksilver through every spoken sentence.

CHAPTER XVI

A WATERSPOUT

Almost imperceptibly, Buck Weaver's relation to his jailers changed. It was still understood that their interests differed, but the personal bitterness was largely gone. He went riding occasionally with the boys, rather as a guest than as a prisoner.

At any time he might have escaped, but for a tacit understanding that he would stay until Menendez was strong enough to be sent home from the Twin Star.

One pleasure, however, was denied him. He saw nothing of Phyllis, save for a distant glimpse or two when she was starting to school or returning from a ride with Larrabie Keller. He knew that her father and her brother were studiously eliminating him, so far as she was concerned. Certain events had been of a nature to induce whispered gossip. Fortunately, such gossip had been nipped in the bud. They intended that there should be no revival of it.

Weaver had sent word to the riders of the Twin Star that there was to be nothing doing in the matter of the feud until his return.

He had at the same time ordered from them a change of linen, a box of his favorite cigars, and certain papers to be found in his desk. These in due time were delivered by Jesus Menendez in person, together with a note from the ranch.

TWIN STAR RANCH, Tuesday Morning.

DERE BUCK: You've sure got us up in the air. The boys was figurring some on rounding up the whole Seven Mile outfit in a big drive, but looks like you got other notions. Wise us if you want the cooperation of

PESKY and the other boys.

With a smile, Weaver showed it to Phil. "Shall I send word to the boys to start on the round-up?"

"It won't be necessary. You don't need their cooperation. Fact is, now Menendez is back, you're free to go. 'Rastus is getting your horse right now."

The cattleman realized instantly that he did not want to go. Business affairs at home pressed for his attention, but he felt extremely reluctant to pull out and leave the field in possession of Larrabie Keller, even temporarily. He could not, however, very well say so.

"Good enough," he said brusquely. "Before I go, we'd better settle the matter of the range. Send for your father, and I'll make him a proposition that looks fair to me."

When Sanderson arrived, he found the cattleman with a map of the county spread before him upon the table. With a pencil he divided the range in a zigzag, twisting line.

"How about that? I'll take all on the valley side. You take

what is in the hills and the parks."

Sanderson looked at him in astonishment. "That's all we've been contending for!"

Buck nodded. "Since you get what you want, you ought to be satisfied," he said gruffly. "Of course, there will have to be some give-and-take about this. My cattle will cross the line. So will yours. That can't be helped. I've worked out this problem of the range feed pretty thoroughly. My territory will feed just about as many as yours. Each year we can arrange together to keep the number of cattle down."

Under his shaggy brows, Sanderson looked at him in perplexity. The proposition was more than generous. It meant that Weaver would have to sell off about a thousand head of cattle, while the hill-men, on the other hand, could increase their holdings.

"What about sheep?" the old man asked bluntly.

Buck's stony gaze met his steadily. "I'm going to leave those sheep on your conscience, Mr. Sanderson. You'll have to settle that matter for yourself."

"You mean you'll not stand in the way, if I want to keep them?"

"That's what I mean. It's up to you."

Phil, who was sitting on the porch sewing on a pair of leather chaps, indulged in a grin. "I see this is where we go out of the sheep business," he said.

"The market's good. I don't know but what it would be the right thing to sell," his father agreed. "I want to meet you halfway in settling this trouble, Mr. Weaver."

The matter was discussed further at some length, after which the cattleman shook hands all round and departed. Out of the tail of his eye he saw Keller saddling a horse at the stables.

"Think I'll beat you out of that ride with the schoolmarm to-day, my friend. A steady diet of rides like that is liable to intoxicate a man," he told himself, with his grim smile. In plain sight of all, he turned the head of his horse toward the road that led to the schoolhouse.

Presently he met pupils galloping home, calling to each other joyously as they rode. Others followed more sedately in buggies. Nearer the schoolhouse he came on one walking.

After Phyllis had looked over some papers, made up her weekly report, and outlined on the board work for next day, she saddled her pony and set out homeward. Not in ten years had the country been so green and lovely as it was now. There had been many winter snows and spring rains, so that the *alfilaria* covered the hills with a carpet of grass. Muddy little rivulets, pouring down arroyos on their way from the mountains, showed that there had been recent rains. These all ran into the Del Oro, a creek which was dry in summer but was now full to its banks.

She followed the river into the canon of the same name, a narrow gulch with sheer precipitous walls. So much water was in the river that the trail along the bank scarce gave the pony footing. Half a mile from the point where she had entered the Del Oro the trail crept up the wall and escaped to the mesa above. Phyllis was nearing the ascent when a sound startled her. She swung round in her saddle, to see a wall of water roaring down the lane with the leap of some terrible wild beast. Somewhere in the hills there had been a waterspout.

She called upon her pony with spur and voice, racing desperately for the place where the trail rose. Of that wild dash for life she remembered nothing afterward save the overmastering sense of peril. She knew that the roan was pounding forward with the best speed in him, and presently she knew too that no speed could save her. The roar of the advancing water grew louder as it swept upon her. With a cry of terror she dragged the pony to its haunches, slipped from the saddle, and attempted to climb the rock face.

Catching hold of outcropping ledges, mesquit, and even cactus bushes, she went up like a mountain goat But the water swept upon her, waist high, and dragged at her. She clung to a quartz knob her fingers had found, but her feet were swept from her by the suction of the torrent. Her hold relaxed, and she slid back into the river.

Like a flash of light a rope descended over her outstretched arms, tightened at her waist, and held her taut. She felt the pain of a tremendous tug that seemed to tear her in two. Dimly her brain reported that somebody was shouting. A long time afterward, as it seemed to her then, a strong arm went round her. Inch by inch she was dragged from the water that fought and wrestled for her. Phyllis knew that her rescuer was working up the cliff wall with her. Then her perceptions blurred.

"I'll never make it this way," he told himself aloud, half way up.

In fact, he had come to an *impasse*. Even without the burden of her weight, the sheer smooth wall rose insurmountable above him. He did the one thing left for him to do. Leaving her unconscious body in a sort of trough formed by the juncture of two strata, he lowered himself into the rushing stream, searched with his foot for a grip, and swung to the left into the niche formed by a mesquit bush growing from the rock. From here, after stiff climbing, he reached the top.

He found, as he had expected, his cow pony with feet braced to keep the rope taut. Old Baldy was practising the lesson learned from scores of roped steers. No man in the Malpais country was stronger than this one. In another minute he had drawn up the girl and laid her on the grass.

Soon she opened her eyes and looked into his troubled face.

"Mr. Weaver," she breathed in faint surprise. "Where am I?"

But her glances were already answering the question. They took in the rope under her arms, followed it to the horn of the saddle, around which the other end was tied, and came back to the leathery weather-beaten face that looked down into hers.

"You have saved my life."

"Not me. Old Baldy did it. I never could have got you out alone. When I roped you, he backed off same as if you had been a steer, and pulled for all there was in him. Between us we got you up."

"Good old Baldy!" She let it go at that for the moment, while she thought it out. "If you hadn't been right here—" She finished her sentence with a shudder.

She could not guess how that thought stabbed him, for he replied cheerfully: "I heard you call, and Baldy brought me on the jump."

Phyllis covered her face with her hands. She was badly shaken and could not quite control herself. "It was awful—

awful." And short staccato sobs shook her.

Buck put his arm around her shoulders, and soothed her gently. "Don't you care, Phyllis. It's all past now. Forget it, little girl."

"It was like some tremendous wild beast—a thousand times stronger and crueller than a grizzly. It leaped at me, and—Oh, if you hadn't been here!"

She caught at his sleeve and clung to it with both hands.

"If a fellow sticks around long enough he is sure to come in handy," Buck told her lightly.

She did not answer, but presently she walked across a little unsteadily and put her arms around the neck of the white-faced broncho. Her face she buried in its mane. Weaver knew she was crying softly, and he wisely left her alone while he recoiled the rope.

Presently she recovered her composure and began to pat the white silken nose of the pony.

"You helped him to save my life, Baldy. Even he couldn't have done it without you. How can I ever pay you for it?"

Weaver had an inspiration. "He's yours from this moment. You can pay him by taking him for your saddle horse. Baldy will never ride the round-up again. We'll give him a Carnegie medal and retire him on a good-service pension so far as the rough work goes."

Without looking at him, the girl answered softly: "Thank you. I know I'm taking from you the best cow-pony in Arizona, but I can't help it."

"A cow-pony is a cow-pony, but a horse that saves the life of Miss Phyllis Sanderson is a gentleman and a hero."

"And what about the man who saves her life?" Her voice was very small and weepy.

"Tickled to death to have the chance. We'll forget that."

Still she did not look at him. "Never! Never as long as I live," she cried vehemently.

It came to him that if he was ever going to put his fortune to the test now was the time. He strode across and swung her round till she faced him.

"As long as you live, Phyllis. And you're only eighteen. Me, I'm thirty-seven. I lack just a year of being twice as old. What about it? Am I too old and too hard and tough for you, little girl?"

"I—don't—understand."

"Yes, you do. I'm asking you to marry me. Will you?"

"Oh, Mr. Weaver!" she gasped.

"I ought to wrap it up pretty, oughtn't I? But there's nothing pretty about me. No woman should marry me if she can help it, not unless her heart brings her to me in spite of herself. Is it that way with you?"

Never before had she met a man like him, so masterful and virile. He took short cuts as if he did not notice the "No Trespassing" sign. She read in him a passion clamped by a will of iron, and there thrilled through her a fierce delight in her power over this splendid type of the male lover. She lived in a world of men, lean, wide-shouldered fellows, who moved and had their being in conditions that made hickory withes of them physically, hard close-mouthed citizens mentally. But even by the frontier tests of efficiency, of gameness, of going the limit, Weaver stood head and shoulders above his neighbors. She had lifted her gaze to meet his, quite sure that her answer was not in doubt, but now her heart was beating like a triphammer. She felt herself drifting from her moorings. It was as though she were drowning forty fathoms deep in those calm, unwinking eyes of his.

"I don't think so," she cried desperately.

"You've got to be sure. I don't want you else."

"Yes—yes!" she cried eagerly. "Don't rush me."

"Take all the time you need. You can't be any too sure to suit me."

"I—I don't think it will be yes," she told him shyly.

"I'm betting it will," he said confidently. "And now, little girl, it's time we started. You'll ride your Carnegie horse and I'll walk."

Her eyes dilated, for this brought to her mind something she had forgotten. "My roan! What do you think has become of it?"

He shook his head, preferring not to guess aloud. As he helped her to the saddle his eyes fell on a stain of red running from the wrist of her gauntlet.

"You've hurt your hand," he cried.

"It must have been when I caught at the cactus."

Gently he slipped off the glove. Cruel thorns had torn the skin in a dozen places. He drew the little spikes out one by one. Phyllis winced, but did not cry out. After he had removed the last of them he tied her handkerchief neatly round the wounds and drew on the gauntlet again. It had been only a small service, nothing at all compared to the great one he had just rendered, but somehow it had tightened his hold on her. She wondered whether she would have to marry Buck Weaver no matter what she really wanted to do.

With her left hand she guided Baldy, while Buck strode beside, never wavering from the easy, powerful stride that was the expression of his sinuous strength.

"Were you ever tired in your life?" she asked once, with a little sigh of fatigue.

He stopped in his stride, full of self-reproach. "Now, ain't that like me! Pluggin' ahead, and never thinking about how played out you are. We'll rest here under these cottonwoods."

He lifted her down, for she was already very stiff and sore from her adventure. An outdoor life had given her a supple strength and a wiry endurance, of which her slender frame furnished no indication, but the reaction from the strain was upon her. To Buck she looked pathetically wan and exhausted. He put her down under a tree and arranged her saddle for a pillow. Again the girl felt a net was being wound round her, that she belonged to him and could not escape. Nor was she sure that she wanted to get away from his possessive energy. In the pleasant sun glow she fell asleep, without any intention of doing so. Two hours later she opened her eyes.

Looking round, she saw Weaver lying flat on his back fifty yards away.

"I've been asleep," she called.

He leaped to his feet and walked across the sand to her.

"I suspected it," he said with a smile.

"I feel like a new woman now."

"Like one of them suffragettes?"

"That isn't quite what I meant," she smiled. "I'm ready to start."

Half an hour later they reached her home. It was close to supper time, but Weaver would not stay.

"See you next week," he said quietly, and turned his horse toward the Twin Star ranch.

CHAPTER XVII

THE HOLD-UP

From the wash where the sink of the Mimbres edges close to Noches two riders emerged in mid-afternoon of a day that shimmered under the heat of a blazing sun. They travelled in silence, the core of an alkali dust cloud that moved with them and lay thick upon them. Well down over their eyes were drawn the broad-rimmed hats. One of them wore sun goggles and both of them had their lower faces covered by silk bandannas as if to keep out the thick dust their ponies stirred. For the rest their costumes were the undistinguished chaps, spurs, shirt, neckerchiefs, and gauntlets of the range.

With one distinction, however: these were better armed than the average cow-puncher jaunting to town for the quarterly spree. Revolver butts peeped from the holsters of their loosely hung cartridge belts. Moreover, their rifles were not strapped beneath the stirrup leathers, but were carried across the pommels of the saddles.

The bell in the town hall announced three o'clock as they reached the First National Bank at the corner of San Miguel and Main Streets. Here one of the riders swung from the saddle, handed the reins and his rifle to the other man, and jingled into the bank. His companion took the horses round to the side entrance of the building, and waited there in such shade as two live oaks offered.

He had scarce drawn rein when two other riders joined him, having come from a direction at right angles to that followed by him. One of them rode an iron-gray, the other a roan with white stockings. Both of these dismounted, and one of them passed through the side door into the bank. Almost instantly he reappeared and nodded to his comrade, who joined him with his own rifle and that of the first man that had gone in.

There was an odd similarity in arms, manner, and dress between these and the first arrivals. Once inside the building, each of them slipped a black mask over his face. Then one stepped quickly to the front door and closed and locked it, while the other simultaneously covered the teller with a revolver.

The cashier, busy in conversation with the first horseman about a loan the other had said he wanted, was sitting with his back to the cage of the teller. The first warning he had of anything unusual was the closing of the door by a masked man. One glance was enough to tell him the bank was about to be robbed.

His hand moved swiftly toward the drawer in his desk which contained a weapon, but stopped halfway to its destination. For he was looking squarely into the rim of a six-shooter less than a foot from his forehead. The gun was in the hands of the client with whom he had been talking.

"Don't do that," the man advised him brusquely. Then, more sharply: "Reach for the roof. No monkeying."

Benson, the cashier, was no coward, but neither was he a fool. He knew when not to take a chance. Promptly his arms shot up. But even while he obeyed, his eyes were carrying to his brain a classification of this man for future identification. The bandit was a stranger to him, a heavy-set, bandy-legged fellow of about forty-five, with a leathery face and eyes as stony as those of a snake.

"What do you want?" the bank officer asked quietly.

"Your gold and notes. Is the safe open?"

Before the cashier could reply a shot rang out. The unmasked outlaw slewed his head, to see the president of the bank firing from the door of his private office. The other two robbers were already pumping lead at him. He staggered, clutched at the door jamb, and slowly sank to the floor after the revolver had dropped from his hand.

Benson seized the opportunity to duck behind his desk and drag open a drawer, but before his fingers had closed on the weapon within, two crashing blows descended with stunning force on his head. The outlaw covering him had reversed his heavy revolver and clubbed him with the butt.

"That'll hold him for a while," the bandit remarked, and dragged the unconscious man across the floor to where the president lay huddled.

One of the masked men, a lithe, sinuous fellow with a polka-dot bandanna round his neck, took command.

"Keep these men covered, Irwin, while we get the loot," he ordered the unmasked man.

With that he and the boyish-looking fellow who had ridden into town with him, the latter carrying three empty sacks, followed the trembling teller to the vault.

No sound broke the dead silence except the loud ticking of the bank clock and an occasional groan from the cashier, who was just beginning to return to consciousness. Twice the man left on guard called down to those in the vault to hurry.

There was need of haste. Somebody, attracted by the sound of firing, had come running to the bank, peered in the big front window, and gone flying to spread the alarm.

Outside a shot and then another shattered the sultry stillness of the day. The man left on guard ran to the door and looked out. An upper window down the street was open, and from it a man with a rifle was firing at the outlaw left in charge of the horses.

The wrangler had taken refuge behind a bulwark of horse-flesh, and was returning the fire.

"Hurry the boys, Brad! Hell's broke loose!" he called to his companion.

The town was alarmed and buzzing like a hornet's nest. Soon they would feel the sting of the swarm unless they beat an immediate retreat. One sweep of his eyes told the bandy-legged fellow as much. He could hear voices crying the alarm, could see men running to and fro farther down the street. Even in the second he stood there a revolver began potting at him.

"Back in a moment," he cried to the wrangler, and disappeared within to shout an urgent warning to the looters.

Three men came up from the vault, each carrying a sack. The teller was pushed into the street first, and the rest followed. A scattering fire began to converge at once upon them. The roan with the white stockings showed a red ridge across its flank where a bullet had furrowed a path.

The teller dropped, wounded by his friends. Two of the robbers loaded the horses, while the others answered the townsmen. In the inevitable delay of getting started, every moment seemed an hour to the harassed outlaws.

But at last they were in the saddle and galloping down the street, firing right and left as they went. At the next street crossing two men, one fat and the other lean, came running, revolvers in hands, to intercept them. They were too late. Before they reached the corner the outlaws had galloped past in a cloud of white dust, still flinging bullets at the invisible they were escaping.

The big lean cow-puncher stopped with an oath as the riders disappeared. "Nothing doing, Budd," he called to the fat man. "The show's moved on to a new stand."

Jim Budd, puffing heavily and glistening with perspiration, nodded the answer he could not speak. Presently he got out what he wanted to say.

"Notice that leading hawss on the nigh side, Slim?" he asked.

"So you noticed it, too, Jim. I could swear to that roan with the four stockings. It's the hawss Mr. Larrabie Keller mavericks around on, durn his forsaken hide! And the man on it wore a polka-dot bandanna. So does Keller. He'll have to go some to explain away that. I reckon the others must be nesters from Bear Creek, too."

"We've got 'em where the wool's short this time," Budd agreed. "They been shootin' around right promiscuous. If anybody's dead, then Keller has put a rope round his own neck."

Men were already saddling and mounting for the first unorganized pursuit. Slim and his friend joined these, and cantered down the dusty street scarce ten minutes after the robbers.

The suburbs of the town fell to the rear, and left them in the fall and rise of the foothills that merged to the left in the wide, flat, shimmering plain of the Malpais, and on the other side in the saw-toothed range that notched the horizon from north to south. Somewhere in that waste of cow-backed hills, in that swell of endless land waves, the trail of the robbers vanished.

Men rode far and wide, carrying the pursuit late into the night, but the lost trail was not to be picked up again. So one by one, or in pairs, under the yellow stars, they drifted back to Noches, leaving behind the black depths of blue-canopied hills that had swallowed the fleeing quartette.

CHAPTER XVIII

BRILL HEALY AIRS HIS SENTIMENTS

To Phyllis, riding from school near the close of a hot Friday afternoon along the old Fort Lincoln Trail, came the voice of Brill Healy from the ridge above. She waved to him the broad-brimmed hat she was carrying in her hand, and he guided his pony deftly down the edge of the steep slope.

"Been looking for some strays down at Three Pines," he explained. "Awful glad I met you."

"Where were you going now?" she asked.

"Home, I reckon; but I'll ride with you to Seven Mile if you don't mind."

She looked at her watch. "It's just five-thirty. We'll be in time for supper, and you can ride home afterward."

"I guess you know that will suit me, Phyllis," he answered, with a meaning look from his dark eyes.

"Supper suits most healthy men so far as I've noticed," she said carelessly, her glance sweeping keenly over him before it passed to the purple shadowings that already edged the mouth of a distant canon.

"I'll bet it does when they can sit opposite Phyl Sanderson to eat it."

She frowned a little, the while he took her in out of half-shut, smoldering eyes, as one does a picture in a gallery. In truth, one might have ridden far to find a living picture more vital and more suggestive of the land that had cradled and reared her.

His gaze annoyed her, without her quite knowing why. "I wish you wouldn't look at me all the time," she told him with the boyish directness that still occasionally lent a tang to her speech.

"And if I can't help it?" he laughed.

"Fiddlesticks! You don't have to say pretty things to me, Brill Healy," she told him.

"I don't say them because I have to."

"Then I wish you wouldn't say them at all. There's no sense in it when you've known a girl eighteen years."

"Known and loved her eighteen years. It's a long time, Phyl."

Her eyes rained light derision on him. "It would be if it were true. But then one has to forget truth when one is senti-mental, I reckon."

"I'm not sentimental. I tell you I'm in love," he answered.

"Yes, Brill. With yourself. I've known that a long time, but not quite eighteen years," she mocked.

"With you," he made answer, and something of sullenness had by this time crept into his voice. "I've got as much right to love you as any one else, haven't I? As much right as that durned waddy, Keller?"

Fire flashed in her eyes. "If you want to know, I despise you when you talk that way."

The anger grew in him. "What way? When I say anything against the rustler, do you mean? Think I'm blind? Think I can't see how you're running after him, and making a fool of yourself about him?"

"How dare you talk that way to me?" she flamed, and gave her surprised pony a sharp stroke with the quirt.

Five minutes later the bronchos fell again to a walk, and Healy took up the conversation where it had dropped.

"No use flying out like that, Phyl. I only say what any one can see. Take a look at the facts. You meet up with him making his getaway after he's all but caught rustling. Now, what do you do?"

"I don't believe he was rustling at all."

"Course you don't *believe* it. That proves just what I was saying."

"Jim doesn't believe it, either."

"Yeager's opinion don't have any weight with me. I want to tell you right now that the boys are getting mighty leary of Jim. He's getting too thick with that Bear Creek bunch."

"Brill Healy, I never saw anybody so bigoted and pig-headed

as you are," the girl spoke out angrily. "Any one with eyes in his head could see that Jim is as straight as a string. He couldn't be crooked if he tried. Long as you've known him I should think you wouldn't need to be told that."

"Oh, *you* say so," he growled sullenly.

"Everybody says so. Jim Yeager of all men," she scoffed. Then, with a flash of angry eyes at him, "How would you like it if your friends rounded on you? By all accounts, you're not quite a plaster saint. I've heard stories."

"What about?"

"Oh, gambling and drinking. What of it? That's *your* business. One doesn't have to believe all the talk that is flying around." She spoke with a kind of fine scorn, for she was a girl of large generosities.

"We've all got enemies, I reckon," he said sulkily.

"You're Phil's friend, and mine, too, of course. I dare say you have your faults like other men, but I don't have to listen to people while they try to poison my mind against you. What's more, I don't."

She had been agile-minded enough to shift the attack and put him upon the defensive, but now Healy brought the question back to his original point.

"That's all very well, Phyl, but we weren't talking about me, but about you. When you found this Keller making his escape you buckled in and helped him. You tied up his wound and took him to Yeager's and lied for him to us. That's bad enough, but later you did a heap worse."

"In saving him from being lynched by you?"

"Before that you made a fuss about him and had to tie up his wounds. I had a cut on *my* cheek, but I notice you didn't tie it up!"

"I'm surprised at you, Brill. I didn't think you were so small; and just because I didn't let a wounded man suffer."

"You can put it that way if you want to," he laughed unpleasantly.

Her passion flared again. "You and your insinuations! Who made you the judge over my actions? You talk as if you were my father. If you've got to reform somebody, let it be yourself."

"I'm the man that is going to be your husband," he said evenly. "That gives me a right."

"Never! Don't think it," she flung back. "I'd not marry you if you were the last man on earth."

"You'll see. I'll not let a scoundrel like Keller come between us. No, nor Yeager, either. Nor Buck Weaver himself. I notice he was right attentive before he went home."

Resentment burned angrily on her cheek. "Anybody else?" she asked quietly.

"That's all for just now. You're a natural-born flirt, Phyllis. That's what's the matter with you."

"Thank you, Mr. Healy. You're the only one of my friends that has been so honest with me," she assured him sweetly.

William MacLeod Raine

"I'm the only one of them that is going to marry you. Don't think I'll let Keller butt in. Not on your life."

Her rage broke bounds. "I never in my life heard of anything so insolent. Never! *You'll* not let me do this or that. Who are you, Brill Healy?"

"I've told you. I'm the man that means to marry you," he persisted doggedly.

"You never will. I'm not thinking of marrying, but when I do I'll not ask for your indorsement. Be sure of that."

"I'll not stand it! He'd better look out!"

"Who do you mean?"

"Keller, that's who I mean. This thing is hanging over his head yet. He's got to come through with proofs he ain't a rustler, or he's got to pull his freight out of the Malpais country."

"And if he won't?"

"We'll finish that little business you interrupted," he told her, riding his triumph roughshod over her feelings.

"You wouldn't, Brill! Not when there is a doubt about it. Jim says he is innocent, and I believe he is. Surely you wouldn't!"

"You'll see."

"If you do I'll never speak to you again! Never, as long as I live; and I'll never rest till I have you in the penitentiary for his murder!" she cried tensely.

"And yet you don't care anything about him. You've just been kind to him out of charity," he mocked.

For some minutes they had seen Seven Mile Ranch lying below them in the faint twilight. They rode the rest of the way in silence, each of them too bitter for speech. When they reached the house, she swung from the saddle and he kept his seat, for both of them considered her supper invitation and his acceptance cancelled.

He bowed ironically and turned to leave.

"Just a moment, Brill," called an excited voice. "I've got a piece of news that will make you sit up."

The speaker was the young mule skinner known as Cuffs. He came running out to the porch and fired his bolt.

"The First National Bank at Noches was held up two hours ago, and the robbers got away with their loot after shooting three or four men!"

"Two hours ago," the girl repeated. "You got it over the phone, of course."

"Yep. Slim called me up just now. He got back right this minute from following their trail. They lost the fellows in the hills. Four of 'em, Slim says, and he thinks they're headed this way."

"What makes him think so?" asked Healy.

"He figures they are Bear Creek men. One of them was recognized. It was that fellow Keller."

"Keller!" Phyllis and Healy cried the word together.

Cuffs nodded. "Slim says he can swear to his hawss, and he's plumb sure about the man, too. He wants we should organize a posse and nail them as they go into the Pass for Bear Creek. He figures we'll have time to do it if we jump. Noches is fifty-five miles from here, and about forty from the Pass.

"With their bronchs loaded they can't make it in much less than five hours. That gives us most three hours to reach the Pass and stop them. What think, Brill? Can we make it?"

"We'll try damned hard. I'm not going to let Mr. Rustler Keller slip through my fingers again!" Healy cried triumphantly.

"I don't believe it was Bear Creek men at all. I'm sure it wasn't Mr. Keller," Phyllis cried, with a face like parchment.

There was an unholy light of vindictive triumph in Healy's face. "We'll show you about that, Miss Missouri. Get the boys together, Cuffs. Call up Purdy and Jim Budd and Tom Dixon on the phone. Rustle up as many of the boys as you can. Start 'em for the Pass just as soon as they get here. I'm going right up there now. Probably I can't stop them, but I may make out who they are. Notify Buck Weaver, so he can head them off if they try to cross the Malpais. And get a move on you. Hustle the boys right along."

And with that he put spurs to his horse and galloped off.

CHAPTER XIX

THE ROAN WITH THE WHITE STOCKINGS

Unerringly rode Healy through the tangled hills toward a saddle in the peaks that flared vivid with crimson and mauve and topaz. A man of moods, he knew more than one before he reached the Pass for which he was headed. Now he rode with his eyes straight ahead, his face creased to a hard smile that brought out its evil lines. Now he shook his clenched fist into the air and cursed.

Or again he laughed exultingly. This was when he remembered that his rival was trapped beyond hope of extrication.

While the sky tints round the peaks deepened to purple with the coming night he climbed canons, traversed rock ridges, and went down and up rough slopes of shale. Always the trail grew more difficult, for he was getting closer to the divide where Bear Creek heads. He reached the upper regions of the pine gulches that seamed the hills with wooded crevasses, and so came at last to Gregory's Pass.

Here, close to the yellow stars that shed a cold wintry light, he dismounted and hobbled his horse. After which he found a soft spot in the mossy rocks and fell asleep. He was a light sleeper, and two hours later he awakened. Horses were laboring up the Pass.

He waited tensely, rifle in both hands, till the heads of the riders showed in the moonlight. Three—four—five of them he counted. The men he saw were those he expected, and he lowered his rifle at once.

"Hello, Cuffs! Purdy! That you, Tom? Well, you're too late."

"Too late," echoed little Purdy.

"Yep. Didn't get here in time myself to see who any of them were except the last. It was right dark, and they were most through before I reached here."

"But you knew one," Purdy suggested.

Healy looked at him and nodded. "There were four of them. I crept forward on top of that flat rock just as the last showed up. He was ridin' a hawss with four white stockings."

"A roan, mebbe," Tom put in quickly.

"You've said it, Tom—a roan, and it looked to me like it was wounded. There was blood all over the left flank."

"O' course Keller was riding it," Purdy ventured.

"Rung the bell at the first shot," Healy answered grimly.

"The son of a gun!"

"How long ago was it, Brill?" asked another.

"Must a-been two hours, anyhow."

"No use us following them now, then."

"No use. They've gone to cover."

They turned their horses and took the back trail. The cow ponies scrambled down rocky slopes like cats, and up steep inclines with the agility of mountain goats. The men rode in single file, and conversation was limited to disjointed fragments jerked out now and again. After an hour's rough going they reached the foothills, where they could ride two abreast. As they drew nearer to the ranch country, now one and now another turned off with a shout of farewell.

Healy accepted Purdy's invitation, and dismounted with him at the Fiddleback. Already the first glimmering of dawn flickered faintly from the serrated range. The men unsaddled, watered, fed, and then walked stiffly to the house. Within five minutes both of them lay like logs, dead to the world, until Bess Purdy called them for breakfast, long after the rest of the family had eaten.

"What devilment you been leading paw into, Brill?" demanded Bess promptly when he appeared in the doorway. "Dan says it was close to three when you got home."

She flung her challenge at the young man with a flash of smiling teeth. Bess was seventeen, a romp, very pretty, and hail-fellow-well-met with every range rider in a radius of thirty miles.

"We been looking for a beau for you, Bess," Healy immediately explained.

Miss Purdy tossed her head. "I can find one for myself, Brill Healy, and I don't have to stay out till three to get him, either."

"Come right to your door, do they?" he asked, as she helped him to the ham and eggs.

"Maybe they do, and maybe they don't."

"Well, here's one come right in the middle of the night. Somehow, I jest couldn't make out to wait till morning, Bess."

"Oh, you," she laughed, with a demand for more of this sort of chaffing in her hazel eyes.

At this kind of rough give and take he was an adept. After breakfast he stayed and helped her wash the dishes, romping with her the whole time in the midst of gay bursts of laughter and such repartee as occurred to them.

He found his young hostess so entertaining that he did not get away until the morning was half gone. By the time he reached Seven Mile the sun was past the meridian, and the stage a lessening patch of dust in the distance.

Before he was well out of the saddle, Phyllis Sanderson was standing in the doorway of the store, with a question in her eyes.

"Well?" he forced her to say at last.

Leisurely he turned, as if just aware of her presence.

"Oh, it's you. Mornin', Phyl."

"What did you find out?"

"I met your friend."

"What friend?"

"Mr. Keller, the rustler and bank robber," he drawled insolently, looking full in her face.

"Tell me at once what you found out."

"I found Mr. Keller riding a roan with four white stockings and a wound on its flank."

She caught at the jamb. "You didn't, Brill!"

"I ce'tainly did," he jeered.

"What—what did you do?" Her lips were white as her cheeks.

"I haven't done, anything—yet. You see, I was alone. The other boys hadn't arrived then."

"And he wasn't alone?"

"No; he had three friends with him. I couldn't make out whether any more of them were college chums of yours."

Without another word, she turned her back on him and went into the store. All night she had lain sleepless and longed for and dreaded the coming of the day. Over the wire from Noches had come at dawn fuller details of the robbery, from her brother Phil, who was spending two or three days in town.

It appeared that none of the wounded men would die, though the president had had a narrow escape. Posses had been out all night, and a fresh one was just starting from Noches. It was generally believed, however, that the bandits would be able to make good their escape with the loot.

Her father was absent, making a round of his sheep camps, and would not be back for a week. Hence her hands were very full with the store and the ranch.

She busied herself with the details of her work, nodded now and again to one of the riders as they drifted in, smiled and chatted as occasion demanded, but always with that weight upon her heart she could not shake off. Now, and then again, came to her through the window the voices of Public Opinion on the porch. She made out snatches of the talk, and knew the tide was running strongly against the nester. The sound of Healy's low, masterful voice came insistently. Once, as she looked through the window, she saw a tilted flask at his lips.

Suddenly she became aware, without knowing why, that something was happening, something that stopped her heart and drew her feet swiftly to the door.

Conversation had ceased. All eyes were deflected to a pair of riders coming down the Bear Creek trail with that peculiar jog that is neither a run nor a walk. They seemed quite at ease with the world. Speech and laughter rang languid and carefree. But as they swung from the saddles their eyes swept the group before them with the vigilance of search-lights in time of war.

Brill Healy leaned forward, his right hand resting lightly on his thigh.

"So you've come back, Mr. Keller," he said.

"As you see."

"But not on that roan of yours, I notice."

"You notice correctly, seh."

"Now I wonder why." Healy spoke with a drawl, but his eyes glittered menacingly.

"I expect you know why, Mr. Healy," came the quiet retort.

"Meaning?"

"That the roan was stolen from the pasture two nights ago. Do you happen to know the name of the thief?"

The cattleman laughed harshly, but behind his laughter lay rising anger. "So that's the story you're telling, eh? Sounds most as convincing as that yarn about the pocketknife you picked up."

"I'm not quite next to your point. Have I got to explain to you why I do or don't ride a certain horse, seh?"

"It ain't necessary. We all know why. You ain't riding it because there is a bullet wound in the roan's flank that might be some hard to explain."

"I don't know what you mean. I haven't seen the horse for two days. It was stolen, as I say. Apparently you know a good deal about that roan. I'd be right pleased to hear what you know, Mr. Healy."

"Glad to death to wise you, Mr. Keller. That roan was in Noches yesterday, and you were on its back."

The nester shook his head. "No, I reckon not."

Yeager broke in abruptly: "What have you got up your sleeve, Brill? Spit it out."

"Glad to oblige you, too, Jim. The First National at Noches was held up yesterday, about half-past three or four, by some masked men. Slim and Jim Budd were around and recognized that roan and its rider."

"You mean—"

"You've guessed it, Jim. I mean that your friend, the rustler, is a bank robber, too."

"Yesterday, you say, at four o'clock?"

"About four, yes."

Yeager's face cleared. "Then that lets him out. I was with him yesterday all day."

"Any one else with him?"

"No. We were alone."

"Where?"

"Out in the hills."

"Didn't happen to meet a soul all day maybe?"

"No; what of it?"

Healy barked out again his hard laugh of incredulity. "Go slow, Jim. That ain't going to let him out. It's going to let you in."

Yeager took a step toward him, fists clenched, and eyes flashing. "I'll not stand for that, Brill."

Healy waved him aside. "I've got no quarrel with you, Jim. I ain't making any charges against you to-day. But when it comes to Mr. Keller, that's different." His gaze shifted to the nester and carried with it implacable hostility. "I back my play. He's not only a rustler, he's a bank robber, too. What's more, he'll never leave here alive, except with irons on his wrists!"

"Have you a warrant for my arrest, Mr. Healy?" inquired Keller evenly.

"Don't need one. Furthermore, I'd as lief take you in dead as alive. You cayn't hide behind a girl's skirts this time," continued Healy. "You've got to stand on your own legs and take what's coming. You're a bad outfit. We know you for a rustler, and that's enough. But it ain't all. Yesterday you gave us surplusage when you shot up three men in Noches. Right now I serve notice that you've reached the limit."

"*You* serve notice, do you?"

"You're right, I do."

"But not legal notice, Mr. Healy."

At sight of his enemy standing there so easy and undisturbed, facing death so steadily and so alertly, Brill's passion seethed up and overflowed. Fury filmed his eyes. He saw red. With a jerk, his revolver was out and smoking. A stop watch could scarce have registered the time before Keller's weapon was answering.

But that tenth part of a second made all the difference. For the first heavy bullet from Healy's .44 had crashed into the shoulder of his foe. The shock of it unsteadied the nester's aim. When the smoke cleared it showed the Bear Creek man sinking to the ground, and the right arm of the other hanging limply at his side.

At the first sound of exploding revolvers, Phyllis had grown rigid, but the fusillade had not died away before she was flying along the hall to the porch.

Brill Healy's voice, cold and cruel, came to her in even tones:

"I reckon I've done this job right, boys. If he hadn't winged me, and if Jim hadn't butted in, I'd a-done it more thorough, though."

Yeager was bending over the man lying on the ground. He looked up now and spoke bitterly: "You've murdered an innocent man. Ain't that thorough enough for you?"

Then, catching sight of Cuffs on the porch of the house, Yeager issued orders sharply: "Get on my horse and ride like hell for Doc Brown! Bob, you and Luke help me carry him into the house. What room, Phyl?"

"My room, Jim. Oh, Cuffs, hurry, please!" With that she was gone into the house to make ready the bed for the wounded man.

Healy picked up the revolver that had fallen from his hand, and slid it back into the holster.

"That's right, boys. Take him in and let Phyl patch up the coyote if she can. I reckon this time, she'll have her hands plumb full. Beats all how a decent girl can take up with a ruffian and a scoundrel."

"That will be enough from you, seh," Yeager told him sharply.

Purdy nodded. "Jim's right, Brill. This man has got what was coming to him. It ain't proper to jump him right now, when he's down and out."

"Awful tender-hearted you boys are. Come to that, I've got a pill in me, too, but of course that don't matter," Healy retorted.

"If he dies you'll have another in you, seh," Yeager told him quietly, meeting his eyes steadily for an instant. "Steady, Bob. You take his feet. That's right."

They carried the nester to the bedroom of Phyllis and laid him down gently on the bed. His eyes opened and he looked about him as if to ask where he was. He seemed to understand what had happened, for presently he smiled faintly at his friend and said:

"Beat me to it, Jim. I'm bust up proper this time."

"He shot without giving warning."

Keller moved his head weakly in dissent. "No, I knew just when he was going to draw, but I had to wait for him."

The big, husky plainsmen undressed him with the tenderness of women, and did their best with the help of Aunt Becky, to take care of his wounds temporarily. After these had been dressed Phyllis and the old colored woman took charge of the nursing and dismissed all the men but Yeager.

It would be many hours before Doctor Brown arrived, and it took no critical eyes to see that this man was stricken low.

All the supple strength and gay virility were out of him. Three of the bullets had torn through him. In her heavy heart the girl believed he was going to die. While Yeager was out of the room she knelt down by the bedside, unashamed, and asked for his life as she had never prayed for anything before.

By this time his fever was high and he was wandering in his head. The wild look of delirium was in his eyes, and faint weak snatches of irrelevant speech on his lips. His moans stabbed her heart. There was nothing she could do for him but watch and wait and pray. But what little was to be done in the way of keeping his hot head cool with wet towels her own hands did jealously. Jim and Aunt Becky waited on her while she waited on the sick man.

About midnight the doctor rode up. All day and most of the night before he had been in the saddle. Cuffs had found him across the divide, nearly forty miles away, working over a boy who had been bitten by a rattlesnake. But he brought into the sick room with him that manner of cheerful confidence which radiates hope. You could never have guessed that he was very tired, nor, after the first few minutes, did he know it himself. He lost himself in his case, flinging himself into the breach to turn the tide of what had been a losing battle.

CHAPTER XX

YEAGER RIDES TO NOCHES

Jim Yeager had not watched through the long day and night with Phyllis without discovering how deeply her feelings were engaged. His unobtrusive readiness and his constant hopefulness had been to her a tower of strength during the quiet, dreadful hours before the doctor came.

Once, during the night, she had followed him into the dark hall when he went out to get some fresh cold water, and had broken down completely.

"Is he—is he going to die?" she besought of him, bursting into tears for the first time.

Jim patted her shoulder awkwardly. "Now, don't you, Phyl. You got to buck up and help pull him through. Course he's shot up a heap, but then a man like him can stand a lot of lead in his body. There aren't any of these wounds in a vital place. Chief trouble is he's lost so much blood. That's where his clean outdoor life comes in to help build him up. I'll bet Doc Brown pulls him through."

"Are you just *saying* that, Jim, or do you really think so?"

"I'm saying it, and I think it. There's a whole lot in gaming a thing out. What we've got to do is to *think* he's going to make it. Once we give up, it will be all off."

"You are such a help, Jim," she sighed, dabbing at her eyes with her little handkerchief. "And you're the *best* man."

"That's right. I'll be the best man when we pull off that big wedding of yours and his."

Her heart went out to him with a rush. "You're the only friend both of us have," she cried impulsively.

With the coming of Doctor Brown, Jim resigned his post of comforter in chief, but he stayed at Seven Mile until the crisis was past and the patient on the mend. Next day Slim, Budd, and Phil Sanderson rode in from Noches. They were caked with the dust of their fifty-mile ride, but after they had washed and eaten, Yeager had a long talk with them. He learned, among other things, that Healy had telephoned Sheriff Gill that Keller was lying wounded at Seven Mile, and that the sheriff was expecting to follow them in a few hours.

"Coming to arrest Brill for assault with intent to kill, I reckon," Yeager suggested dryly.

Phil turned on him petulantly. "What's the use of you trying to get away with that kind of talk, Jim? This fellow Keller was recognized as one of the robbers."

"That ain't what Slim has just been telling, Phil. He says he recognized the hawss, and thinks it was Keller in the saddle. Now, I don't think anything about it. I *know* Keller was with me in the hills when this hold-up took place."

"You're his friend, Jim," the boy told him significantly.

"You bet I am. But I ain't a bank robber, if that's what you mean, Phil."

His clear eyes chiselled into those of the boy and dominated him.

"I didn't say you were," Phil returned sulkily. "But I reckon we all recall that you lied for him once. Whyfor would it be a miracle if you did again?"

Jim might have explained, but did not, that it was not for Keller he had lied. He contented himself with saying that the roan with the white stockings had been stolen from the pasture before the holdup. He happened to know, because he was spending the night in Keller's shack with him at the time.

Slim cut in, with drawling sarcasm: "You've got a plumb perfect alibi figured out for him, Jim. I reckon you've forgot that Brill saw him riding through the Pass with the rest of his outfit."

"Brill says so. I say he didn't," returned Yeager calmly.

Toward evening Gill arrived and formally put Keller under arrest. Practically, it amounted only to the precaution of leaving a deputy at the ranch as a watch, for one glance had told the sheriff that the wounded man would not be in condition to travel for some time.

It was the following day that Yeager saddled and said good-by to Phyllis.

"I'm going to Noches to see if I cayn't find out something. It don't look reasonable to me that those fellows could disappear, bag and baggage, into a hole and draw it in after them."

"What about Brill's story that he saw them at the Pass?" the girl asked.

"He may have seen four men, but he ce'tainly didn't see Larrabie Keller. My notion is, Brill lied out of whole cloth, but of course I'm not in a position to prove it. Point is, why did he lie at all?"

Phyllis blushed. "I think I know, Jim."

Yeager smiled. "Oh, I know that. But that ain't, to my way of thinking, motive enough. I mean that a white man doesn't try to hang another just because he—well, because he cut him out of his girl."

"I never was his girl," Phyllis protested.

"I know that, but Brill couldn't get it through his thick head till a stone wall fell on him and give him a hint."

"What other motive are you thinking of, Jim?"

He hesitated. "I've just been kinder milling things around. Do you happen to know right when you met Brill the day of the robbery?"

"Yes. I looked at my watch to see if we would be in time for supper. It was five-thirty."

"And the robbery was at three. The fellows didn't get out of town till close to three-thirty, I reckon," he mused aloud.

"What has that got to do with it? You don't mean that—" She stopped with parted lips and eyes dilating.

He shook his head. "I've got no right to mean that, Phyllie. Even if I did have a kind of notion that way I'd have to give it up. Brill's got a steel-bound, copper-riveted alibi. He couldn't have been at Noches at three o'clock and with you two hours later, fifty-five miles from there. No hawss alive could do it."

"But, Jim—why, it's absurd, anyway. We've known Brill always. He couldn't be that kind of a man. How could he?"

"I didn't say he could," returned her friend noncommittally. "But when it comes to knowing him, what do you know about him—or about me, say? I might be a low-lived coyote without you knowing it. I might be all kinds of a devil. A good girl like you wouldn't know it if I set out to keep it still."

"I could tell by looking at you," she answered promptly.

"Yes, you could," he derided good-naturedly. "How would you know it? Men don't squeal on each other."

"Do you mean that Brill isn't—what we've always thought him?"

"I'm not talking about Brill, but about Jim Yeager," he evaded. "He'd hate to have you know everything that's mean and off color he ever did."

"I believe you must have robbed the bank yourself, Jim," she laughed. "Are you a rustler, too?"

He echoed her laugh as he swung to the saddle. "I'm not

giving myself away any more to-day."

Brill Healy rode up, his arm in a sling. Deep rings of dissipation or of sleeplessness were under his eyes. He looked first at Yeager and then at the young woman, with an ugly sneer. "How's your dear patient, Phyl?"

"He is better, Brill," she answered quietly, with her eyes full on him. "That is, we hope he is better. The doctor isn't quite sure yet."

"Some of us don't hope it as much as the rest of us, I reckon."

She said nothing, but he read in her look a contempt that stung like the lash of a whip.

"He'll be worse again before I'm through with him," the man cried, with a furious oath.

Phyllis measured him with her disdainful eye, and dismissed him. She stepped forward and shook hands with Yeager.

"Take care of yourself, Jim, and don't spare any expense that is necessary," she said.

For a moment she watched her friend canter off, then turned on her heel, and passed into the house, utterly regardless of Healy.

Yeager reached Noches late, for he had unsaddled and let his horse rest at Willow Springs during the heat of the broiling day.

After he had washed and had eaten, Yeager drifted to the Log Cabin Saloon and gambling house. Here was gathered the varied and turbulent life of the border country. Dark-skinned Mexicans rubbed shoulders with range riders baked almost as brown by the relentless sun. Pima Indians and Chinamen and negroes crowded round the faro and dice tables. Games of monte and chuckaluck had their devotees, as had also roulette and poker.

It was a picturesque scene of strong, untamed, self-reliant frontiersmen. Some of them were outlaws and criminals, and some were as simple and tender-hearted as children. But all had become accustomed to a life where it is possible at any moment to be confronted with sudden death.

A man playing the wheel dropped a friendly nod at Jim. He waited till the wheel had stopped and saw the man behind it rake in his chips before he spoke. Then, as he scattered more chips here and there over the board, he welcomed Yeager with a whoop.

"Hi there, Malpais! What's doing in the hills these yere pleasant days?"

"A little o' nothin', Sam. The way they're telling it you been having all the fun down here."

Sam Wilcox gathered the chips pushed toward him by the croupier and cashed in. He was a heavy-set, bronzed man, with a bleached, straw-colored mustache. Taking his friend by the arm, he led him to one end of the bar that happened for the moment to be deserted.

"Have something, Jim. Oh, I forgot. You're ridin' the water wagon and don't irrigate. More'n I can say for some of you Malpais lads. Some of them was in here right woozy the other day."

"The boys will act the fool when they hit town. Who was it?"

"Slim and Budd and young Sanderson."

"Was Phil Sanderson drunk?" Yeager asked, hardly surprised, but certainly troubled.

"I ain't sure he was, but he was makin' the fur fly at the wheel, there. Must have dropped two hundred dollars."

Jim's brows knit in a puzzled frown. He was wondering how the boy had come by so much money at a time.

"Who was he trailin' with?"

"With a lad called Spiker, that fair-haired guy sitting in at the poker table. He's another youngster that has been dropping money right plentiful."

"Who is he?"

"He's what they call a showfer. He runs one o' these automobiles; takes parties out in it."

"Been here long? Looks kind o' like a tinhorn gambler."

"Not long. He's thick with some of you Malpais gents. I've seen him with Healy a few."

"Oh, with Healy."

Jim regarded the sportive youth more attentively, and presently dropped into a vacant seat beside him, buying twenty dollars worth of chips.

Spiker was losing steadily. He did not play either a careful or a brilliant game. Jim, playing very conservatively, and just about holding his own, listened to the angry bursts and the boastings of the man next him, and drew his own conclusions as to his character. After a couple of hours of play the Malpais man cashed in and went back to the hotel where he was putting up.

He slept till late, ate breakfast leisurely, and after an hour of looking over the paper and gossiping with the hotel clerk about the holdup he called casually upon the deputy sheriff. Only one thing of importance he gleaned from him. This was that the roan with the white stockings had been picked up seven miles from Noches the morning after the holdup.

This put a crimp in Healy's story of having seen Keller in the Pass on the animal. Furthermore, it opened a new field for surmise. *Brill Healy said that he had seen the horse with a wound in its flank.* Now, how did he know it was wounded, since Slim had not mentioned this when he had telephoned? It followed that if he had not seen the broncho—and that he had seen it was a sheer physical impossibility—he could know of the wound only because he was already in close touch with what had happened at Noches.

But how could he be aware of what was happening fifty miles away? That was the sticker Jim could not get around. His alibi was just as good as that of the horse. Both of them rested on the assumption that neither could cover the ground between two given points in a given time. There was one other possible explanation—that Healy had been in telephonic communication with Noches before he met Phyllis. But this seemed to Jim very unlikely, indeed. By his own story he had been cutting trail all afternoon and had seen nobody until he met Phyllis.

Yeager called on the cashier, Benson, later in the day, and

had a talk with him and with the president, Johnson. Both of these were now back at their posts, though the latter was not attempting much work as yet. Jim talked also with many others. Some of them had theories, but none of them had any new facts to advance.

The young cattleman put up at the same hotel as Spiker and struck up a sort of intimacy with him. They sometimes loafed together during the day, and at night they were always to be seen side by side at the poker table.

CHAPTER XXI

BREAKING DOWN AN ALIBI

Keller found convalescence under the superintendence of Miss Sanderson one of the great pleasures of his life. Her school was out for the summer and she was now at home all day. He had never before found time to be lazy, and what dreaming he had done had been in the stress of action. Now he might lie the livelong day and not too obviously watch her brave, frank youth as she moved before him or sat reading. For the first time in his life he was in love!

But as the nester grew better he perceived that she was withdrawing herself from him. He puzzled over the reason, not knowing that her brother, Phil, was troubling her with flings and accusations thrown out bitterly because his boyish concern for her good name could find no gentler way to express itself.

"They're saying you're in love with the fellow—and him headed straight for the pen," he charged.

"Who says it, Phil?" she asked quietly, but with flaming cheeks.

He smote his fist on the table. "It don't matter who says it.

252   William MacLeod Raine

You keep away from him. Let Aunt Becky nurse him. You haven't any call to wait on him, anyhow. If he's got to be nursed by one of the family, I'll do it."

He tried to keep his word, and as a result of it the wounded man had to endure his sulky presence occasionally. Keller was man of the world enough to be amused at his attitude, and yet was interested enough in the lad's opinion of him to keep always an even mood of cheerful friendliness. There was a quantity of winsome camaraderie about him that won its way with Phil in spite of himself. Moreover, all the boy in him responded to the nester's gameness, the praises of which he heard on all sides.

"I see you have quite made up your mind I'm a skunk," the wounded man told him amiably.

"You robbed the bank at Noches and shot up three men that hadn't hurt you any," the boy retorted defiantly.

"Not unless Jim Yeager is a liar."

"Oh, Jim! No use going into that. He's your friend. I don't know why, but he is."

"And you're Brill Healy's. That's why you won't tell that he was carrying your sister's knife the day I saw you and him first."

The boy flashed toward the bed startled eyes. Keller was looking at him very steadily.

"Who says he had Phyl's knife?"

"Hadn't he?"

"What difference does that make, anyhow? I hear you're telling that you found the knife beside the dead cow. You ain't got any proof, have you?" challenged young Sanderson angrily.

"No proof," admitted the other.

"Well, then." Phil chewed on it for a moment before he broke out again: "I reckon you cayn't talk away the facts, Mr. Keller. We caught you in the act—caught you good. By your own story, you're the man we came on. What's the use of you trying to lay it on me and Brill?"

"Am I trying to lay it on you?"

"Looks like. On Brill, anyhow. There's nothing doing. Folks in this neck of the woods is for him and against you. Might as well *sabe* that right now," the lad blurted.

"I *sabe* that some of them are," the other laughed, but not with quite his usual debonair gayety. For he did not at all like the way things looked.

But though Phil had undertaken to do all the nursing that needed to be done by the family, he was too much of an outdoors dweller to confine himself for long to the four walls of a room. Besides, he was often called away by the work of looking after the cattle of the ranch. Moreover, both he and his father were away a good deal arranging for the disposal of their sheep. At these times her patient hoped, and hoped in vain, that Phyllis would take her brother's place.

Came a day when Keller could stand it no longer. In Becky's absence, he made shift to dress himself, bit by bit, lying on the bed in complete exhaustion after the effort of getting into each garment. He could scarce finish what he had undertaken, but at last he was clothed and ready for the journey. Leaning on a walking stick, he dragged himself into the passage and out to the porch, where Phyllis was sitting alone.

She gave a startled cry at sight of him standing there, haggard and white, his clothes hanging on his gaunt frame much as if he had been a skeleton.

"What are you doing?" she cried, running to his aid.

After she had got him into her chair, he smiled up at her and panted weakly. He was leaning back in almost complete exhaustion.

"You wouldn't come to see me, so—I came—to see you," he gasped out, at last.

"But—you shouldn't have! You might have done yourself a great injury. It's—it's criminal of you."

"I wanted to see you," he explained simply.

"Why didn't you send for me?"

"There wasn't anybody to send. Besides, you wouldn't have stayed. You never do, now."

She looked at him, then looked away. "You don't need me now—and I have my work to do."

"But I do need you, Phyllie."

It was the first time he had ever spoken the diminutive to her. He let out the word lingeringly, as if it were a caress. The girl felt the color flow beneath her dusky tan. She changed the subject abruptly.

"None of the boys are here. How am I to get you back to your room?"

"I'll roll a trail back there presently, ma'am."

She looked helplessly round the landscape, in hope of seeing some rider coming to the store. But nobody was in sight.

"You had no business to come. It might have killed you. I thought you had better sense," she reproached.

"I wanted to see you," he parroted again.

Like most young women, she knew how to ignore a good deal. "You'll have to lean on me. Do you think you can try it now?"

"If I go, will you stay with me and talk?" he bargained.

"I have my work to do," she frowned.

"Then I'll stay here, thank you kindly." He settled back into the chair and let her have his gay smile. Nevertheless, she saw that his lips were colorless.

"Yes, I'll stay," she conceded, moved by her anxiety.

"Every day?"

"We'll see."

"All right," he laughed weakly. "If you don't come, I'll take a *pasear* and go look for you." She helped him to his feet and they stood for a moment facing each other.

"You must put your hand on my shoulder and lean hard on me," she told him.

But when she saw the utter weakness of him, her arm slipped round his waist and steadied him.

"Now then. Not too fast," she ordered gently.

They went back very slowly, his weight leaning on her more at every step. When they reached his room, Keller sank down on the bed, utterly exhausted. Phyllis ran for a cordial and put it to his lips. It was some time before he could even speak.

"Thank you. I ain't right husky yet," he admitted.

"You mustn't ever do such a thing again," she charged him.

"Not ever?"

"Not till the doctor says you're strong enough to move."

"I won't—if you'll come and see me every day," he answered irrepressibly.

So every afternoon she brought a book or her sewing, and sat by him, letting Phil storm about it as much as he liked. These were happy hours. Neither spoke of love, but the air was electrically full of it. They laughed together a good deal at remarks not intrinsically humorous, and again there were conversational gaps so highly charged that she would rush at them as a reckless hunter takes a fence.

As he got better, he would be propped up in bed, and Aunt Becky would bring in tea for them both. If there had been any corner of his heart unwon it would have surrendered then. For to a bachelor the acme of bliss is to sit opposite a girl of whom he is very fond, and to see her buttering his bread and pouring his tea with that air of domesticity that visualizes the intimacy of which he has dreamed. Keller had played a lone hand all his turbulent life, and this was like a glimpse of Heaven let down to earth for his especial benefit.

It was on such an occasion that Jim Yeager dropped in on them upon his return from Noches. He let his eyes travel humorously over the room before he spoke.

"Why for don't I ever have the luck to be shot up?" he drawled.

"Oh, you Jim!" Keller called a greeting from the bed. Phyllis came forward, and, with a heightened color, shook hands with him.

"You'll sit down with us and have some tea, Jim," she told him.

"Me? I'm no society Willie. Don't know the game at all, Phyl. Besides, I'm carrying half of Arizona on my clothes. It's some dusty down in the Malpais."

Nevertheless he sat down, and, over the biscuits and jam, told the meagre story of what he had found out.

The finding of the stocking-footed roan near Noches so soon after the robbery disposed of Healy's lie, though it did not prove that Keller had not been riding it at the time of the holdup. As for Healy, Yeager confessed he saw no way of implicating him. His alibi was just as good as that of any of them.

But there was one person his story did involve, and that was

Spiker, the tinhorn, tenderfoot sport of Noches. During the absence of this young man at the gaming table, Jim and his friend, Sam Weaver, had got into his room with a skeleton key and searched it thoroughly. They had found, in a suit case, a black mask, a pair of torn and shiny chaps, a gray shirt, a white, dusty sombrero, much the worse for wear, and over three hundred dollars in bills.

"What does he pretend his business is?" Keller asked, when Jim had finished.

"Allows he's a showfer. Drives folks around in a gasoline wagon. That's the theory, but I notice he turned down a mining man who wanted to get him to run him into the hills on Monday. Said he hadn't time. The showfer biz is a bluff, looks like."

The nester made no answer. His eyes, narrowed to slits, were gazing out of the window absently. Presently he came from deep thought to ask Yeager to hand him the map he would find in his inside coat pocket. This he spread out on the bed in front of him. When at last he looked up he was smiling.

"I reckon it's no bluff, Jim. He's a chauffeur, all right, but he only drives out select outfits."

"Meaning?"

The map lying in front of Keller was one of Noches County. The nester located, with his index finger, the town of that name, and traced the road from it to Seven Mile. Then his finger went back to Noches, and followed the old military road to Fort Lincoln, a route which almost paralleled the one to the ranch.

The eyes of Phyllis were already shining with excitement. She divined what was coming.

"Is this road still travelled, Jim?"

"It goes out to the old fort. Nobody has lived there for most thirty years. I reckon the road ain't travelled much."

"Strikes through Del Oro Canon, doesn't it, right after it leaves Noches?"

"Yep."

"I reckon, Jim, your friend, Spiker, drove a party out that way the afternoon of the holdup," the nester drawled smilingly. "By the way, is your friend in the lockup?"

"He sure is. The deputy sheriff arrested him same night we went through his room."

"Good place for him. Well, it looks like we got Mr. Healy tagged at last. I don't mean that we've got the proof, but we can prove he might have been on the job."

"I don't see it, Larry. I reckon my head's right thick."

"I see it," spoke up Phyllis quickly.

Keller smiled at her. "You tell him."

"Don't you see, Jim? The motor car must have been waiting for them somewhere after they had robbed the bank," she explained.

"At the end of Del Oro Canon, likely," suggested the nester.

She nodded eagerly. "Yes, they would get into the canon before the pursuit was in sight. That is why they were not seen by Slim and the rest of the posse."

Yeager looked at her, and as he looked the certainty of it grew on him. His mind began to piece out the movements of the outlaws from the time they left Noches. "That's right, Phyl. His car is what he calls a hummer. It can go like blazes—forty miles an hour, he told me. And the old fort road is a dandy, too."

"They would leave the automobile at Willow Creek, and cut across to the Pass," she hazarded.

"All but Brill. Being bridlewise, he rode right for Seven Mile to make dead sure of his alibi, whilst the others made their getaway with the loot. When he happened to meet you on the way, he would be plumb tickled, for that cinched things proper for him. You would be a witness nobody could get away from."

"And what about their hawsses? Did they bring the bronchs in the car, too?" drawled Keller, an amused flicker in his eyes.

The others, who had been swimming into their deductions so confidently, were brought up abruptly. Phyllis glanced at Jim and looked foolish.

"The bronchs couldn't tag along behind at a forty per clip. That's right," admitted Yeager blankly.

"I hadn't thought about that. And they had to have their horses with them to get from Willow Creek to the Pass. That spoils everything," the girl agreed.

Then, seeing her lover's white teeth flashing laughter at her, she knew he had found a way round the difficulty. "How would this do, partners—just for a guess: The car was waiting for them at the end of the Del Oro Cañon. They dumped their loot into it, then unsaddled and threw all the saddles in, too. They gave the bronchs a good scare, and started them into the hills, knowing they would find their way back home all right in a couple of days. At Willow Creek they found hawsses waiting for them, and Mr. Spiker hit the back trail for Noches, with his car, and slid into town while everybody was busy about the robbery."

"Sure. That would be the way of it," his friend nodded. "All we got to do now is to get Spiker to squeal."

"If he happens to be a quitter."

"He will—under pressure. He's that kind."

A knock came on the door, and Tom Benwell, the store clerk, answered her summons to come in.

"It's Budd, Miss Phyl. He came to see about getting-that stuff you was going to order for a dress for his little girl," the storekeeper explained.

Phyllis rose and followed the man back to the store. When she had gone, Jim stepped to the door and shut it. Returning, he sat down beside the bed.

"Larry, I didn't tell all I know. That hat in Spiker's room had the initials P.S. written on the band. What's more, I knew the hat by a big coffee stain splashed on the crown. It happens I made that stain myself on the round-up onct when we were wrastling and I knocked the coffeepot over."

Keller looked at his friend gravely. "It was Phil Sanderson's hat?"

Yeager nodded assent. "He must have loaned his old hat to Spiker for the holdup."

"You didn't turn the hat over to the sheriff?"

"Not so as you could notice it. I shoved it in my jeans and burnt it over my camp fire next day."

"This mixes things up a heap. If Phil is in this thing—and it sure looks that way—it ties our hands. I'd like to have a talk with Spiker before we do anything."

"What's the matter with having a talk with Phil? Why not shove this thing right home to him?"

The nester shook his head. "Let's wait a while. We don't want to drive Healy away yet. If the kid's in it he would go right to Healy with the whole story."

Yeager swore softly. "It's all Brill's fault. He's been leading Phil into devilment for two years now."

"Yes."

"And all the time been playing himself for the leader of us fellows that are against the rustlers and that Bear Creek outfit," continued Jim bitterly. "Why, we been talking of electing him sheriff. Durn his forsaken hide, he's been riding round asking the boys to vote for him on a promise to clean out the miscreants."

"You can oppose him, of course. But we have no absolute proof against him yet. We must have proof that nobody can doubt."

"I reckon. And'll likely have to wait till we're gray."

"I don't think so. My guess is that he's right near the end of his rope. We're going to make a clean-up soon as I get solid on my feet."

"And Phil? What if we catch him in the gather, and find him wearing the bad-man brand?"

Keller's eyes met those of his friend. "There never was a rodeo where some cattle didn't slip through unnoticed, Jim."

CHAPTER XXII

SURRENDER

The weeks slipped away and brought with them healing to the wounded man at Seven Mile. He moved from the bed where at first he had spent his days to a lounge in the living room, and there, from the bay window, he could look out at the varied life of the cattle country. Men came and went in the dust of the drag drive, their approach heralded by the bawl of thirsty cattle. Others cantered up and bought tobacco and canned goods. The stage arrived twice a week with its sack of mail, and always when it did Public Opinion gathered upon the porch of the store, as of yore. Phil Sanderson he saw often, Yeager sometimes, and once or twice he caught a glimpse of Healy's saturnine face.

A scarcity of beef and a sharp rise in prices brought the round-up earlier than usual. Every spare man was called upon to help comb the hills for the wild steers that ran the wooded water-sheds, as untamed as the deer and the lynx. Even the storekeeper, Benwell, was pressed into the service. 'Rastus and the nester were the only men about the place, the deputy sheriff having been recalled to Noches on the collapse of Healy's story.

The removal to a distance of the rest of her admirers did not have the effect of throwing Keller alone with Phyllis more often. The young mistress of the ranch invited Bess Purdy to visit her, and now he never saw her except in the presence of her other guest.

Bess took him in at once, evidencing her approval of him by entering upon a spirited war of repartee with him. She had not been in the house twenty-four hours before she had unbosomed herself of a derisive confidence.

"I don't believe you're a bank robber, at all! I don't believe you are even a rustler! You're a false alarm!"

Both Keller and Miss Sanderson smiled at the daring of the girl's challenge. But the former defended himself with apparent heat.

"What makes you think so? Why should you undermine my reputation with such an assertion? You can't talk that way about me without proving it, Miss Purdy."

"Well, I don't. You don't *look* it."

"I can't help that. You ask Mr. Healy. He'll tell you I am."

"You'll need a better witness than Brill before I'll believe it."

"And I thought you were going to like me," he lamented.

"I like a lot of people who aren't ruffians, but of course I can't admire you so much as if you were a really truly bad man."

"But if I promise to be one?"

"Oh, anybody can *promise*," she flung back, eyes bubbling

with laughter.

"Wait till I get on my feet again."

A youth galloped up to the house in a cloud of alkali dust.

"There's Cuffs," announced Phyllis, smiling at Bess.

That young woman blushed a little, supposed, aloud, she must go out to see him, and withdrew in seeming reluctance.

"He wants Bess to go with him to the Frying Pan dance. He sent a note over from the round-up to ask her. She hasn't had a chance yet to tell him that she would," explained her friend.

"How will he take her?" asked the nester, his eyes quickening.

"In the surrey, I suppose. Why?"

"The surrey will hold four."

She made no pretense of not understanding. Her look met his in a betrayal of the pleasure his invitation gave her. Yet she shook her head.

"No, thank you."

"But why—if I may ask?"

"Ah! But you mayn't," she smiled.

He considered that. "You like to dance."

"Most girls do."

"Then it is because of me," he soliloquized aloud.

"Please," she begged lightly.

"My reputation, I suppose."

She began to roll up the embroidery upon which she was busy. But he got to the door before her.

"No, you don't."

"You are not going to make me tell you why I can't go with you, are you?"

"That, to start with. Then I'm going to make you tell me some other things."

"But if I don't want to tell?" Her eyes were wide open with surprise, for he had never before taken the masterful line with her. Deep down, she liked it; but she had no intention of letting him know so.

"There are times not to tell, and there are times to tell. This will be one of the last kind, Phyllis."

She tried mockery. "When you throw a big chest like that I suppose you always get what you want."

"You act right funny, girl. I never see you alone any more. We haven't had a good talk for more than a week. Now, why?"

She thought of telling him she had been too busy; then, moved by an impulse of impatience, met his gaze fully, and told him part of the truth.

"I should think you would understand that a girl has to be careful of what she does!"

"You mean about us being friends?"

"Oh, we can be friends, but—If you can't see it, then I can't tell you," she finished.

"I can see it, I reckon. You saved my life, and I expect some human cat got his claws out and said it was because you were fond of me.

"Then you saved it again by your nursing. No two ways about that. Doc Brown says you and Jim did. I was so sick folks knew it had to be. But now I'm getting well, you have to show them you're not interested in me. Isn't that about it?"

"Yes."

"But you don't have to show me, too, do you?"

"Am I not—courteous?"

"I ain't worrying any about your courtesy. But, look here, Phyllie. Have you forgotten what happened in the kitchen that night you helped me to escape?"

She flashed him one look of indignant reproach. "I should think you would be the last person in the world to remind me of it."

"I've got a right to mention it because I've asked you a question since that ain't been answered. That week's been up ten days."

"I'm not going to answer it now."

And with that she slipped past him and from the room.

He ran a hand through his curls and voiced his perplexity. "Now, if a woman ain't the strangest ever. Just as a fellow is ready to tell her things, she gets mad and hikes."

Nevertheless he smiled, not uncheerfully. What experience he had had with young women told him the signs were not hopeless for his success. He was not sure of her, not by a good deal. He had captured her imagination. But to win a girl's fancy is not the same as to storm her heart. He often caught himself wondering just where he stood with her. For himself, he knew he was fathoms deep in love.

She was in his thoughts when he fell asleep.

He awoke in the darkness, and sat upright in the bed, a feeling of calamity oppressing him. Something pungent tickled his nostrils.

A faint crackling sounded in the air.

Swiftly he slipped on such clothes as he needed and stepped into the passage. A heavy smoke was pouring up the back stairway. He knocked insistently upon the door where Phyllis and her guest were sleeping.

"What is it?" a voice demanded.

"Get up and dress, Miss Sanderson! The house is on fire! You have plenty of time, I think. If there's any hurry I'll let you know after I've looked."

He went down the front stairs and found that the fire was in the back part of the house. Already volumes of smoke with spitting tongues of flame were reaching toward the foot of the stairs. He ran up to the room where the girls were dressing, and called to them:

"Are you ready?"

"Yes."

The door opened, to show him two very pale girls, each carrying a bundle of clothes. They were only partially dressed, but wrappers covered their disarray. Keller went to the clothes closet, emptied it with a sweep and lift of his arm, and returned, to lead the way downstairs.

"Take a breath before you start. The smoke's bad, but there is no real danger," he told them as he plunged forward.

At the foot of the stairs he stopped to see that they were following him closely, then flung open the outer door and let in a rush of cool, sweet air. In another moment they were outside, safe and unhurt.

Phyllis drew a long breath before she said:

"The house is gone!"

"If there is anything you want particularly from the living room I can get in through the window," Keller told her.

She shuddered. Flame jets were already shooting out here and there. "I wouldn't let you go back for the world. We didn't get out too soon."

"No," he agreed.

A sniveling voice behind them broke in: "Where is Mr. Phil? I yain't seen him yet."

Larrabie swung round on 'Rastus like a flash. "What do you mean? He's at the round-up, of course."

The little fellow began to bawl: "No, sah. He done come home late last night. Aftah you-all had gone to bed. He's in his room, tha's where he is."

Phyllis caught at the arm of Keller to steady her. She was colorless to the lips.

"Oh, God! Oh, God!" she cried faintly.

The nester pushed her gently into the arms of her guest.

"Take care of her, Bess. I'll get Phil."

He ran round the house to the back. The bedroom occupied by young Sanderson was on the first floor. The ranger caught up a stick, smashed the window, and tore out the frame by main strength. Presently he was inside, groping through the dense smoke toward the bed.

Flames leaped at him from out of it like darting serpents. His hair, his face, his clothes, caught fire before he had discovered that the bed had been used, but was now empty. The door into the hall was open, and through it were pouring billows of smoke. Evidently Phil must have tried to escape that way and been overpowered.

The young man caught up a towel and wrapped it around his throat and mouth, then plunged forward into the caldron of the passage. The smoke choked him and the intense heat peeled his face and made the endurance of it an agony.

He stumbled over something soft, and discovered with his hands that it was a body. Smothered and choked, half frantic with the heat, he struggled back into the bedroom with his burden.

Somehow he reached the window, stumbled through it, and dragged the inanimate body after him. Then, with Phil in his arms, he reeled forward into the fresh air beyond.

With a cry Phyllis broke from Bess and ran toward him. But before she had reached the rescuer and the rescued, Keller went down in total collapse. He, too, was unconscious when she knelt beside him and began with her hands to crush out the smoldering fire in his clothes.

He opened his eyes and smiled faintly when he saw who it was.

"How's the boy?" he asked.

"He is breathing," cried Bess joyfully, from where she was bending over Sanderson.

"You go attend to him. I'm all right now."

"Are you truly?"

"Truly."

He proved it by sitting up, and presently by rising and joining with her the group gathered around Phil. For Aunt Becky had now emerged from her cabin and taken charge of affairs.

Phil was supported to the bunk house and put to bed by Keller and 'Rastus. It was already plain that he would be none the worse for his adventure after a night's good sleep. Aunt Becky applied to his case the homely remedies she had used before, while the others stood around the bed and helped as best they could. Strangely enough, he was not burned at all. In this he had escaped better than Keller, whose hair and eyebrows and skin were all the worse for singeing.

The nester noticed that Phyllis, in handing a bowl of water to Bess, used awkwardly her left hand. The right one, he observed, was held with the palm concealed against the folds of her skirt.

Presently Phyllis, her anxiety as to Phil relieved, left Aunt Becky and Bess to care for him, while she went out to make arrangements for disposing of the party until morning. The nester followed her into the night and walked beside her toward the house of the foreman. The darkness was lit up luridly by the shooting flames of the burning house.

"The store isn't going to catch fire. That's one good thing," Keller observed, by way of comfort.

"Yes." There was a catch in her voice, for all the little treasures of her girlhood, gathered from time to time, were going up in smoke.

"You're insured, I reckon?"

"Yes."

"Well, it might be worse."

She thought of the narrow escape Phil had had, and nodded.

"You'll have to sleep in the bunk house. Take any of the beds you like. Bess and I will put up at the foreman's," she explained.

As is the custom among bachelors who attend to their own domestic affairs, they found the bed just as the foreman had stepped out of it two weeks before. While Keller held the lantern, Phyllis made it up, and again he saw that she was using her right hand very carefully and flinching when it touched the blankets. Putting the lantern down on the table, he walked up to her.

"I'll make the bed."

She stepped back, with a little laugh. "All right."

He made it, then turned to her at once.

"I want to see your hand."

She gave him the left one, even as he had done on the occasion of their second meeting. He took it, and kept it.

"Now the other."

"What do you want with it?"

"Never mind." He reached down and drew it from the folds of her skirt, where it had again fallen. Very gently he turned it so that the palm was up. Ugly blisters and a red seam showed where she had burned herself. He looked at her without speaking.

"It's nothing," she told him, a little hysterically.

For an instant her mind flashed back to the time when Buck Weaver had drawn the cactus spines out of that same hand.

His voice was rough with feeling. "I can see it isn't. And you got it for me—putting out the fire in my clothes. I reckon I cayn't thank you, you poor little tortured hand." He lifted the fingers to his lips and kissed them.

"Don't," she cried brokenly.

"Has it got to be this way always, Phyllie—you giving and me taking?" His hand tightened on hers ever so slightly, and a spasm of pain shot across her face. He looked at the burned fingers again tenderly. "Does it hurt pretty bad, girl?"

"I wish it was ten times as bad!" she broke out, with a sob. "You saved Phil's life—at the risk of your own. I wish I could tell you how I feel, what I think of you, how splendid you are." In default of which ability, she began to cry softly.

He wasted no more time. He did not ask her whether he might. With a gesture, his arm went around her and drew her to him.

"Let me tell what I think of you, instead, girl o' mine. I cayn't tell it, either, for that matter, but I reckon I can make out to show you, honey."

"I didn't mean—that way," she protested, between laughter and tears.

"Well, that's the way I mean."

Neither spoke again for a minute. Than: "Do you really— love me?" she murmured.

"What do you think?" He laughed with the sheer unconquerable boyish delight in her.

"I think you're pretending right well," she smiled.

"If I am making believe."

"If you are." Her arms slipped round his neck with a swift impulse of love. "But you're not. Tell me you're not, Larry."

He told her, in the wordless way lovers have at command, the way that is more convincing than speech.

So Phyllis, from the troubled waters of doubt, came at last to safe harborage.

CHAPTER XXIII

AT THE RODEO

There was an exodus from Seven Mile the second day after the fire. Keller went up Bear Creek, Phyllis accepted the invitation of Bess to stay with her at the Fiddleback, and her brother returned to the round-up.

The riders were now combing the Lost Creek watershed. Phil knew the camp would be either at Peaceful Valley or higher up, near the headwaters of the creek. Before he reached the valley the steady bawl of cattle told him that the outfit was camped there. He topped the ridge and looked down upon Cattleland at its busiest. Just below him was the remuda, the ponies grazing slowly toward the hills under the care of three half-grown boys.

Beyond were the herded cattle. Here all was activity. Within the fence of riders surrounding the wild creatures the cutting out and the branding were being pushed rapidly forward. Occasionally some leggy steer, tail up and feet pounding, would make a dash to break the cordon. Instantly one of the riders would wheel in chase, head off the animal, and drive it back.

Brill Healy, boss of the rodeo by election, was in charge. He

William MacLeod Raine

was an expert handler of cattle, one of the best in the country. It was his nature to seek the limelight, though it must be said for him that he rose to his responsibilities. The owners knew that when he was running the round-up few cattle would slip through the net he wound around them.

"Hello, Brill!" shouted the young man as he rode up.

"Hello, son! Too bad about the fire. I'll want to hear about it later. Looking for a job?" he flung hurriedly over his shoulder. For he had not even a minute to spare.

"I reckon."

Phil did not wait to be assigned work, but joined the calf branders.

Not until night had fallen and they were gathered round in a semicircle leaning against their saddles did Phil find time to tell the story of the fire. There was some haphazard comment when he had finished, after which Slim spoke.

"So the nester hauled you out. Ce'tainly looks like he's plumb game. You said he was afire when he got you into the open, didn't you, Phil?"

The boy nodded. "And all in. He fainted right away."

"With him still burning away like the doctor's fire there," murmured Healy ironically, with a slight gesture toward the cook.

Phil looked at him angrily. "I didn't say that. Some one put the fire out."

"Oh, some one! Might a man ask who?"

Phil had not had any intention of telling, but he found himself letting Healy have it straight.

"Phyllis."

"About what I thought!" Healy said it significantly, and with a malice that overrode his discretion.

"What do you mean?" demanded the boy fiercely.

"I ain't said anything, have I?" Healy came back smoothly.

Yeager's quiet voice broke the silence that followed, while Phil was trying to voice the resentment in him.

"You mean what we're all thinking, Brill, I reckon—that she is the sort to forget herself when somebody needs her help. Ain't that it?"

The eyes of the two met steadily in a clash of wills. Healy's gave way for the time, not because he was mastered, but because he did not wish to alienate the rough, but fair-minded, men sitting around.

"You're mighty good at explaining me to the boys, Jim. I expect that is what I mean," he answered sullenly.

"Sure," put in Purdy, with amiable intent.

"But when it comes to Mr. Keller I can explain myself tol'able well. I don't need any help there, Jim, not even if he is yore best friend."

"If you've got anything to say against him, I'll ask you to say it when I'm not around," broke in Phil. "You'll recollect, please, that he's *my* friend, too."

"That so? Since, when, Phil?" the rodeo boss retorted sarcastically.

"Since he went into the fire after me and saved my life. Think I'm a coyote to round on him? I tell you he's a white man clear through. In my opinion, he's neither a rustler nor a bank robber." He was flushed and excited, but his gaze met that of his former friend and challenged him defiantly.

Healy's eyes narrowed. He gazed at the boy darkly, as if he meant to read him through and through. For years he had dominated Phil, had shaped him to his ends, had led him into wild, lawless courses after him. Now the anchors were dragging. He was losing control of him. He resolved to turn the screws on him, but not at this time and place.

"I've always been considered a full-grown man, Phil. What I think I aim to say out loud when the notion hits me. That being so, I go on record as having an opinion about Keller. You think he's on the square, and you give him a white-washed certificate as a bony-fidy Sunday-school scholar.

"Different here. I think him a coyote and a crook, and so I say it right out in meeting. Any objections?" The gaze of the boss shifted from Sanderson to Yeager, and fastened.

"None in the world. You think what you like, Brill, and we'll stick to our opinions," Yeager replied cheerfully.

"And when I get good and ready I'll act on mine," Healy replied with an evil grin.

"If you find it right convenient. I expect Keller ain't exactly a wooden cigar Indian. Maybe he'll have a say-so in what's doing," suggested Yeager.

"About as much as he had last time," sneered the round-up boss. With which he rose, stretched himself, and gave orders. "Time to turn in, boys. We're combing Old Baldy to-morrow, remember."

"And Old Baldy's sure a holy terror," admitted Slim.

"Come three more days and we'd ought to be through. I'm not going to grieve any when we are. This high life don't suit me too durned well," put in Benwell.

"Yet when you come here first you was a right sick man, Tom. Now, you're some healthy. Don't that prove the outside of a hawss is good for the inside of a man, like the docs say?" grinned Purdy.

"Tom's notion of real living is sassiety with a capital S," explained Cuffs. "You watch him cut ice at the Frying Pan dance next week. He'll be the real-thing lady-killer. All you lads going, I reckon. How about you, Jim?"

Yeager said he expected to be there.

"With yore friend the rustler?" asked Healy insolently over his shoulder.

"I haven't got any friend that's a rustler."

"I'm speaking of Mr. Larrabie Keller." There was a slurring inflection on the prefix.

"He'll be there, I shouldn't wonder."

"I'd wonder a heap," retorted Healy. "You'll see he won't show his face there."

"That's where you're wrong, Brill. He told me he was going," spoke up Phil triumphantly.

"We'll see. He's wise to the fact that this country knows him for an out-and-out crook. He'll stay in his hole."

"You going, Slim?" asked Purdy amiably, to turn the conversation into a more pacific channel.

"Sure," answered that young giant, getting lazily to his feet. "Well, sons, the boss is right. Time to pound our ears."

They rolled themselves in their blankets, the starry sky roofing their bedroom. Within five minutes every man of them was asleep except the night herders—and one other.

Healy lay a little apart from the rest, partially screened by some boxes of provisions and a couple of sacks of flour. His jaw was clamped tight. He looked into the deep velvet sky without seeing. For a long time he did not move. Then, noiselessly, he sat up, glanced around carefully to make sure he was not observed, rose, and stole into the darkness, carrying with him his saddle and bridle.

One of his ponies was hobbled in the mesquite. Swiftly he saddled. Leading the animal very carefully so as to avoid rustling the brush, he zigzagged from the camp until he had reached a safe distance. Here he swung himself on and rode into the blur of night, at first cautiously, but later with swift-pounding hoofs. He went toward the northwest in a bee line without hesitation or doubt. Only when the lie of the ground forced a detour did he vary his direction.

So for hours he travelled until he reached a canon in which squatted a little log cabin. He let his voice out in the howl of a coyote before he dismounted. No answer came, save the echo from the cliff opposite. Again that mournful call sounded, and this time from the cabin found an answer.

A man came sleepily to the door and peered out. "Hello! That you, Brill?"

Healy swung off, trailed his rein, and followed the man into the cabin. "Don't light up, Tom. No need."

For ten minutes they talked in low tones. Healy emerged from the cabin, remounted, and rode back to the cow camp. He reached it just as the first, faint streaks of gray tinged the eastern sky.

Silently he unsaddled, hobbled his pony, and carried his saddle back to the place where he had been lying. Once more he lay down, glanced cautiously round to see all was quiet, and fell asleep as soon as his head touched the saddle.

William MacLeod Raine

CHAPTER XXIV

MISSING

From all over the Malpais country, from the water-sheds where Bear and Elk and Cow creeks head, from the halfway house far out in the desert where the stage changes horses, men and women dribbled to the Frying Pan for the big dance after the round-up. Great were the preparations. Many cakes and pies and piles of sandwiches had been made ready. Also there was a wash boiler full of coffee and a galvanized tub brimming with lemonade. For the Frying Pan was doing itself proud.

Phil and his sister drove over together. The boy had asked Bess to go with him, but Cuffs had beaten him to it. The distance was only twenty-five miles, a neighborly stroll in that country of wide spaces and desert stretches filled with absentees.

When Phyllis came into the big room where the dancing was in progress, her dark eye swept the room without finding him for whom she looked. There were many there she knew, not more than two or three whom she had never met, but among them all she looked at none who was a magnet for her eyes. Keller had not yet arrived.

Before she had taken her seat she had three engagements to dance. Jim Yeager had waylaid her; so, too, had Slim and Curly. She waltzed first with Phil, and after he had done his duty he left her to the besiegings of half a score of riders for various ranches who came and went and came again. She joked with them, joined the merry banter that went on, laughed at them when they grew sentimental, always with a sprightly devotion to the matter in hand.

Nevertheless, though they did not know it, her mind was full of him who had not yet appeared. Why was he late? Could he have missed the way by any chance? And later—as the hours passed without bringing him—could anything have happened to him? More than once her troubled gaze fell upon Brill Healy with a brooding question in it. The man had received only the day before his party's nomination for sheriff, and he was doing the gracious to all the women and children.

He had many of the qualities that make for popularity, even though he was often overbearing, revengeful, and sullen. When he chose he could be hail fellow well met in a way Malpais found flattering to its vanity. Now he was apparently having the time of his life. Wherever he moved an eddy of laughter and gayety went with him. The eyes of men as well as women admiringly followed his dark, lithe, picturesque figure.

Phyllis had declined to dance with him, giving as an excuse a full programme, and for an instant his face had blazed with the suppressed rage in him. He had bowed and swaggered away with a malicious sneer. Her judgment told her it was folly to connect this man with the absence of her lover, but that look of malevolent triumph had none the less shaken her heart. What had he meant? It seemed less a threat for the future than a gloating over some evil already done.

When she could endure them no longer she carried her fears to Jim Yeager. They were dancing, but she made an excuse of fatigue to drop out.

"First time I ever knew you to play out at a dance, Phyl," he rallied her.

"It isn't that. I want to say something to you," she whispered.

He had a guess what it was, for his own mind was not quite easy.

"Do you think anything could have happened, Jim?" she besought pitifully when for a moment they were alone in a corner.

"What *could* have happened, Phyllie? Do you reckon he fell off his hawss, and him a full-size man?" he scoffed.

"Yes, but—you don't know how Brill looked at me. I'm afraid."

"Oh, Brill!" His voice held an edge of scorn, but none the less it concealed a real fear. He was making as much concession to it as to her when he added lightly: "Tell you what I'll do, Phyl. I'll saddle up and take a look back over the Bear Creek trail. Likely I'll meet him, and we'll come in together."

Her eyes met his, and he needed no other thanks. "You'll lose the dance," was her only comment.

Jim followed the road until it branched off to join the Bear Creek trail. Here he deflected toward the mountains, taking the zigzag path that ran like a winding thread among the rocks as it mounted. Now for the first time there came to him the faint rhythmic sound of a galloping horse's hoofs. He did not stop, and as he picked his way among the rocks he heard for some time no more of it.

"Mr. Hurry-up-like-hell kept the road, I reckon," Jim ruminated aloud, and even as he spoke he caught again the echo of an iron shoe striking a rock.

He stopped and listened. Some one was climbing the trail behind him.

"Mebbe he's a friend, and then mebbe he isn't. We'll let him have the whole road to himself, eh, Keno?"

Yeager guided his pony to the left, and took up a position behind some huge bowlders from whence he could see without being seen. The pursuer toiled into sight, a slim, wiry youth on a buckskin. He came forward out of the shadows into the fretted moonlight.

Yeager gave a glad whoop of recognition. "Hi-yi, Phil!"

"You're there, are you? Did I scare you off the trail, Jim?"

"That's whatever, boy. What are you doing here?"

"Sis sent me. She got worried again, and we figured I'd better join you."

"I reckon there's nothing serious the matter. Still, it ain't like Larry to say he would come and then not show up."

"Brill is back there bragging about it." Phil nodded his head toward the lights of the Frying Pan glimmering far below. "Says he knew the waddy wouldn't show his head. You don't reckon, Jim, he's turned a trick on Keller, do you?"

"That's what we have got to find out, Phil."

"Looks funny he'd be so durned sure when we all know how game Keller is," the boy reflected aloud.

"I don't expect you're armed, Phil?" Jim put the statement as a question.

"Nope. Are you?"

"No, I ain't. Didn't think of it when I started. Oh, well, we'll make out. Like enough there will be no need of guns."

A gray light was sifting into the sky, and still they rode, winding up toward the peaks of the divide. Jim, leading the way, drew rein and pointed to a cactus bush beside the trail. Among its spines lay a gray felt hat. From it his eye wandered to the very evident signs of a struggle that had taken place. Moss and cactus had been trampled down by boot heels. To the cholla hung here and there scraps of cloth. A blood splash stared at them from an outcropping slope of rock.

Jim swung from the saddle and rescued the hat from the spines. Inside the sweat band were the initials L.K. Silently he handed the hat to Phil.

"It's his hat," the boy cried.

"It's his hat," Jim agreed. "They must have laid for him here. He put up a good scrap. Notice how that cholla is cut to ribbons. Point is, what did they do to him?"

They searched the ground thoroughly, and discovered no body hidden in the brush.

"They've taken him away. Likely he's alive," Yeager decided aloud at last.

"Brill couldn't have been in this. He was at the Frying Pan before I was."

"I reckon he ordered it done. If that's correct they will be holding Larry till Brill gets there to give further orders."

Phil entered an objection. "That doesn't look to me like Brill's way. He's not scared of any man that lives. When he squares accounts with Keller he'll be on the job himself."

"That's so, too," admitted Yeager. "Still, I figure this is Healy's work. Maybe he gave out there was to be no killing. He was at the ranch himself, big as coffee, so as to be sure of his alibi."

"What does he care about an alibi? When he gets ready to go gunnin' after Keller he won't care if the whole Malpais sees him. There's something in this I don't *sabe*."

"There sure is. We've got to run the thing down *muy pronto*. No use both of us going ahead without arms, Phil. My notion is this: You burn a shuck back to the Frying Pan and round up some of our friends on the q.t. Don't let Brill get a notion of what's in the air. Better make straight for Gregory's Pass. I'm going to follow this trail we've cut and see what's doing. Once I find out I'll double back to the Pass and meet you. Bring along an extra gun for me."

"I don't reckon I will, Jim. What's the matter with me going on instead of you? I can follow this trail good as you can. I announce right here that I'm not going back. I've got first call on this job. Keller went into the fire after me. I'm going to follow this trail to hell if I have to."

Yeager tried persuasion, argument, appeal. The lad was as fixed as Gibraltar.

"I'm not going to go buttin' in where I'm not wanted any more than you would, Jim. I'll play this hand out with a cool head, but I'm going to play it my ownself."

"All right. It's your say-so. I'll admit you've got a claim. But you want to remember one thing—if anything happens to you I cayn't square it with Phyl. Go slow, boy!"

Without more words they parted, Jim to ride swiftly back for help, and young Sanderson to push on up the trail with his eyes glued to it. Ever since he could swing himself to a saddle he had been a vaquero in the cow country.

He was therefore an expert at reading the signs left by travellers. What would have been invisible to a tenderfoot offered evidence to him as plain as the print on a primer. Mile after mile he covered with a minute scrutiny that never wavered.

CHAPTER XXV

LARRY TELLS A BEAR STORY

Keller rode blithely down the piney trail while the sun flung its brilliant good-bye over the crotch of the mountains behind which it was slipping. The western sky was a Turner sublimated to the *nth* degree, a thing magnificent and indescribable. The young man rode with his crisp curls bared to the light, grateful breeze that came like healing from the great peaks. From the joyous, unquenchable youth in him bubbled snatches of song and friendly smiles scattered broadcast over a world that pleased him mightily.

He was going to see his girl, going down to the Frying Pan to take her in his arms and whirl her into the land of romance to the rhythm of the waltz. He wanted to shout it out to the chipmunks and the quails. Ever and again he broke out with a line or two of a melody he had heard once from a phonograph. No matter if he did not get the words exactly. He was sure of the sentiment. So the hills flung back his lusty:

"I love a lassie,
A bonnie Hieland lassie,
She's as pure as the lily of the dell."

William MacLeod Raine

Disaster fell upon him like a bolt out of a June sky. His pony stumbled, went down heavily with its weight on his leg. From the darkness men surged upon him. Rough hands dragged at him. The butt of a weapon crashed down on his hat and stunned him.

He became dimly aware that his leg was free from the horse, that he was struggling blindly to rise against the force that clamped him down. He knew that he reached his feet, that he was lashing out furiously with both hands, that even as he grappled with one assailant a gleam of steel flashed across the moonlight and shot through him with a zigzag pain that blotted out the world.

As his mind swam back to consciousness through troubled waters a far-away voice came out of the fog that surrounded him.

"He's coming to, looks like. I reckon you ain't bust his head, after all, Brad."

Vague, grinning gargoyles mocked him from the haze. Slowly these took form. Features stood out. The masks became faces. They no longer floated detached in space, but belonged definitely to human beings.

"It ain't our fault if you're stove up some, pardner. You're too durned anxious to whip yore weight in wildcats," one of the men grinned.

"Right you are, Tom. He shore hits like a kicking mule," chimed in a third, nursing a cheek that had been cut open to the bone.

A fourth spoke up, a leather-faced vaquero with hard eyes of jade. "No hard feelings, friend. All in the way of business."

With which he gave a final tug at the knot that tied the hands of his prisoner.

"I've got Mr. Healy to thank for this, I expect," commented the nester quietly.

"We've got no rope on yore expectations, Mr. Keller; but this outfit doesn't run any information bureau," answered the heavy-set, sullen fellow who had been called Brad.

There were four of them, all masked; but the ranger was sure of one of them, if not two. The first speaker had been Tom Dixon; the last one was Brad Irwin, a rider belonging to the Twin Star outfit.

They helped the bound man to his horse and held a low-voiced consultation. Three of his captors turned their horses toward the south, while Irwin took charge of Keller. With his rifle resting across the horn of his saddle, the man followed his charge up the trail, winding among the summits that stood as sentinels around Gregory's Pass. Through the defile they went, descending into the little-known mountain parks beyond.

This region was the heart of the watershed where Little Goose Creek heads. The peaks rose gaunt above them. Occasionally they glimpsed wide vistas of tangled, wooded canons and hills innumerable as sea billows. Into this maze they plunged ever deeper and deeper. Daylight came, and found them still travelling. The prisoner did not need to be told that this inaccessible country was the lurking place of the rustlers who had preyed so long upon the Malpais district. Nor did he need evidence to connect the sinister figure behind him with the gang of outlaws who rode in and out of these silent places on their nefarious night errands while honest folks kept their beds.

William MacLeod Raine

The sun was well up to its meridian before they came through a thick clump of quaking aspens to the mouth of a gulch opening from the end of a little mountain park. On one of the slopes of the gulch a cabin squatted, half hidden by the great boulders and the matting of pine boughs in front. Here Brad swung stiffly from the saddle.

"We'll 'light hyer," he announced.

"Time, too," returned Keller easily. "If anybody asks you, tell them I usually eat breakfast some before ten o'clock."

"You'll do yore eating from now on when I give the word," his guard answered surlily.

He was a big, dark man with a grouch, one who took his duties sourly. Not by any stretch of imagination could he be considered a brilliant conversationalist. What he had to say he growled out audibly enough, but for the rest his opinions had to be cork-screwed out of him in surly monosyllables.

There was a good deal of the cave man about him. The heavy, slouching shoulders, the glare of savagery, the long, hairy arms, all had their primordial suggestion. Given a club and a stone ax, he might have been set back thousands of years with no injustice to his mentality.

The man soon had a fire blazing in the stove, and from it came a breakfast of bacon, black coffee, and biscuits. He freed the hands of the nester and sat opposite him at the table, a revolver by the side of his plate for use in an emergency.

Keller smiled. "This is one of those fashionable dinners where they have extra hardware beside the plates," he suggested.

"Get gay, and I'll blow the top of yore head off!" the cow-puncher swore with gusto.

"Thanks. Under the circumstances, I reckon I'll not get gay. I'm in no hurry to put you in the pen, seh. Plenty of time. I'm going to need the top of my head to testify against you."

Irwin swore violently.

"For two cents I'd pump you full of holes right now," he glared.

Keller laughed, meeting him eye to eye pleasantly.

"Those aren't the orders, friend. I'm to be held here till the boss shows up or gives the signal."

The big jaw of his captor fell from astonishment. "Who told you that?"

The prisoner helped himself to more bacon and laughed again. He had made a guess, but he knew now that he had hit the bull's-eye with his shot in the dark.

"Some things don't need telling. I don't have to be told, for instance, that if things get too hot for Brill Healy he will slide out and leave you to settle the bill with the law."

Irwin's eyes glared angrily at his smiling ones. The unabashed impudence, the unfluttered aplomb, but above all the uncanny prescience of this youth disturbed him because he could not understand them. Moreover, it happened that his suspicious mind had lingered on the chance of a betrayal at the hands of his chief. For which very reason he broke into angry denial.

William MacLeod Raine

"That's a lie! Brill ain't that sort. He'd stand pat to a finish." Then, tardily, came the instinct for caution. "And there's nothing to tell, anyways," he finished sulkily.

"Sure. What's a little rustling and a little bank robbing among friends?" Keller wanted to know cheerfully.

For just an instant he thought he had gone too far. The big ruffian opposite choked over his biscuit, the while rage purpled his face. He caught up the revolver, and his fingers itched at the trigger.

His prisoner, leaning back in the chair, held him with quiet, unwavering eyes. "Steady! Steady!" he drawled.

"That will be about enough from you," Irwin let out through set teeth. "You padlock that mouth of yours, mister."

Keller took his advice temporarily, but it was not in him to long repress the spirit of adventure that bubbled in him. The temptation to bait this bear drew him irresistibly. He could not let him alone, the more that he sensed the danger to himself of the prods he sent home through the thick skin.

Lying carelessly on the bed with his head on his arm, or perhaps sitting astride a chair with his hands crossed on the back support, he would smile with childlike innocence and sent his barbs in gayly. And Irwin, murder in his dull brain, would glare at him like a maniac.

"Now would be a good time to blow off the top of my cocoanut," the nester suggested more than once to the infuriated cave man. "I'm allowing, you know, to send you to Yuma as soon as I get out of this. Nothing like grabbing your opportunity by the forelock."

"And when are you expecting to get out of here?" his guard demanded huskily.

Keller waved his hand with airy persiflage. "No exact information obtainable, my friend. Likely to-day. Maybe not till to-morrow. The one dead-sure point is that I'll make my getaway at the right time."

"There's one more dead-sure point—that I'm going to blow holes in you at the right time," retorted the other.

"Like to bet on which of us is a true prophet?"

Brad relapsed into black, sulky silence.

The hours followed each other, and still nobody came to relieve the guard. Keller could not understand the reason for this, any more than he could fathom an adequate one for his abduction. There was of course something behind it— something more potent than mere malice. If the intention had been merely to kill him, the thing could have been done without all this trouble. But though he searched his brain for an explanation, he could not find one that satisfied.

The answer came to him later in the day. In the middle of the afternoon a horse pounded up the draw to the cabin. Irwin went to the door, his eye still on his prisoner, except for a swift glance at the newcomer.

"How's yore five-thousand-dollar beauty, Brad?" inquired a voice that the nester recognized.

"Finer than silk, boss."

The rider swung from the saddle, trailed his rein, and came with jingling spurs into the cabin.

"Good evening, Mr. Keller," he said with derisive respect.

The nester, lying sideways on the bed with his head on his hand, nodded a greeting.

"I didn't know you and Mr. Irwin had doubled up and were bunkies," continued the jubilant voice. "When did you-all patch up the partnership?"

"About eight o'clock last night, Mr. Healy," returned the prisoner, eying him coolly. "And of course I knew it would be a surprise to you when you learned it."

"Expecting to stay long with him?"

"He seems right hospitable, but I don't reckon I'll outstay my welcome."

Healy laughed, with mockery and not amusement. "Brad's such a pressing host there's no telling when he'll let you go."

He was as malevolent as ever, but it was plain to be seen that he was riding high on a wave of triumph. Affairs were plainly going to his liking.

"The way I heard it you were expected down at the Frying Pan last night. Changed yore mind about going, I reckon," he went on insolently.

"I reckon."

"Had business that detained you, maybe."

"You're a good guesser."

"Folks were right anxious down there, according to the say-so that reached me."

Keller's cool eye measured him in silence, at which his enemy laughed contemptuously and turned on his heel.

Healy drew his confederate to one side of the room and held a whispered talk with him. Apparently he did not greatly care whether his foe caught the drift of it or not, for occasionally his voice lifted enough so that scraps of sentences reached the man lounging on the bed.

"—close to two hundred head—by the Mimbres Pass—the boys are ce'tainly pushing the drive—out of danger by midnight—wait for the signal before you turn him loose—"

"So-long, Mr. Keller. I cayn't spare the time to stay longer with you," their owner jeered.

"Just a moment, Mr. Healy. I want to know why you are keeping me here."

The man grinned. "Am I keeping you here, seh? Looks to me like it was Brad that's a-keeping you. Make a break for a getaway, and I'll not do a thing to you. Course I cayn't promise what Brad won't do. He's such a plumb anxious host."

"You're his brains. What you tell him to do he does. I hold you responsible for this!"

"You don't say!"

"And right now I'll add, for all the devilment that has been going on in these parts for years. You've about reached the end of your rope, though."

"I'll bet dollars to doughnuts you reach the end of one inside of forty-eight hours, Mr. Rustler," flashed back Healy.

And with an evil, significant grin he was gone. They heard the sound of retreating hoofs die in the distance.

But his visit had told the prisoner two things. A hurried wholesale drive of rustled cattle was being made across the line into Sonora, and it was being done in such a way as to fasten the suspicion of it upon the nester who had not appeared at the dance and had not been seen since that time. The irony of the thing was superb in its audacity. Healy and his friends would get the profit from the stolen cattle, and they would visit the punishment for the crime upon him. Evidence would be cooked up of course, and the retribution would be so swift that his friends would not be able to save him. This time his enemy would take no chances. He would be wiped out like a troublesome insect. The thing was diabolic in the simplicity of its cleverness.

Keller watched his jailer now like a hawk. He was ready to take the first chance that offered, no matter how slight a one it seemed. But the man was vigilant and wary. He never let his hand wander a foot from the handle of the weapon he carried.

Silently Irwin cooked a second meal. They sat down to it opposite each other, Keller facing the open window. While his jailer plied the knife, his revolver again lay on the oilcloth within reach.

"While I'm your guest and eating at your expense, I want to be properly grateful," the nester told his vis-a-vis. "Some folks might kick because the me-an'-you wasn't more varied, but I ain't that kind. You're doing your best, and nobody could do more."

"The which?" asked Irwin puzzled.

"The me-an'-you. It's French for just plain grub. For breakfast we get bacon and coffee and biscuits. For supper there's a variety. This time it is biscuits and coffee and bacon. To-morrow I reckon—"

Keller stopped halfway in his sentence, but took up his drawling comment again instantly. Only an added sparkle in his eyes betrayed the change that had suddenly wiped out his indolence and left him tense and alert. For while he had been speaking a head had slowly raised itself above the window casement and two eyes had looked in and met his. They belonged to Phil Sanderson.

Never had the brain of the prisoner been more alert. While his garrulous tongue ran aimlessly on, he considered ways and means. The boy held up empty hands to show him that he was unarmed. The nester did not by the flicker of an eyelash betray the presence of a third party to the man at table with him. Nevertheless his chatter became from that moment addressed to two listeners. To one it meant nothing in particular. To the other it was pregnant with meaning.

"No, seh. Some might complain because you ain't better provided with grub and fixings, but what I say is *to make out the best we can with what we've got*," the slow, drawling voice continued. "Some folks cayn't get along unless things are up to the Delmonico standard. That's plumb foolishness. Reminds me of a friend of mine that happened on a grizzly onct while he was cutting trail.

"Not expecting to meet Mr. Bear, he didn't have any gun along. Mr. Bear was surely on the wah-path that day. He made a bee line for my friend to get better acquainted. Nothing like presence of mind. That cow-puncher got his rope coiled in three shakes of a maverick's tail, his pinto bucking for fair to make his getaway. The rope drapped over Mr. Bear's head just as the puncher and the hawss separated company.

"Things were doing right sudden then. My friend grabbed the end of that rope and twisted it round and round a young live oak. Then he remembered an appointment and lit out, Mr. Bear after him on the jump. *Muy pronto* that grizzly came up awful sudden. The more he jerked the nearer he was to being choked. You better believe Mr. Puncher was hitting that trail right willing in the meanwhile."

"You talk too much with yore mouth," growled Irwin.

"It's a difference of opinion that makes horse races. I was just aiming to show you that *if my friend hadn't happened to have a rope along he would have been in a bad fix.* But, you notice, he used his brains, *and a rope did just as well as a gun.*"

The eyes just above the window casing disappeared. Brad attended to the business in hand, which was that of getting away with bacon and biscuits while he kept an eye on the man opposite. His prisoner also did justice to his supper, to his flow of conversation, and to the window behind the unconscious jailer.

In that open window were presently framed again the head and shoulders of young Sanderson. Irwin pushed back his chair to get some more coffee, and the picture in the frame shot instantly down. The guard, his coffee cup, and his revolver went to the stove and returned. Phil reappeared at the window, his rope coiled for action. It slid gracefully forward, dropped over the head of Brad, and was instantly jerked tight.

Keller vaulted across the table, and flung himself upon the struggling man. Brad's arms were entangled in the rope, but one leg shot out and hurled back the nester. But before he could free himself from the taut loop his prisoner was upon him again and had borne him to the ground.

Of the two, Irwin was far the more powerful, Keller the more agile and supple. He knew every trick of the wrestling game, whereas the other was clumsy and muscle-bound. By main strength the older man got to his feet again. Over went the table as they surged against it.

A chair, stamped into kindling, was hurled aside by the force of their impact. The stove rocked, and the bed collapsed as the locked figures crashed down upon it. The ranger, twisting as they fell, landed on top and his fingers instantly found the throat of his foe. Simultaneously Phil came to his assistance.

Even then, taken at an advantage, with two much younger men against him, the big jailer fought to the finish like a bear. Not till he was completely exhausted and they nearly so did he give up and lie quiet. All three of them panted heavily, the allies lying across his chest and legs. The nester managed to draw the loop taut about Irwin's neck and insert his knuckles so that he could use them as a tourniquet if necessary.

"Gather up the other end of the rope, loop it, and tie his feet together," the nester ordered, getting his sentence out in fragmentary jerks.

Phil did so, deftly and expertly, after which, in spite of renewed struggles, they tied the hands of their prisoner behind his back.

"Looks like a cyclone had hit the room," said the boy,

glancing at the debris.

Larrabie laughed. "He's the most willing mixer I ever saw."

"What are you going to do with him?"

"We'll leave him tied right where he is. When we get down into the settlement we'll notify his friends, though I reckon they'll find him without any help from us."

In order to make sure they went over the knots again, tightening them here and there. The revolver and the rifle of the bound man they appropriated. The nester's horse was in a little corral back of the house. He saddled, and shortly the two were on the back trail. Phil knew the country as a golfer knows his links. To him Keller put the question in his mind:

"How far is the Mimbres Pass from here, and in what direction?"

The younger man looked at him in surprise. "A dozen miles, I reckon. See that cleft over there? That's the Mimbres."

His friend drew rein and looked with level eyes at him.

"Phil, it's come to a show-down! Are you for Brill Healy or are you for me?"

"I'm through with Brill."

"Dead sure of that?"

"Dead sure. Why?"

"Because you've got to make your choice to-night whether you're going to stand with honest men or thieves. Healy's gang is rustling a bunch of cows gathered at the round-up. They're heading for Mimbres Pass. I'm going to stop them if I can."

"I'm with you, Larry."

"Good! I was sure of you, Phil."

The boy flushed, but his eyes did not waver. "I want to tell you something. That day we most caught you over the dead cow of the C.O. outfit Brill was carrying Phyl's knife. I had lent it to him the night before."

Keller nodded. "I had figured it out that way."

"But that ain't all. Once when I was cutting trail in the hills— must have been about six months before that time—I happened on Brill driving a calf still bleeding from the brand he had put on it.

"I didn't think anything of that, but I noticed he was anxious to have me turn and join him. But I kept on the way I was going, and just by a miracle my pony almost stumbled over a dead cow lying in the brush. That set me thinking. That night I rode over to Healy's and asked an explanation.

"He had one ready. Some one else must have killed the cow. He found the calf wandering about alone, and branded it. Somehow his story didn't quite satisfy me, but I wasn't ready then to think him a coyote. I liked him—always had. And it flattered me that he had picked me out to be his best friend. So I said nothing, and figured it out that he was on the square. Of course I knew he was reckless and wild, but I didn't like him any the less for that. I reckon nobody ever accused him of not being game."

"Hardly," smiled Keller. "He'll stand the acid that way."

"The thing that stuck in my craw was his lying about seeing you on the night of the bank robbery. He said you were riding the roan with white stockings. Later we found out that couldn't be true. Then I knew Jim was telling the truth about you being with him in the hills at the time. It kind of sifted to me by degrees that you were a white man and he was a skunk."

"And then?"

"Then we had it out one day. He had his reason for wanting to stand well with me. I reckon you know what it is."

"I know his reason. No man could have a better. I reckon I've a right to think so, Phil, because she has promised to marry me."

The boy shook hands with him impulsively. "I'm right glad to hear it—and I want to say they don't make girls any better than Phyl."

"That's not news to me. I have known it since the first time I saw her."

Sanderson returned to the order of the day. "Well, Brill and I had had one or two tiffs, mostly about you and Phyl. He saw I was changed toward him, and he wanted to know why. I let him have it straight, and since then we haven't been friends."

"I'm glad of that. It makes plain sailing for me. He's got to be run down and caged, Phil. Healy is at the head of all this rustling that has been troubling the Malpais country. His gang stuck up the Diamond Nugget stage, killed Sheriff Fowler, and robbed the Noches Bank."

"How could he have robbed the bank when he was seen fifty miles from there not two hours afterward?"

Keller briefly explained his theory then pushed on at once to his plans.

"I'm going to make straight for the Mimbres Pass while you go back and rustle help. I'll try to keep them from getting through the Pass until you close in on them behind."

"That don't look good to me. How do I know how long it will be before I can gather the boys together or find Jim and his outfit? You might be massacred before I got back."

"A man has to take his fighting chance."

"Then let me take mine. We'll hold the pass together. I'll bet we can. Don't you reckon?"

"What use would you be without a rifle? No, Phil, you'll have to bring up the reinforcements. That's the best tactics."

Sanderson protested eagerly, but in the end was overborne. They turned their backs upon each other, one headed for the Mimbres and the other for the trail that ran down to the Malpais country.

CHAPTER XXVI

THE MAN-HUNT

When Jim Yeager separated from Phil after their discovery of Keller's hat and the deductions they drew from it, the former turned his pony toward the Frying Pan. Daylight had already broken before he came in sight of it, but sounds of revelry still issued boisterously from the house.

As he drew near there came to him the squeal of sawing riddles, the high-pitched voice of the dance caller in sing-song drawl, the shuffling of feet keeping time to the rhythm of the music. For though a new day was at hand, the quadrilles continued with unflagging vigor, one succeeding another as soon as the floor was cleared.

The cow country takes its amusements seriously. A dance is infrequent enough to be an event. Men and women do not ride or drive from thirty to fifty miles without expecting to drink the last drop of pleasure there may be in the occasion.

As Jim swung from the saddle, a slim figure in white glided from the shadow of the wild cucumber vines that rioted over one end of the porch.

"Well, Jim?"

The man came to the point with characteristic directness. "He has been waylaid, Phyl. We found his hat and the place where they ambushed him."

"Is he—" Her voice died at the word, but her meaning was clear.

"I don't think it. Looks like they were aiming to take him prisoner without hurting him. They might easily have shot him down, but the ground shows there was a struggle."

"And you came back without rescuing him?" she reproached.

"Phil and I were unarmed. I came back to get guns and help."

"And Phil?"

"He's following the trail. I wanted him to let me while he came back. But he wouldn't hear to it. Said he had to square his debt to Larry."

"Good for Phil!" his sister cried, eyes like stars.

"Is Brill still here?" he asked.

"No. He rode away about an hour ago. He was very bitter at me because I wouldn't dance with him. Said I'd curse myself for it before twenty-four hours had passed. He must have Larry in his power, Jim."

"Looks like," he nodded, and added grimly: "If you do any regretting there will be others that will, too."

She caught the lapels of his coat and looked into his face with extraordinary intensity. "I'm going back with you, Jim. You'll let me, won't you? I've waited—and waited. You can't think what an awful night it has been. I can't stand it any longer! I'll go mad! Oh, Jim, you'll take me, I know!" Her hands slipped down to his and clung to them with passionate entreaty.

"Why, honey, I cayn't. This is likely to be war before we finish. It ain't any place for girls."

"I'll stay back, Jim. I'll do whatever you say, if you'll only let me go."

He shook his head resolutely. "Cayn't be done, girl. I'm sorry, but you see yourself it won't do."

Nor could all her beseechings move him. Though his heart was very tender toward her he was granite to her pleadings. At last he put her aside gently and stepped into the house.

Going at once to the fiddlers, he stopped the music and stood on the little rostrum where they were seated. Surprised faces turned toward him.

"What's up, Jim?" demanded Slim, his arm still about the waist of Bess Purdy.

"A man was waylaid while coming to this dance and taken prisoner by his enemies. They mean to do him a mischief. I want volunteers to rescue him."

"Who is it?" several voices cried at once.

"The man I mean is Larrabie Keller."

A pronounced silence followed before Slim drawled an answer:

"Cayn't speak for the other boys, but I reckon I haven't lost any Kellers, Jim."

"Why not? What have you got against him?"

"You know well enough. He's under a cloud. We don't say he's a rustler and a bank robber, but then we don't say he ain't."

"I say he isn't! Boys, it has come to a show-down. Keller is a member of the Rangers, sent here by Bucky O'Connor to run down the rustlers."

Questions poured upon him.

"How do you know?"

"How long have you known?"

"Who told you?"

"Why didn't he tell us so himself, then?"

Jim waited till they were quiet. "I've seen letters from the governor to him. He didn't come here declaring his intentions because he knew there would be nothing doing if the rustlers knew he was in the neighborhood. He has about done his work now, and it's up to us to save him before they bump him off. Who will ride with me to rescue him?"

There was no hesitation now.

Every man pushed forward to have a hand in it.

"Good enough," nodded Yeager. "We'll want rifles, boys. Looks to me like hell might be a-popping before mo'ning grows very ancient. We'll set out from Turkey Creek Crossroads two hours from now. Any man not on hand then will get left behind.

"And remember—this is a man hunt! No talking, boys. We don't want the news that we're coming spread all over the hills before we arrive."

As Jim descended from the rostrum, his roving gaze fell on Phyl Sanderson standing in the doorway. Her fears stolen the color even from her lips, but the girl's beauty had never struck him more poignantly.

Misery stared at him out of her fine eyes, yet the unconscious courage of her graceful poise—erect, with head thrown back so that he could even see the pulse beat in the brown throat—suggested anything but supine surrender to her terror. Before he could reach her she had slipped into the night, and he could not find her.

Men dribbled in to the Turkey Creek Crossroads along as many trails as the ribs of a fan running to a common centre. Jim waited, watch open, and when it said that seven o'clock had come he snapped it shut and gave the word to set out.

It was a grim, business-like posse, composed of good men and true who had been sifted in the impartial sieve of life on the turbid frontier. Moreover, they were well led. A certain hard metallic quality showed in the voice and eye of Jim Yeager that boded no good for the man who faced him in combat to-day. He rode with his gaze straight to the front, toward that cleft in the hills where lay Gregory's Pass. The others fell in behind, a silent, hard-bitten outfit as ever took the trail for that most dangerous of all big game—the hidden outlaw.

The little bunch of riders had not gone far before Purdy, who was riding in the rear, called to Yeager.

"Somebody coming hell-to-split after us, Jim."

It turned out to be Buck Weaver, who had been notified by telephone of what was taking place. A girl had called him up out of his sleep, and he had pounded the road hard to get in at the finish.

Jim explained the situation in a few words and offered to yield command to the owner of the Twin Star ranch. But Buck declined.

"You're the boss of this *rodeo*, Yeager. I'm riding in the ranks to-day."

"How did you hear we were rounding-up to-day?" Jim asked.

"Some one called me up," Buck answered briefly, but he did not think it necessary to say that it was Phyllis.

Behind them, unnoticed by any, sometimes hidden from sight by the rise and fall of the rough ground, sometimes silhouetted against the sky line, rode a slim, supple figure on a white-faced cow pony. Once, when the fresh morning wind swept down a gulch at an oblique angle, it lifted for an instant from the stirrup leather what might have been a gray flag. But the flag was only a skirt, and it signalled nothing more definite than the courage and devotion of a girl who knew that the men she loved best on earth were in danger.

CHAPTER XXVII

THE ROUND-UP

The Mimbres Pass narrows toward the southern exit where Point o' Rocks juts into the canon and commands it like a sentinel. Toward this column of piled boulders slowly moved a cloud of white dust, at the base of which crept a band of hard-driven cattle. Swollen tongues were out, heads stretched forward in a bellow for water taken up by one as another dropped it. The day was still hot, though the sun had slipped down over the range, and the drove had been worked forward remorselessly. Every inch that could be sweated out of them had been gained.

For those that pushed them along were in desperate hurry. Now and again a rider would twist round in his saddle to sweep back a haggard glance. Dust enshrouded them, lay heavy on every exposed inch; but through it seams of anxiety crevassed their leathern faces. Iron men they were, with one exception. Fight they could and would to the last ditch. But behind the jaded, stony eyes lay a haunting fear, the never-ending dread of a pursuit that might burst upon them at any moment. Driven to the wall, they would have faced the enemy like tigers, with a fierce, exultant hate. It was the never-ending possibility of disaster that lay heavily upon them.

Just as they entered the pass, a man came spurring up the steep trail behind them. The drag drivers shouted a warning to those in front and waited alertly with weapons ready. The man trying to overtake them waved a sombrero as a flag of truce.

"Keep an eye on him, Tom. If he makes a move that don't look good to you, plug him!" ordered the keen-eyed man beside one of the drag drivers.

"I'm bridle wise, boss." But though he spoke with bravado Dixon shook like an aspen in a breeze.

The man he had called boss looked every inch a leader. He rode with the loose seat and the straight back of the Westerner to the saddle born. Just now he was looking back with impassive, reddened eyes at the approaching figure.

"Hold on, Tom! Don't shoot! It's Brad," he decided. "And I wonder what in Mexico he is doing here."

The leader of the outlaws was soon to learn. Irwin told the story of the strategy that had changed him from jailer to prisoner and of the way he had later freed himself from the rope that bound him.

Healy unloaded his sentiments with an emphasis that did the subject justice. Nevertheless he could not see that their plans were seriously affected.

"It's a leetle premature, but his getaway doesn't cut any ice. What we want to do is to nail him, clamp the evidence home, and put him out of business before his friends can say Jack Robinson. The story now is that he was caught driving a little bunch of cows to met the big bunch his pals were rustling, and that we left him in charge of Brad while we tried to run down the other waddies. Understand, boys?"

They did, and admired the more the versatility of a leader who could make plans on the spur of the moment to meet any emergency.

"We'll push right on, boys. Once we get through the pass it will trouble anybody to find us. Before mo'ning you'll be across the line."

"And you, Brill?"

"I'm going back to settle accounts for good and all with Mr. Keller," answered Healy grimly between set teeth. "I've got a notion about him. I believe he's a spy."

Just before Point o' Rocks a defile runs into the Mimbres Pass at right angles. The leaders of the cattle, pushed forward by the pressure from behind, stopped for a moment, and stood bawling at the junction. A rider spurred forward to keep them from attempting the gulch. Suddenly he dragged his pony to its haunches, so quickly did he stop it. For a clear voice had called down a warning as if from the heavens:

"You can't go this way! The Pass is closed!"

The rider looked up in amazement, and beheld a man standing on the ledge above with a rifle resting easily across his forearm.

"By Heaven, it's Keller!" the rustler muttered.

He wheeled as on a half dollar, pushed his way back along the edge of the wall past the cattle, and shouted to his chief:

"We're trapped, Brill!"

None of the outlaws needed that notification. Five pair of eyes had lifted to the ledge upon which Keller stood. The shock of the surprise paralyzed them for an instant. For it occurred to none of the five that this man would be standing there so quietly unless he were backed by a posse sufficient to overpower them. He had not the manner of a man taking a desperate chance. The situation was as dramatic as life and death, but the voice that had come down to them had been as matter-of-fact as if it had asked some one to pass him a cup of coffee at the breakfast table.

The temper of the outlaws' metal showed instantly. Dixon dropped his rifle, threw up his hands, and ran bleating to the cover of some large rocks, imploring the imagined posse not to shoot. Others found silently what shelter they could. Healy alone took reckless counsel of his hate.

Flinging his rifle to his shoulder, he blazed away at the figure on the ledge—once, twice, three times. When the smoke cleared the ranger was no longer to be seen. He was lying flat on his rock like a lizard, where he had dropped just as his enemy whipped up his weapon to fire. Cold as chilled steel, in spite of the fire of passion that blazed within him, Healy slid to the ground on the far side of his horse and, without exposing himself, slowly worked to the loose boulders bordering the edge of the canon bed.

The bawling of the cattle and the faint whimpering of Dixon alone disturbed the silence. Healy and his confederates were waiting for the other side to show its hand. Meanwhile the leader of the outlaws was thinking out the situation.

"I believe there's only two of them, Bart," he confided in a low voice to the big fellow lying near. "Keller must have heard us when we talked it over at the shack. I reckon he and Phil hit the trail for here immediate. They hadn't time to go back and rustle help and still get here before us.

"We'll make Mr. Keller table his cards. I'm going to try to rush the cattle through. We'll see at once what's doing. If they are too many for us to do that we'll break for the gulch and fight our way out—that is, if we find we're hemmed in behind, too."

He called to the rest of the bandits and gave crisp instructions. At sound of his sharp whistle four men leaped into sight, each making for his horse. Dixon alone did not answer to the call. He lay white and trembling behind the rock that sheltered him, physically unable to rise and face the bullets that would rain down upon him.

Keller, watching alertly from above, guessed what they would be at. His rifle cracked twice, and two of the horses staggered, one of them collapsing slowly. He had to show himself, and for three heartbeats stood exposed to the fire of four rifles. One bullet fanned his cheek, a second plunged through his coat sleeve, a third struck the rock at his feet. While the echoes were still crashing, he was flat on his rock again, peering over the edge to see their next move.

"He's alone," cried Healy jubilantly. "Must have sent the kid back for help. Bart, get Dixon's gun, steal up the ravine, and take him in the rear. I'd go myself, but I can't leave the boys now."

Slowly the cattle felt the impetus from behind, and began to move forward. The voice above shouted a second warning. Healy answered with a derisive yell. Keller again stood exposed on the ledge.

Rifles cracked.

This time the cattle detective was firing at men and not at horses, and they in turn were pumping at him fast as they could work the levers. One man went down, torn through and through by a rifle slug in his vitals. Healy's horse twitched and staggered, but the rider was unhurt. The officer on the ledge, a perfect target, was the heart of a very hail of lead, but when he sank again to cover he was by some miracle still unhurt.

"They'll try a flank attack next time," Keller told himself.

Up to date the honors were easily his. He had put three horses out of commission and disabled one of the outlaws so badly that he would prove negligible in the attack. Peering down, he could see Healy, with superb contempt for the marksman above, slowly and carefully carry his wounded comrade to shelter. The other men were already driven back to cover. The cattle, excited by the firing, were milling round and round uneasily.

Healy laid the wounded man down, knelt beside him, and gave him water from his flask. The man was plainly hard hit, though he was not bleeding much.

"Where is it, Duke? Can I do anything for you, old fellow?"

The dying man shook his head and whispered hoarsely: "I've got mine, Brill. Shot to pieces. I'm dying right now. Get out while you can. Don't mind me."

His chief swore softly. "We'll get him right, Duke. Brad's after him now. Buck up, old pard. You'll worry through yet."

"Not this time, Brill. I've played rustler once too often."

Keller, far up on the precipice, became aware of approaching riders long before the outlaws below could see them. He counted eight—nine—ten men, still black dots in a cloud of dust. This he knew must be Phil's posse.

If he could hold the rustlers for ten minutes more they would be caught like rats in a trap. Once or twice he glanced behind him as a precaution against some one of the enemy climbing Point o' Rocks from the defile, but he gave this little consideration. He had not seen Brad when he disappeared into the mesquite, and he supposed all of the rustlers were still in the Pass five hundred feet below him.

What he had expected was that they would force their way up the defile for a quarter of a mile and strike the easy trail that ran from the rear to the top of the Point. He wondered that this had not occurred to Healy.

In point of fact it had, but the outlaw leader knew that as they picked their way among the broken boulders of the gulch bottom the enemy would have them in the open for more than a hundred yards of slow going. He had chosen the alternative of sending Brad quietly up the rough face of the cliff. The other plan would do as a last resource if this failed.

Healy believed that his enemy had been delivered into his hands. After Keller had been killed they would toss his body down into the Pass, and while his companions continued the drive to Mexico, Healy would return to get help for Duke and spread the story he wanted to get out. The main features of that tale would be that he and Duke had cut their trail by accident, suspected rustling, and followed as far as the Mimbres Pass, where Keller had shot Duke and been in turn shot by Healy.

It was a neat plan, and one that would have been fairly sure of success but for one unforeseen contingency—the approach of Yeager's posse a half hour too soon. Healy heard them coming, knew he was trapped, and attempted to force an escape through the narrows in front of Point o' Rocks.

The milling cattle had jammed the gateway. Keller, shooting down one or two of them, blocked the exit still more. Healy and his confederates could not get through, and turned to try the defile just as the first of the posse came flying down the Pass.

Young Sanderson was in the van, a hundred yards in front of Yeager, dashing over the uneven ground in a reckless haste that Jim's slower horse could not match. Loose shale was flying from his pony's hoofs as it pounded forward. The outlaws just beat him to the mouth of the intersecting gulch. Dragging his broncho to a slithering halt, he fired twice at the retreating men. He had taken no time to aim, and his bullets went wild.

Brill laughed in mockery, covered him deliberately with his rifle, and just as deliberately raised the barrel and fired into the air. The distance was scarce a hundred yards. Phil could not doubt that his former friend had purposely spared his life. The boy's rifle dropped from his shoulder.

"Brill wouldn't shoot at me! I couldn't kill him!" he shouted to Weaver, as the latter rode up.

Buck nodded. "Let me have him!" And he plunged into the gorge after the men that had disappeared.

Twice Keller's rifle spat at Healy and his companion as they plowed forward across the boulder bed, but the difficulty of shooting from far above at moving figures almost directly below saved the rustlers. They reached a thick growth of aspens and disappeared. Healy parted company with his ally at the place where the trail to the summit of Point o' Rocks led up.

"Break south when you get out of the gulch, Sam. In half an hour it will be night, and you'll be safe. So-long."

"Where you going, Brill?"

"I'm going to settle accounts with that dashed spy!" answered Healy, with an epithet. "Inside of half an hour either Keller or I will be down and out!"

The outlaw took the stiff incline leisurely, for he knew Keller could come down only this way, and he had no mind to let himself get so breathed as to disturb the sureness of his aim. The aspen grove ran like a forked tongue up the ridge for a couple of hundred yards. As Healy emerged from it he saw a rider just disappearing over the shoulder of the hill in front of him. For an instant he had an amazed impression that the figure was that of a woman, but he dismissed this as absurd. He went the more cautiously, for he now knew that there would be two for him to deal with on the Point instead of one—unless Brad reached the scene in time to assist him.

The sound of a shot drifted down to him, followed presently by a far, faint cry of terror. What had happened was this:

Keller, turning away from the overhanging ledge from which he had seen the outlaws vanish into the grove, looked down the long slope preliminary to descending. He was surprised to see a horse and rider halfway between him and the aspen tongue. To him, too, there came a swift impression that it was a woman, and almost at once something in the poise of the gallant figure told him what woman. His heart leaped to meet her. He waved a hand, and broke into a run.

But only for two strides. For there had come to him a warning. He swung on his heel and waited. Again he heard the light rumble of shale, and before that had died away a sinister click. Alert in every fiber, his gaze swept the bluff— and stopped when it met a pair of beady eyes peering at him over the edge of the precipice.

The two pair of eyes fastened for what seemed like an eternity, but could have been no longer than four ticks of a clock. Neither of the men spoke. The outlaw fired first— wildly, for the arm which held the rifle was cramped for space. Keller's revolver flashed an answer which tore through Irwin's teeth and went out beneath his ear. With a furious oath the man dropped his weapon and flung himself upward and forward, landing in a heap almost at the feet of the detective.

"Don't move!" ordered the latter.

Brad writhed forward awkwardly, knew the shock of another heavy bullet in his shoulder, and catching his foe by the legs dragged him from his feet. Keller's revolver was jerked over the edge of the precipice as he let go of it to close with the burly ruffian.

Both of them were unarmed save for the weapons nature had given them. The detailed purpose of the struggle defined itself at once. Irwin meant by main strength to fling the detective into the gulf that descended sheer for five hundred feet. The other fought desperately to save himself by dragging his infuriated antagonist back from the edge.

They grappled in silence, save for the heavy panting that evidenced the tension of their efforts. Each tried to bear the other to the ground, to establish a grip against which his foe would be helpless. Now they were on their knees, now on their sides. Over and over they rolled, first one and then the other on top, shifting so fast that neither could clinch any temporary advantage.

Yet Keller, with a flying glance at the cliff, knew that he was being forced nearer the gulf by sheer strength of muscle. Irwin, his jaw shattered and his shoulder torn, was not fighting to win, but to kill. He cared not whether he himself also went to death. He was obsessed by the old primeval lust to crush the life out of this lusty antagonist, and his whole gigantic force was concentrated to that end. He scarce knew that he was wounded, and he cared not at all. Backward and forward though the battle went, on the whole it moved jerkily toward the chasm.

The end came with a suddenness of which Larrabie had but an instant's warning in the swift flare of joy that lit the madman's face. His foot, searching for a brace as he was borne back, found only empty space. Plunged downward, the nester clung viselike to the man above, dragged him after, and by the very fury of Irwin's assault flung him far out into the gulf head-first.

It was Phyl Sanderson's cry of horror that Healy heard. She had put her horse up the steep at a headlong gallop, had seen the whole furious struggle and the tragic end of it that witnessed two men hurled over the precipice into space. She slipped from the saddle, and sank dizzily to the ground, not daring to look over the cliff at what she would see far below. Waves of anguish shot through her and shook her very being.

A man bent over her, and gave a startled cry.

"My heaven, it's Phyl!" he cried.

"Yes." She spoke in a flat, lifeless voice he could not have recognized as hers.

"Where is he? What's become of him?" Healy demanded.

She told him with a gesture, then flung herself on the turf, and broke down helplessly. The outlaw went to the edge and looked over. The gulf of air told no story except the obvious one. No wingless living creature could make that descent without forfeiture of life. He stepped back to the girl and touched her on the shoulder.

"Come."

She looked up, shuddering, and asked, "Where?"

"With me."

"With you? It was you that drove him to his death, and I loved him!"

"Never mind that now. Come."

"I hate you! I should kill you when I got a chance! Why should I go with you?" she asked evenly.

He did not know why. He had no definite plan. All he knew was that his old world lay in ruins at his feet, that he must fly through the night like a hunted wolf, and that the girl he loved was beside him, forever free from the rival who lay crushed and lifeless at the foot of the cliff. He could not give her up now. He would not.

The old savage instinct of ownership rose strong in him. She was his. He had won her by the fortune of war. He would keep her against all comers so long as he had life to fight. Night was falling softly over the hills. They would go forth into it together to a new heaven and a new earth.

He lifted her to her feet and brought up her horse. She looked at him in a silence that stripped him of his dreams.

"Come!" he said again, between clenched teeth.

"Not with you. I don't know you. Leave me alone. You killed him! You're a murderer!"

He stretched hands toward her, but she shrank from him, still in the dull stupor of horror that was on her spirit.

"Go away! Don't touch me! You and your miscreants killed him!" And with that she flung herself down again, and buried her face from the sight of him.

He waited doggedly, helpless against her grief and her hatred of him, but none the less determined to take her with him. Across the border he would not be a hunted man with a price on his head. They could be married by a padre in Sonora, and perhaps some day he would make her love him and forget this man that had come between them. At all events, he would be her master and would tie her life inextricably to his. He stooped and caught her shoulder. She had fainted.

A footfall set rolling a pebble. He looked up quickly, and almost of its own volition, as it seemed, the rifle leaped to both of his hands. A man stood looking at him across the plateau of the summit. He, too, held a rifle ready for instant action.

"So it's you!" Healy cried with an oath.

"Have you killed him?"

The outlaw lied, with swift, unblazing passion: "Yes, Buck Weaver, and tossed his body to the buzzards. Your turn now!"

"Then who is that with you there?"

"The woman you love, the woman that turned you and him down for me," taunted his rival. "After I've killed you we're going off to be married."

"Only a coyote would stand behind a woman's skirts and lie. I can't kill you there, and you know it."

Healy asked nothing better than an even break. He might have killed with impunity from where he stood. Yet pantherlike, he swiftly padded six paces to the left, never lifting his eyes from his antagonist.

Buck waited, motionless. "Are you ready?"

The outlaw's weapon flashed to the level and cracked. Almost simultaneously the other answered. Weaver felt a bullet fan his cheek, but he knew that his own had crashed home.

The shock of it swung Healy half round. The man hung in silhouette against the sky line, then the body plunged to the turf at full length. Buck moved forward cautiously, fearing a trick, his eyes fastened on the other. But as he drew nearer he knew it was no ruse. The body lay supine and inert, as lifeless as the clay upon which it rested.

Once sure of this Buck turned immediately to Phyllis. A faint crackling of bushes stopped him. He waited, his eyes fixed on the edge of the precipice from which the sound had come. Next there came to him the slipping of displaced rubble. He was all eyes and ears, tense and alert in every pulse.

From out of the gulf a hand appeared and groped for a hold. Weaver stepped noiselessly to the edge and looked down. A torn and bleeding face looked up into his.

"Good heavens, Keller!"

Buck was on his knees instantly. He caught the ranger's hand with both of his and dragged him up. The rescued man sank breathless on the ground and told his story in gasped fragments.

"—caught on a ledge—hung to some bushes growing there—climbed up—lay still when Healy looked over—a near thing—makes me sick still!"

"It was a millionth chance that saved you—if it was a chance."

"Where's Healy?"

Weaver pointed to the body. "We fought it out. The luck was with me."

A faint, glad, terrified little cry startled them both. Phyllis was staring with dilated eyes at the man restored to her from the dead. He got up and walked across to her with outstretched hands.

"My little girl."

"Oh, Larry! I don't understand. I thought—"

He nodded. "I reckon God was good to us, sweetheart."

Her arms crept up and round his neck. "Oh, boy—boy—boy. I thought you were—I thought you were—"

She broke down, but he understood. "Well, I'm not," he laughed happily. Catching sight of Buck's grim, set face, Larrabie explained what scarce needed an explanation. "You'll have to excuse us, I reckon. It's my day for congratulations."

Phyllis freed herself and walked across to her other lover. "My friend, I know the answer now," she told him.

"I see you do."

"Don't—please don't be hurt," she begged. "I have to care for him."

The hard, leathery face softened. "I lose, girl. But who told you I was a bad loser? The best man wins. I've got no kick to register."

"Not the best man," Keller corrected, shaking hands with his rival.

Phyllis summed it up in woman fashion: "My man, whether he is the best or not. It's just that a girl goes where her heart goes."

Weaver nodded. "Good enough. Well, I'll be going. I expect you'll not miss me."

He turned and went down the hill alone. At the foot of it he met Jim Yeager.

"What about Brill?" the younger man asked quickly.

"He'll never rustle another cow," Buck answered gravely. "I killed him on the top of Point o' Rocks after an even break."

"Duke has cashed in. Game to the last. Wouldn't say a word to implicate his pals. But Tom has confessed everything. The boys slipped a noose over his head, and he came through right away.

"Says he and Duke and Irwin helped Healy rob the Noches Bank and do a lot of other deviltry. It was just like Keller figured. The automobile was waiting for the bunch with the showfer, and took them out the old Fort Lincoln Road. Dixon knows where the gold is hidden, and is going to show the boys."

"That clears up everything, then. I judge we've made a pretty thorough gather."

Jim looked up and indistinctly saw the lovers coming slowly down through the grove. Dusk had fallen and soon the cloak of night would be over the mountains.

"Who is that?"

Buck did not look round. "I reckon it's Keller and his sweetheart. She followed us here."

"I told her not to come."

"I expect she takes her telling from Mr. Keller." He changed the subject abruptly. "We'll go on down to the boys and see what's doing. They'll be some glad, I shouldn't wonder, at making a gather that cleans out the worst bunch of cutthroats and rustlers in the Malpais. Don't you reckon?"

"I reckon," answered Yeager briefly.

Choose from Thousands of 1stWorldLibrary Classics By

A. M. Barnard
Ada Leverson
Adolphus William Ward
Aesop
Agatha Christie
Alexander Aaronsohn
Alexander Kielland
Alexandre Dumas
Alfred Gatty
Alfred Ollivant
Alice Duer Miller
Alice Turner Curtis
Alice Dunbar
Allen Chapman
Alleyne Ireland
Ambrose Bierce
Amelia E. Barr
Amory H. Bradford
Andrew Lang
Andrew McFarland Davis
Andy Adams
Angela Brazil
Anna Alice Chapin
Anna Sewell
Annie Besant
Annie Hamilton Donnell
Annie Payson Call
Annie Roe Carr
Annonaymous
Anton Chekhov
Archibald Lee Fletcher
Arnold Bennett
Arthur C. Benson
Arthur Conan Doyle
Arthur M. Winfield
Arthur Ransome
Arthur Schnitzler
Arthur Train
Atticus
B.H. Baden-Powell
B. M. Bower
B. C. Chatterjee
Baroness Emmuska Orczy
Baroness Orczy
Basil King
Bayard Taylor
Ben Macomber
Bertha Muzzy Bower
Bjornstjerne Bjornson

Booth Tarkington
Boyd Cable
Bram Stoker
C. Collodi
C. E. Orr
C. M. Ingleby
Carolyn Wells
Catherine Parr Traill
Charles A. Eastman
Charles Amory Beach
Charles Dickens
Charles Dudley Warner
Charles Farrar Browne
Charles Ives
Charles Kingsley
Charles Klein
Charles Hanson Towne
Charles Lathrop Pack
Charles Romyn Dake
Charles Whibley
Charles Willing Beale
Charlotte M. Braeme
Charlotte M. Yonge
Charlotte Perkins Stetson
Clair W. Hayes
Clarence Day Jr.
Clarence E. Mulford
Clemence Housman
Confucius
Coningsby Dawson
Cornelis DeWitt Wilcox
Cyril Burleigh
D. H. Lawrence
Daniel Defoe
David Garnett
Dinah Craik
Don Carlos Janes
Donald Keyhoe
Dorothy Kilner
Dougan Clark
Douglas Fairbanks
E. Nesbit
E. P. Roe
E. Phillips Oppenheim
E. S. Brooks
Earl Barnes
Edgar Rice Burroughs
Edith Van Dyne
Edith Wharton

Edward Everett Hale
Edward J. O'Biren
Edward S. Ellis
Edwin L. Arnold
Eleanor Atkins
Eleanor Hallowell Abbott
Eliot Gregory
Elizabeth Gaskell
Elizabeth McCracken
Elizabeth Von Arnim
Ellem Key
Emerson Hough
Emilie F. Carlen
Emily Bronte
Emily Dickinson
Enid Bagnold
Enilor Macartney Lane
Erasmus W. Jones
Ernie Howard Pie
Ethel May Dell
Ethel Turner
Ethel Watts Mumford
Eugene Sue
Eugenie Foa
Eugene Wood
Eustace Hale Ball
Evelyn Everett-green
Everard Cotes
F. H. Cheley
F. J. Cross
F. Marion Crawford
Fannie E. Newberry
Federick Austin Ogg
Ferdinand Ossendowski
Fergus Hume
Florence A. Kilpatrick
Fremont B. Deering
Francis Bacon
Francis Darwin
Frances Hodgson Burnett
Frances Parkinson Keyes
Frank Gee Patchin
Frank Harris
Frank Jewett Mather
Frank L. Packard
Frank V. Webster
Frederic Stewart Isham
Frederick Trevor Hill
Frederick Winslow Taylor

Friedrich Kerst
Friedrich Nietzsche
Fyodor Dostoyevsky
G.A. Henty
G.K. Chesterton
Gabrielle E. Jackson
Garrett P. Serviss
Gaston Leroux
George A. Warren
George Ade
Geroge Bernard Shaw
George Cary Eggleston
George Durston
George Ebers
George Eliot
George Gissing
George MacDonald
George Meredith
George Orwell
George Sylvester Viereck
George Tucker
George W. Cable
George Wharton James
Gertrude Atherton
Gordon Casserly
Grace E. King
Grace Gallatin
Grace Greenwood
Grant Allen
Guillermo A. Sherwell
Gulielma Zollinger
Gustav Flaubert
H. A. Cody
H. B. Irving
H.C. Bailey
H. G. Wells
H. H. Munro
H. Irving Hancock
H. R. Naylor
H. Rider Haggard
H. W. C. Davis
Haldeman Julius
Hall Caine
Hamilton Wright Mabie
Hans Christian Andersen
Harold Avery
Harold McGrath
Harriet Beecher Stowe
Harry Castlemon
Harry Coghill
Harry Houidini

Hayden Carruth
Helent Hunt Jackson
Helen Nicolay
Hendrik Conscience
Hendy David Thoreau
Henri Barbusse
Henrik Ibsen
Henry Adams
Henry Ford
Henry Frost
Henry James
Henry Jones Ford
Henry Seton Merriman
Henry W Longfellow
Herbert A. Giles
Herbert Carter
Herbert N. Casson
Herman Hesse
Hildegard G. Frey
Homer
Honore De Balzac
Horace B. Day
Horace Walpole
Horatio Alger Jr.
Howard Pyle
Howard R. Garis
Hugh Lofting
Hugh Walpole
Humphry Ward
Ian Maclaren
Inez Haynes Gillmore
Irving Bacheller
Isabel Cecilia Williams
Isabel Hornibrook
Israel Abrahams
Ivan Turgenev
J.G.Austin
J. Henri Fabre
J. M. Barrie
J. M. Walsh
J. Macdonald Oxley
J. R. Miller
J. S. Fletcher
J. S. Knowles
J. Storer Clouston
J. W. Duffield
Jack London
Jacob Abbott
James Allen
James Andrews
James Baldwin

James Branch Cabell
James DeMille
James Joyce
James Lane Allen
James Lane Allen
James Oliver Curwood
James Oppenheim
James Otis
James R. Driscoll
Jane Abbott
Jane Austen
Jane L. Stewart
Janet Aldridge
Jens Peter Jacobsen
Jerome K. Jerome
Jessie Graham Flower
John Buchan
John Burroughs
John Cournos
John F. Kennedy
John Gay
John Glasworthy
John Habberton
John Joy Bell
John Kendrick Bangs
John Milton
John Philip Sousa
John Taintor Foote
Jonas Lauritz Idemil Lie
Jonathan Swift
Joseph A. Altsheler
Joseph Carey
Joseph Conrad
Joseph E. Badger Jr
Joseph Hergesheimer
Joseph Jacobs
Jules Vernes
Julian Hawthrone
Julie A Lippmann
Justin Huntly McCarthy
Kakuzo Okakura
Karle Wilson Baker
Kate Chopin
Kenneth Grahame
Kenneth McGaffey
Kate Langley Bosher
Kate Langley Bosher
Katherine Cecil Thurston
Katherine Stokes
L. A. Abbot
L. T. Meade

L. Frank Baum
Latta Griswold
Laura Dent Crane
Laura Lee Hope
Laurence Housman
Lawrence Beasley
Leo Tolstoy
Leonid Andreyev
Lewis Carroll
Lewis Sperry Chafer
Lilian Bell
Lloyd Osbourne
Louis Hughes
Louis Joseph Vance
Louis Tracy
Louisa May Alcott
Lucy Fitch Perkins
Lucy Maud Montgomery
Luther Benson
Lydia Miller Middleton
Lyndon Orr
M. Corvus
M. H. Adams
Margaret E. Sangster
Margret Howth
Margaret Vandercook
Margaret W. Hungerford
Margret Penrose
Maria Edgeworth
Maria Thompson Daviess
Mariano Azuela
Marion Polk Angellotti
Mark Overton
Mark Twain
Mary Austin
Mary Catherine Crowley
Mary Cole
Mary Hastings Bradley
Mary Roberts Rinehart
Mary Rowlandson
M. Wollstonecraft Shelley
Maud Lindsay
Max Beerbohm
Myra Kelly
Nathaniel Hawthrone
Nicolo Machiavelli
O. F. Walton
Oscar Wilde
Owen Johnson
P.G. Wodehouse
Paul and Mabel Thorne

Paul G. Tomlinson
Paul Severing
Percy Brebner
Percy Keese Fitzhugh
Peter B. Kyne
Plato
Quincy Allen
R. Derby Holmes
R. L. Stevenson
R. S. Ball
Rabindranath Tagore
Rahul Alvares
Ralph Bonehill
Ralph Henry Barbour
Ralph Victor
Ralph Waldo Emmerson
Rene Descartes
Ray Cummings
Rex Beach
Rex E. Beach
Richard Harding Davis
Richard Jefferies
Richard Le Gallienne
Robert Barr
Robert Frost
Robert Gordon Anderson
Robert L. Drake
Robert Lansing
Robert Lynd
Robert Michael Ballantyne
Robert W. Chambers
Rosa Nouchette Carey
Rudyard Kipling
Saint Augustine
Samuel B. Allison
Samuel Hopkins Adams
Sarah Bernhardt
Sarah C. Hallowell
Selma Lagerlof
Sherwood Anderson
Sigmund Freud
Standish O'Grady
Stanley Weyman
Stella Benson
Stella M. Francis
Stephen Crane
Stewart Edward White
Stijn Streuvels
Swami Abhedananda
Swami Parmananda
T. S. Ackland

T. S. Arthur
The Princess Der Ling
Thomas A. Janvier
Thomas A Kempis
Thomas Anderton
Thomas Bailey Aldrich
Thomas Bulfinch
Thomas De Quincey
Thomas Dixon
Thomas H. Huxley
Thomas Hardy
Thomas More
Thornton W. Burgess
U. S. Grant
Upton Sinclair
Valentine Williams
Various Authors
Vaughan Kester
Victor Appleton
Victor G. Durham
Victoria Cross
Virginia Woolf
Wadsworth Camp
Walter Camp
Walter Scott
Washington Irving
Wilbur Lawton
Wilkie Collins
Willa Cather
Willard F. Baker
William Dean Howells
William le Queux
W. Makepeace Thackeray
William W. Walter
William Shakespeare
Winston Churchill
Yei Theodora Ozaki
Yogi Ramacharaka
Young E. Allison
Zane Grey

William MacLeod Raine